KILLING IT IN PARIS

AN AMERICAN IN PARIS MYSTERY BOOK 5

SUSAN KIERNAN-LEWIS

SAN MARCO PRESS

Ella Out of Time
Swept Away
Carried Away
Stolen Away

The French Women's Diet

1

I swear that whenever I step into Monoprix, that Mecca of shopping and trendy French procurement, I feel so much more Parisienne than I can ever really be. I'm not sure why that is exactly. Maybe it's the sheer assortment and variety of colors. As if a mind-numbing plethora of stationery and yogurt isn't enough, they have to come, *mais bien sûr!* in every gradation of the rainbow.

It was a little past five o'clock and the place was packed as Parisiennes filled the supermarket's aisles to pick up last-minute goose *confit* and hand-rolled chicken enchiladas. I walked slowly to allow the more determined shoppers to get on with what they needed for their evening meals.

It's not that I don't have a life. I assure you I do and a busy one at that.

I am after all sixty-three years old with an eighteen-month-old baby to care for, a full-time job, and I live in a country where my language skills are iffy at best. When I'm not working or changing diapers, I'm studying how to ask for wine-by-the-box using the correct article and tense.

As it turns out, mine is a full and exhausting life in the last third of my years.

"The organic sheep's milk yoghurt?"

I broke out of my thoughts to look up at the beautiful young woman wearing an oversized wool coat over vintage cropped jeans and Converse sneakers who stood in front of me. Gigi held my ward Robbie in her arms, his face sticky with the cheese-curd tart she had just fed him while we waited in line for the register. Gigi was looking into our small grocery basket with a frown.

"I'll pick it up tomorrow," I said.

"Are you sure?" Gigi glanced behind me which suggested she'd be happy to dash back to the dairy aisle for the yoghurt.

But I was tired and ready to go home. I'd spent the day surveilling a new client and working with Laura Murphy of the Paris Expat Group on some upcoming privacy issues that she needed my advice on. As an English-speaking private investigator, I make a very good living off the myriad problems of the expats of Paris, most of whom I find through Laura.

I don't think I ever imagined I'd find myself at my age still working full-time. I was tired. I wanted to put my feet up, open a bottle of Pinot Noir, and have someone else cook dinner.

Unfortunately, although a competent au pair who was thoroughly adored by my young charge, Gigi didn't cook or, if she did, she didn't cook for me.

When our turn in line came, Gigi deftly unloaded the boxes and bags of groceries while also holding Robbie. I pushed his empty stroller until it was time to pay, then Gigi loaded up the groceries into the stroller and we headed for home.

Home for me was a two-hundred-year-old two-bedroom apartment in a classic Haussmann building in the ninth arrondissement of Paris.

The details of how I came to live in such an amazing apartment are simple—and trust me, even at seven hundred square feet, for Paris, it's an amazing apartment. My stepfather died two years ago and left it to me along with a comfortable stipend. That combined with the money I made from my work as an investigator enabled me to support myself. After my late husband had raided our retirement funds and savings, I'd been left with nothing. Thanks to my stepfather's generosity—while I wasn't rich—I was comfortable. And saying that while living in Paris was truly saying something.

The street my apartment was on was today covered in a dirty blanket of slush. The cars that parked up and down its length were draped in white. Every now and then a stiff breeze blew a puff of white from the rooftops to sprinkle on the three of us as we walked.

In the nearly two years that I've lived in Paris, I've improved my French language skills, possibly fallen in love, and solved no fewer than four criminal cases, three of them murder and one a bona fide serial killing. I say *possibly* fallen in love because the situation in question never had the opportunity to really bloom before it was cut down.

The "rose" in question was a senior detective with the Central Directorate of the Judicial Police in Paris whom I met when he was investigating the murder of my husband two years ago.

Gigi punched in the security code outside the wrought-iron grill door of my building and I pushed the stroller full of groceries inside. I tried to remember how I had done any of this without Gigi just a few weeks ago.

After walking through the door, we hurried across the courtyard pavers to the heavy oak door that led into my apartment building. Inside the foyer was the ancient pre-World War II elevator. The majority of Paris elevators in nineteenth-century buildings were retrofitted to the available space so elevators were often crammed into the shaft in the middle of spiral staircases leading to the upper floors. Depending on the size of the original staircase, this often meant very small elevators only able to comfortably accommodate one person at a time.

One very slim person.

Although even after two years of a steady diet of pastry and rich wine sauces I can still fit into the typical Parisienne elevator, I usually don't bother. Today, Gigi—with the vigor and limitless energy of youth—bounded up the wide, smooth stairs with Robbie giggling and shrieking with delight in her arms while I wheeled the grocery-laden stroller into the elevator and closed the protective grill door.

Gigi and Robbie were waiting for me at my apartment door when the elevator finally wheezed its way to the third floor. I'd given her a key but she'd lost it a few times. I wasn't sure if the reason she had waited for me to arrive was because she'd lost it again, but I was too tired to care.

I'd found Gigi through Laura Murphy who'd found her through one of the British expats who had used her for their twin girls. The family was moving back to the UK, and so Laura matched me with Gigi. She was in big demand, not just because she was perfectly capable, but also because she was French.

Most expats looking for childcare preferred one who could also help their children learn the language. It would be a few years before Robbie would benefit from a native French speaker, but Gigi was great with him in all other aspects, so I had jumped at the opportunity.

I unlocked the apartment door to the sounds of my extremely vocal French bulldog Izzy barking her greeting to us. Gigi took Robbie straight to her bedroom so she could change him. She lived with us in my guest room as Robbie's fulltime caretaker, which in itself had made such a difference in the workload for me—especially mornings and nights.

Which made it all the more unfortunate that I intended to fire her at the end of the week.

2

I used to make *coq au vin* in my other life back in Atlanta but it was always an all-day affair reserved for special occasions. These days I make it frequently—usually when it's cold outside since it's so warming and hearty—and I can't remember what the fuss was all about.

It's true I chopped the carrots, onions and garlic days earlier so I just needed to pull them out and toss them in a casserole pan on the stove. Browning the chicken pieces then took ten minutes tops. When the whole thing mixes together—with a healthy dose of good red wine—I have thirty minutes to kick off my shoes, put on some nice music, pour myself a glass of something, and relax before I need to set the table.

Like I said, I can't for the life of me remember what all the hassle was about.

I was midway into my thirty minutes, having already enjoyed a nice hot shower and changed clothes when Geneviève arrived.

My eighty-plus year old neighbor from downstairs Geneviève is probably my closest friend and confidant in France—well, honestly in the world. When I came out to check on how dinner looked in the pot, she had already finished setting the table and was feeding Robbie cooked sweet potato puree with peas in his highchair. He was intermittently tossing down bits of torn baguette to Izzy, who sat patiently on the floor beside his chair, and allowing Geneviève to feed him.

Gigi had asked for the night off. Again. It was annoying, of course, but since she was history soon, I didn't feel right about telling her no. Besides, living with someone in your house is a strain. A part of me actually welcomed the evening without her.

Geneviève came into the kitchen while I was plating up the *coq au vin*. She always looked immaculate—even for just a family supper upstairs. Her short hair was styled in silver waves and she had large brown eyes. She typically wore a lot of cardigans but also vintage designer pieces even when she was just sitting around watching television.

Ever since her British husband had died a decade earlier she'd lived alone. Because my stepfather and stepmother used to live in my apartment before my stepfather died and willed it all to me, Geneviève knew both of them well.

My stepfather—Claude Lapin—was a generally affable man and had always been pleasant to me the few times I'd seen him growing up. But the woman he married—whom I refer to as my stepmother but of course that's not right since Claude wasn't my biological father—is a witch of the first order. Even Geneviève said the rest of the building residents avoided her imperious glares for years.

"Have you heard from Jean-Marc, *chérie*?" Geneviève asked.

I nearly dropped the serving dish at her question. I turned and cocked an eyebrow at her.

"What brought that up?" I asked, handing her the plate I'd just filled.

"Just wondering."

Geneviève liked Jean-Marc. Heck, *I* liked Jean-Marc. But

after what had happened with his wife last summer I wasn't at all surprised when he cut off all ties with me and moved to Nice.

Well, frankly I was a little surprised. It was hard to imagine Jean-Marc in shorts let alone a bathing suit. He was a veteran Paris police detective and had just been in the process of resuscitating his career and his reputation when he became a widower. Now he was a senior homicide detective in the south of France and the chances of my ever seeing him again would probably necessitate me driving down to Nice to murder someone.

I'm not ruling it out, but it's probably not likely.

I brought my plate into the dining room and glanced at Robbie. He'd stopped eating and was now essentially scraping his food onto the carpet for Izzy. I'd need to do a better job of coordinating our mealtimes. Unfortunately just when I wanted to sit down and relax at the dinner table, it was time to release the gremlin.

"He will be fine, *chérie*."

"The place isn't really babyproofed, Geneviève," I said.

"So American," she scoffed.

I glanced around the room taking in the marble-base lamp with its irresistible-to-a-child silk fringe shade, the imminently breakable glass figurines on the side table, not to mention the sharp-edged wrought-iron screen in front of the fireplace. At least I'd covered up the wall sockets but there were still a hundred different ways the child could kill himself before Geneviève and I finished our salads.

Robbie kicked his highchair tray and squealed. I sighed and went to over to him. He was already reaching for me with his sticky fingers. I picked up the wet cloth I kept in a bowl on the table and cleaned him up first before taking off the highchair tray. Instantly I saw that it had been hiding a cup's worth of carrots and peas which were now embedded into his overalls.

"Please start eating," I said to Geneviève. "I need to change him."

"Nonsense. A few peas and carrots will not harm him. Unless you are going to give him another bath now too?"

I glanced back longingly at my plate of *coq au vin*, the steam curling from it beside a large goblet of Pinot.

Screw it, I thought, lifting Robbie out of his chair and settling him on the floor.

"You're in charge," I said to Izzy who looked at me with her big eyes blinking at me as if gravely considering my edict.

I came back to the table and sat down as I watched Robbie crawl over to where a pile of his toys sat in the middle of the living room. I'm not sure how the French do it but surely they don't lose that many infants to *après* dinner playtime? I took a big slug of wine and turned back to my plate.

Geneviève passed me the breadbasket.

"Have you heard from Catherine?" she asked.

My daughter Catherine had come over for an extended visit last summer—just in time for all the horror and drama of Robbie's abduction. She had become very fond of him during her stay—especially when she learned that he was actually her half-brother. For a while I thought it might work out for her to bring him back to the States. But Catherine's husband was not on board with the idea and, when Catherine told me she was confident she could force him to accept the situation, I knew that *I* couldn't be on board with it.

Robbie was an amazingly sweet and compliant child. He deserved more than someone who had to be forced to accept him. And that left me, amazingly, at age sixty-three to raise the child of my husband's mistress.

"Where is Mademoiselle Gigi tonight?" Geneviève asked.

"She asked for the night off."

"Again? I thought she did that several times last week."

"Yeah, well, she's a popular girl."

"You will have to talk with her."

"Or I could just let her go."

"Is that fair, *chérie*? Robbie loves her so."

I glanced at Robbie where he sat with his plush toys on the carpeted floor. He'd set a couple of the pieces on top of Izzy's head and she was being careful not to dislodge them.

"He'll love the next one too," I said.

I thought for a moment that Geneviève was going to say something more but she let it go. For now. I knew her too well. She definitely wasn't done with the topic just yet.

Later that night after dinner I shooed Geneviève back to her own place because if I didn't she'd insist on doing the dishes and I'd already leaned on her too much. Plus, I knew that with my determination to sack Gigi, there would likely be more than a few times in the future when I'd need to lean on her again as back-up childcare.

That night it took forever to get Robbie to go down to sleep —the whole nighttime ritual had become increasingly more involved the older he got. Routinely, after his bath, either Gigi or I read to him—even though of course he didn't understand a word. But like Catherine when she was his age, he loved turning the pages and pointing to the pictures.

Unfortunately the night routine was a lot easier when I was thirty than it was now after a long day of work and cooking. Plus I still had a couple of hours of online research I wanted to do tonight for a French American company who had hired me to check out their latest hires. It was easy work and only promised to take just a day or two but I needed to do a good job. The easy work gigs took the sting out of all the hours spent standing on street corners or stationed in cafés waiting for some cheating spouse to walk by so I could take their picture.

When I did this sort of work back in Atlanta, which like most American cities is designed around roadways, my surveillance was done from the comfort of my car. While I don't usually attract too much attention sitting in a café with a long-zoom lens camera—this is Paris after all, the most popular tourist destination in the world—an open-air café wasn't nearly as comfortable as sitting in a private car would have been.

At eighteen months old, Robbie was still sleeping in a crib. But it wouldn't be long before I'd need to move him to a proper bed. My original idea was to swap out the crib for a child's bed and keep it in the guest room with the au pair. But the three weeks living with Gigi had me thinking twice about the whole live-in idea.

Yes, it meant she was up with him early, changing him, singing to him and preparing his breakfast, allowing me to either sleep in, meet someone for coffee, walk Izzy or just have some time to myself. That was all very well and a great convenience. After all, it had been over twenty years since I'd had to accommodate my schedule for a child.

But having a stranger in your house when you're used to living alone is not an easy transition. I half wondered if the real reason I wanted to let Gigi go wasn't because I just needed my place back to myself again. As I looked down at Robbie in my arms, his eyes finally closed and his breathing slow and regular as he succumbed to sleep, I realized that I was not going to get my place back to myself for at least another eighteen years. There was every possibility I might just have to get used to it.

I leaned down and kissed his cheek and waited a few more minutes before lifting him into his bed and arranging his teddy bears and blankets around him.

I tiptoed out of the room, making sure the baby monitor was on, and retreated to the kitchen to do the dishes. Thirty minutes later, I settled down on the couch with my laptop and a final glass of Pinot. I kicked off my shoes and curled up on the couch, tucking my feet under me. It was chilly in the room but I was too tired to get up and fiddle with the thermostat.

I dragged a chunky cashmere throw across my legs and was about to open my laptop when my phone buzzed.

I saw the picture of Adele appear on the screen. I met Adele, a forensic tech thirty years my junior, two summers ago when the simultaneous tragedies of her brother's and my husband's murders coincided. The DNA laboratory she worked for was used to relieve the workload in the forensics department of the Paris homicide division, making Adele a treasure trove of information for me on various criminal cases.

But aside from that and our age differences, we just really liked each other.

Lately she'd been very busy with her latest beau and we hadn't gotten together in a while.

"Hey," I said, answering the phone. "I'm surprised to hear from you."

"I know. I'm a terrible friend."

Instantly I could tell she was down. Adele was French and the French don't make friends or get close easily. The deaths of the two men we loved had leapfrogged us over the typical norms of French friendship.

"Is everything okay?" I asked.

"I broke up with Michel."

"Oh, no. Why?"

"I caught him with someone else."

"Oh, Adele, that's the worst," I said with a sigh.

And I should know. My husband cheated on me with Robbie's mother—a social media specialist in the ad agency he co-owned back in Atlanta. I didn't know about it until after he died.

"No, it's fine. It's good in fact," she said.

"Well, since he was a cheat. It's definitely good to find out now. But still not pleasant."

"It just goes to show, you know?"

"What's that?"

"You don't always know the people closest to you."

"Truer words, my friend."

"Can you meet for lunch tomorrow?"

Tomorrow wasn't good for me. I had three appointments and each of them was going to be a squeeze. But I couldn't say no to her. She was hurting.

"Can we make it dinner?" I asked. "Or drinks?"

The French take their *apéros* very seriously. Drinks were nearly as *de rigueur* as dinner.

"I'm working tomorrow evening," she said with a sigh.

"Let's stay in touch tomorrow. I might be able to swing by and meet you after my first appointment."

And if I can't, I'll cancel it, I thought.

"Okay," she said in a flat, monotone voice.

"Chin up, *chérie*. There are so many more *poissons* in *la mer*."

"Save it for when I have a drink in my hand," she said with a small laugh.

After we hung up, I finished off my wine and decided the day had been full enough without finishing it by working late. I pushed my laptop away and looked at Izzy who had been curled up by my hip throughout my conversation with Adele. She looked at me now, alert and ready.

"We'll just go down and back up, yeah?" I said to her, prompting her to race to the front door where her leash was hanging.

I stood up with a groan and felt around for my shoes.

Just one last thing to do and then all my responsibilities would be done, I thought as I went to the door and took my quilted winter jacket off the hook.

Oh, how wrong I was.

3

I don't know what time Gigi got home that night. She must have been exceedingly quiet because not only did I not awake but neither did Robbie. I'm sure Izzy noticed when she came in but she also knew it wasn't necessary to alert the household over the fact. Izzy loved Gigi. Of course she did. Everyone did.

By the time I'd showered and dressed and entered the dining room, Robbie was already dressed for the day and in the process of having his breakfast wiped from his face by Gigi. Whatever she'd done last night, she must not have danced and drunk until dawn because her face was cheery and rosy and her eyes bright when she greeted me.

"I have made your coffee, Claire," she said cheerfully indicating the pot of French press coffee in the kitchen.

I felt a twinge of guilt.

"Thank you, Gigi. So what are your plans for the day?"

Gigi was like most French girls in that her clothes were always stylish but looked absolutely effortless. The look nowadays is not polished but thrown together, so her uniform of cropped jeans, sneakers and oversized winter coat was one I saw every day in every section of Paris. Gigi was a pretty girl and like most French women was scrupulous about her skin care. She wore a ponytail loose and long down her back in a further I-don't-care affect. But the result was stunning.

"I think we are going to the Jardin des Champs-Élysées," she said, turning to look at Robbie. "*Oui, ma petite*? I am meeting my boyfriend at Café Denzel before we go."

"Oh?" I said, suddenly wary. "Your boyfriend?"

Of course she'd talked about him on and off since she moved in last month, but I'd never met him. Until right now when she was suggesting he might be spending the day with Robbie, I hadn't seen the need.

"Jean-Bernard has the day off and he suggested we might go to the Place de la Concorde and then the park." She turned back to Robbie. "You will love it, *chérie!*" she said, releasing him from his highchair and swinging him onto her hip.

I bit my lip. I didn't want to be a kill joy but neither did I feel good about her plans for the day.

"If you don't mind," I said to her, hating myself for being so mealy mouthed, "I think I'd like to meet Jean-Bernard first." I forced myself not to repeat *If you don't mind*. I'd never mentioned to Gigi about what had happened with Robbie last summer. I didn't think I needed to explain myself.

But I was still reluctant to let them go.

"Oh, Claire, you must come with us! You will love Jean-Bernard! Come to the café! Do you have time?"

I should have just told her not to go with Jean-Bernard, not if she had Robbie with her. I should have just found a spine and told her I didn't have time to meet him and I wasn't comfortable with her bringing Robbie if Jean-Bernard was along.

But I didn't do any of that.

"Sure," I said. "Let me just run Izzy down to the courtyard."

By that time, Gigi had Robbie in his snowsuit and was tucking him into his stroller.

"Meet us there," she said. "I don't want to rush Mademoiselle Izzy." She gave the French bulldog an affectionate tousle around the ears, then stood up and held the door open for me and Izzy to pass through.

I took the stairs as she maneuvered Robbie's stroller into the elevator. I felt my stomach constrict as I descended.

Why couldn't I have just told her no?

I'd been to Café Denzel on rue de l'ancienne comédie a few times. It was a classic Parisienne café with polished wooden floors and lace curtains reflected in floor-to-ceiling gilded mirrors.

Because of the cold weather, Gigi was sitting inside. Izzy had taken forever to do her business this morning in the courtyard but because I was going to be gone for the day I really didn't feel like I could rush her. As a result, when I finally made it to the café, Gigi and her boyfriend already had an assortment of coffee cups and croissant plates on their table.

I entered the café and signaled to the waiter that I was with the table in the front window.

"Claire! Over here!" Gigi called.

As I walked over, Jean-Bernard stood up and smiled broadly. Robbie was in his stroller, gnawing on a biscotti.

Jean-Bernard held out his hand.

"Bonjour, Claire," he said.

At easily six foot five, Jean-Bernard loomed over all three of us at the table. He was clean-shaven with dark hair and sharp features and piercing blue eyes.

First let me say that I'm as bad as anyone when it comes to responding to attractive people. I tend to give them the benefit of the doubt—often in spite of what I know for a fact to be true about them.

"Bonjour, Jean-Bernard," I said. "I can't stay." I looked over at Gigi. "I have a meeting in fifteen minutes."

"Gigi told me you were a private investigator," Jean-Bernard said, clearly not about to sit down if I wasn't going to. "Very sexy work, *non*?"

I laughed. "Well, I don't know about that. But it pays the bills." I glanced down at Robbie. "Are you sure you don't mind sharing your day off with an eighteen-month old?"

He turned to look at Robbie and if possible grinned even wider.

"*Ah, mais non!*" he said. "I love the children. And Robert is so *agrèable, non*?"

I looked at Robbie and felt a strong urge to pick him up and give him a hug, sticky fingers and all.

"Well, okay. If you're sure."

"Do not worry, Claire," Gigi said. "Robbie will have the most wonderful of days today. *Je promis!*"

I leaned over and kissed Robbie on the cheek.

"Have fun, little man," I said before giving both Gigi and Jean-Bernard one last smile before leaving the café.

I never even asked her where they'd finally decided to go for the day.

4

Laura led me to the leopard-patterned velvet sofa in her sun-flooded salon. The walls around us were rose-tinted with cream shelving that displayed a series of six blue-and-white porcelain Asian vases and ginger jars.

The effect was elegant and also Parisienne but not quite warm and welcoming.

Married to a charming but often sickly Texan who had died a few years back, Laura had opted to stay in the gorgeous Haussmann apartment he'd left her and remain in Paris. She'd been the director of the popular American and British Parisienne expat group for nearly eight years. Blonde, petite and nearly always smiling, Laura had no children and appeared to have little interest in remarrying.

While I waited for her to return to the living room with a tray of tea and cookies, I texted Gigi that I thought Jean-Bernard was very nice and I hoped they had a great day.

<Remember to keep R bundled up!> I wrote and threw in a couple of emojis about Eskimo's and hot chocolate to soften the edict. But I knew Gigi would make sure he was warm. She was very good with him.

Although I had no doubt that Robbie's own mother had loved him she had been mostly distracted when it came to Robbie.

I waited but received no answering text from Gigi.

"How are things working out with Gigi?" Laura asked as she came back into the room and set down the large tea tray on the coffee table in front of me. I realized I was steeling myself for this conversation.

Gigi wasn't the first au pair that Laura recommended to me that I'd decided to toss back.

"Gigi is a great girl," I said reaching for a Calisson cookie— redolent of sweet almonds—while Laura poured the Earl Gray into a cup.

"But?"

I forced myself not to look at my phone to see if Gigi had responded in the last three seconds. Honestly, the fact that I found myself constantly calling or texting her throughout the day for updates on Robbie seemed to underscore for me the feeling that I just wasn't comfortable with the girl.

"It's hard to put my finger on it," I said.

"I'd ask you to try," Laura said as she handed me a teacup and saucer. "She was in very big demand before the Hendersons."

"Great. So you'll have no trouble placing her."

I hated to put into words why it was I wanted to try someone new. It was all so subjective and ambivalent and I really depended on Laura seeing me as an objective, cogent investigator. Not as some wishy-washy helicopter parent who wasn't going to like anyone taking care of her baby.

Not that Robbie was *my* baby of course. But still, now that his mother and father were both dead I was all he had. I often looked into his serious little face, usually so ready to break into a smile or infectious giggles with Izzy, and when I did I saw

Bob. I saw the man I thought I knew. I saw the generous, loving man I'd married, the man I'd lived with for twenty-two years in Atlanta and had raised an adored daughter with.

I didn't see a hint of the man who ended up dead in a Paris hotel because he'd tried to proposition the hotel maid while I was out shopping for souvenirs.

"I do have one possibility," Laura said with a sigh. "But if you're not happy with Gigi I can't imagine you'll be satisfied with Haley."

"American?"

"Yes. Both her parents work for Accenture. She goes to the American School. Decent grades but not amazing."

"Why the hesitancy?"

"Just certain things that were said about her from other babysitting jobs. She's a little rough around the edges."

"Have you met her?"

"No. So do you want me to send her over for an interview?"

I hesitated, not ready to commit to another version of Gigi —pleasant as she might be.

"Can you have her come over some evening?" I hedged.

"I'll give you her number, shall I? And then you can make arrangements yourself."

Laura and I had a prickly history, made even more prickly by the fact that last winter I'd accused her of murdering a mutual acquaintance.

I was lucky she was still giving me jobs, let alone trying to help with my childcare needs.

"She's only thirteen," Laura said, jotting down a number on a piece of paper. "So she won't qualify as a live-in."

"That's fine," I said, taking the paper. "She might work as an interim sitter in that case. Can you keep looking for someone else?"

"Of course."

I put Haley's contact info into my phone, and noted with a pulse of misgiving that Gigi had still not responded to my text message.

5

I worked the kink out of my back, sorry I'd worn my favorite Ralph Lauren trousers since I'd spent more time kneeling in them than standing. My morning had vacillated between watching the front entrance of the Franco-American language school in Montmartre for the man whose wife was paying me to see if he was really attending classes—and racing across town in the Latin Quarter to watch the apartment of his possible girlfriend.

I got a bingo at the girlfriend's apartment but by the time I lined up and got focused for a decent shot, my quarry had pulled up his collar, jerked down his sunglasses and was gone.

I was frustrated that I didn't get my picture since I had nothing to show for my morning's effort and now it was too late to slip away to see Adele. Fortunately, by the time I texted her that I wasn't going to be able to make it today she sounded—at least in writing—much better, telling me not to worry about it, we'd try again tomorrow.

By the time I finally watched my mark climb the stairs to the apartment he shared with his wife—my client—I saw I'd received a text from Gigi from an hour earlier saying she and Robbie were at the Eiffel Tower and she would call soon.

That helped somewhat but still didn't assuage the fact that she hadn't responded immediately when I'd phoned earlier. Regardless of the fact that Gigi wasn't long for my employ, she and I were going to have a serious *tête-à-tête* tonight when I got home.

It was just after six o'clock and I was already tired. Since Gigi had gone out the previous night I never did get to put my feet up. Tonight I had my heart set on both a hot bath and an early bedtime—I might even beat Robbie to bed—plus I had a good James Patterson book I wanted to get into.

When I got home I was surprised to see that I'd beat Gigi home. My surprise immediately gave way to annoyance which seemed to be my default attitude around Gigi these days. Poor Izzy had been trapped in the apartment all day and was desperate to get outside and water the pavers in the courtyard. If I'd known that Gigi was going to be gone all day, I would've asked Geneviève to come up and let the poor dog out.

No, this arrangement was definitely not working.

After I returned upstairs with Izzy and set about unpacking the *murgh makhani* and tandoori chicken that I'd picked up on the way home, I called Gigi again. My call went straight to voicemail. That was the moment I knew I was going to fire her the second she crossed the threshold.

It wasn't just anger or spite or even the culmination of the day's frustrations but ever since that terrible time last summer when Robbie had been snatched in Parc Monceau until the moment he was found six hours later, I have felt uneasy about letting him out of my sight. Since I can't enjoy any kind of a life under those conditions, finding someone I can trust to care for him was paramount.

I walked away from the kitchen table with the cartons of jasmine rice and *dal makhani*, and found myself wringing my hands. I felt as if a panicked bird was trapped in my chest. My heart began to pound and a light sheen of sweat developed on my top lip.

They should be home by now.

Gigi wasn't answering her phone and I had no idea where Robbie was.

I tapped in the emergency number to the police on my phone, feeling a swarm of emotions: anger that I couldn't call Jean-Marc, embarrassment because I was probably overreacting, terrified that something had happened to Robbie, and furious with myself that I'd once more allowed someone else to watch him and had lost him. Again.

I thought back to last summer and my determined belief that it was my father—that shadowy sinister presence so committed to upending and disrupting my life who'd orchestrated Robbie's kidnapping. In fact, even in the face of no real evidence to support it, there is no way I will ever believe that my father wasn't responsible for it.

How's that for some gold standard intuitive detective work?

"Paris police department," the operator intoned on the line.

"Yes," I said breathlessly, "I'd like to report...my sitter left this morning with my child and hasn't returned or called."

"Name?"

Before I could ask whether she was asking for my name or Gigi's, there was a knock at the door. Thinking that it must be Gigi who'd lost her key again, I quickly thanked the operator and disconnected as I ran to the door, fully ready to blast into the girl.

It wasn't Gigi at the door. It was two policewomen, one of whom was holding Robbie in her arms.

Robbie instantly held out his arms to me.

"*Maman!*" he yelped, flexing his fingers as if that would get him to me faster.

I went to him and the policewoman handed him over. Just

the feel of him in my arms instantly eased my anxiety. I held him close and breathed in his familiar baby smell.

I looked behind the policewomen for Gigi and felt my heart flutter when she wasn't there.

"What has happened?" I asked, stepping back into my apartment. "Where is Gigi?"

One of the policewomen pulled out an electronic tablet. The other looked around my apartment, her eyes coming to rest on the cartons of uneaten Indian food on the dining table.

I looked at Robbie who looked no worse for wear. No scratches or bruises and he was already kicking his little feet to be set down to go play with Izzy. I held him close not willing to let him go just yet.

"Where is the young woman who was caring for my child?" I asked, my heart racing.

"Gigi Rozen was arrested this afternoon," the policeman said.

"Arrested? What in the world for? Where is she? I'll stand bail for her. Why hasn't she been allowed her phone call?"

"That will be up to her representation to determine," the policewoman said.

"What are you talking about? Why would she need representation?"

The policewoman peered around my apartment before turning her cold gaze back on me.

"Mademoiselle Rozen was charged with pushing her boyfriend to his death from the top of the Eiffel Tower."

6

N ow that is a phrase you don't hear too often.

Charged with pushing her boyfriend off the Eiffel Tower.

I still didn't know what to think of it and I'd been parroting it inside my head the whole drive downtown from my apartment to the Paris police station.

The *Préfecture de Police* was situated in an ancient building in the Place Louis Lépine on the Île de la Cité. Upon entering the building, one is presented with a vast waiting room and a receptionist's station. Past this was a long hallway that led to the detectives bureau and interview stations.

I sat in the hallway and watched as the various detectives and police officers milled past me. I recognized none of them although I could tell many of them recognized me. I'd been in this police station many times over the past two years. A couple of those times as a suspect in a murder investigation.

I would have met most of these people when Jean-Marc worked here, but because of an unfortunate brain anomaly that I was born with called prosopagnosia, I am not able to recall facial features or recognize people from one minute to the next.

It is a singularly unfortunate defect for a private investigator, I can tell you.

In any case, I have long since stopped trying to remember faces. The fact is I can't do it and there's an end to it. The faces who glanced at me—largely unfriendly I have to say—were very likely people I'd been out to dinner with or had spent a good amount of time discussing cases with.

It didn't matter. My brain couldn't recall them.

I was waiting to talk to the detective on Gigi's case, a Capitaine Vincent Muller. I knew nothing about the man except that he'd taken over much of Jean-Marc's responsibilities even though their ranks were not the same. Unless he'd been busted down—something Jean-Marc had had happen to him *twice*—Capitaine Muller was probably middle-aged, or at least certainly not young, and definitely nowhere near Jean-Marc's or my age.

As soon as the policewomen in my apartment left I'd bundled Robbie up, added extra diapers and a couple jars of his baby food, and took him and Izzy downstairs to Geneviève's apartment to watch for me until I could return. I told her in just a few words all that I knew—that Gigi had been arrested and that there'd been some kind of accident at the Eiffel Tower.

Wordlessly, Geneviève took the stroller and Izzy's leash, her face tranquil and impassive. Behind her I could hear the nightly news was on and several times I heard the words "*Tour Eiffel.*" Geneviève clearly knew even more about what had happened at the Eiffel Tower than I did. But I didn't have time to stop and ask her.

"I'll be back as soon as I can," I said, giving Robbie a quick kiss before hurrying out the door.

I'd looked up the news story on my phone as my taxi took me to the police station.

Security precautions to prevent falling off the Eiffel Tower failed today when a man fell to his death from the second platform of the steel structure. The police identified the victim as Jean-Bernard Simon, 29 years old.

As I waited in the hallway at the Préfecture de Police, I continued to search the Internet for any information on what had happened today, reading over and over again any brief newstory I could find. But there was very little.

Why did the police arrest Gigi in connection with this terrible accident? And why are they calling it murder?

"Madame Baskerville?" A gruff male voice broke me out of my focus on my smartphone. I jerked my head up and saw a burly middle-aged man, balding with a droopy mustache and squinty eyes approaching me. Capitaine Muller did not offer to shake my hand. Assuming we would go to his office to speak, I gathered up my purse and stood up.

He simply stood in the hall. Flustered, I faced him.

"I'm here for information on Gigi Rozen," I said. "She is my employee and I—"

"I can tell you nothing, Madame," he said, his eyes dropping to my chest even though I was wearing at least three layers of clothing plus a coat.

I felt heat flushing through my body as I struggled to tamp down my growing anger.

"Well, you can at least tell me why you're holding her," I said.

"Madame, this is an active murder investigation and I am not at liberty to comment on it." He began to turn away.

I'd waited nearly two hours for this? I grabbed his sleeve which made him stop and stare at my hand on his arm. I quickly removed it and he turned to face me again, this time openly inspecting my lower half.

"A man tragically falls from the top of the Eiffel Tower," I began, trying to keep my voice calm and composed, "in spite of heightened security measures and you arrest a young woman in connection with it? That makes no sense!"

His eyes finally made their way back to mine and his lip twitched beneath his moustache into a sneer.

"The man did not 'tragically fall,' Madame," he said. "He was pushed."

"That's impossible," I said in bewilderment.

"*Non*? Tell that to the five eye-witnesses who saw her do it."

7

I sat in the back of the Uber as it drove me home, completely stunned. Muller had refused me any contact with Gigi even by phone. He further refused to give me any information on where she was being held, or who, if anyone, was representing her. By the time I stumbled back out into the cold night to wait for my ride, I was numb with distress and indecision.

How could this have happened? How could a girl be arrested for what was quickly becoming an international news headline event and yet no one was allowed contact with her?

The first thing I had done when I got in the back of my Uber was call Laura Murphy. The call went to voicemail. With building frustration I texted her.

<Have you heard about what happened to Gigi? Who is her next of kin?>

It appeared there was nothing I could do for Gigi tonight. In the meantime, I had no idea where she was or how she was being treated.

I looked back at my phone to see if there was any more information on the Eiffel Tower accident and found a few more bits and pieces. The victim—Jean-Bernard—had fallen or jumped—that part wasn't clear—from the second floor platform above the restaurant Altitude 95. He landed on the roof of the restaurant over the heads of nearly two hundred diners.

I squeezed the terrible image out of my mind. How could it have happened? How was it even possible?

As soon as the Uber reached my apartment building, I hurried inside and ran up the stairs to Geneviève's apartment and tapped lightly on the door. It was only a little after midnight and I knew she would be waiting up for me.

She opened the door in her dressing gown and drew me inside.

"Poor *chérie*," she murmured. "Come in. I have brandy."

"How's Robbie?" I asked as Izzy ran over to me from where she'd been asleep on the couch.

"Sound asleep of course," Geneviève said as I walked to the couch where she poured our drinks.

"I can't believe this is happening," I said. "Have you heard anything on the TV news?"

"Just that there was an accident at the tower today. It was Gigi's young man?"

"Yes. And the cops think she pushed him."

"How is that even possible? I thought the security measures made it impossible to get near the edge."

I drank the brandy and felt it burn all the way down my throat. It actually felt good the way it hurt.

"Well, it happened," I said. "I guess we'll hear more as the days go by."

"What are you going to do about it?"

I looked at her. "What do you mean?"

"You will help her of course."

"In what way? I don't know anything about what happened."

"You know that girl did not push a grown man off the Eiffel Tower!"

I looked at Geneviève. *Did* I know that? Really? Did I know anything?

After a few more minutes of conversation with Geneviève in which she made it clear that, innocent or not, Gigi needed me to have her back on this, I brought Izzy back upstairs to my apartment but left Robbie sleeping. I'd collect him in the morning.

If I thought the long horrible day would at least guarantee me a deep restorative sleep, I was sadly mistaken. After I'd let Izzy out one last time and then went through my nighttime ritual of washing off my makeup, brushing and flossing, I decided I was too tired to take a shower. It could wait until morning. But unfortunately I was not tired enough to actually fall asleep.

The numbers on my bedside digital clock read one thirty in the morning which is the middle of the night for most people. But for someone like Adele it's barely even dinner time. I picked up the phone and called her. Because she works for a commercial forensic company that makes most of its money picking up the slack on work for the Paris police department's in-house forensics team, there was a good chance she would have been working on the Eiffel Tower crime scene. She did say she was working tonight and this job would be a major one because of where it happened.

My call went to voicemail. If she *was* working the scene she was likely still there with no time to chat with me on the phone. That was actually good news because it meant that when I did get hold of her, I'd have firsthand inside information about what had happened.

Something I certainly wasn't going to get from Detective Muller.

Izzy curled up against my hip and because it was a cold night I tucked her inside the covers with me. She reacted with a satisfied sigh before closing her eyes.

My brain buzzed with the events of the day and my emotions were jangling guiltily over how focused I'd been on trying to get rid of Gigi.

No, sleep wouldn't come easily tonight.

The next morning, I jumped in the shower and quickly dressed before attaching Izzy's leash to her collar and hurrying downstairs. I wanted to relieve Geneviève from baby duty as soon as possible. Normally I'd have walked Izzy down the street and collected some *pains aux chocolat* and a couple of coffees but I knew Geneviève would have coffee on.

When I knocked on her door she was ready for me with two steaming cups of freshly brewed coffee. I swear I could smell it through the thick oaken door to her apartment. As soon as I stepped across the threshold I heard Robbie squeal as he toddled over to both me and Izzy. He reached Izzy first and shrieked with pleasure as she went to work cleaning his breakfast off his face with her tongue.

I dropped her leash and sat down on the couch with my coffee.

"I'm sorry," I said. "I wanted to get here before he woke up."

"Monsieur Robbie is an early riser," Geneviève said cheerfully, watching Robbie play with Izzy.

As much as I sometimes regretted defaulting to Geneviève for childcare, I reminded myself that she had no grandchildren. Caring for Robbie gave her something she wouldn't otherwise have.

That's what I keep telling myself anyway.

I sipped my coffee and began to feel the cobwebs of my spotty night's sleep begin to break up. I pulled out my phone and dialed the French criminal courts again while Geneviève went into the kitchen. By the time she came back into the living room, I had the name of the attorney who'd been assigned to Gigi's case.

"Did you know that over here the courts just appoint someone to defend a person who can't afford their own counsel?" I said. "And it's usually someone who has just graduated from law school."

"Oh?" Geneviève said, setting a plate down with little pots of butter and jam. She handed a piece of bread to Robbie and also Izzy, both of whom swarmed the coffee table.

I turned my phone around so she could see the photo of Pierre Berger. Geneviève studied the picture and frowned before looking at me.

"He is young," she said.

"Yeah. He just passed his law examination to become an *avocat*. Totally inexperienced."

"That is not good."

"It doesn't make sense," I said. "This is the *Eiffel Tower*. There should be hundreds of lawyers wanting a piece of this."

"Perhaps nobody wants a piece of anything that would involve defending the woman who would defame the Iron Lady like this," Geneviève said.

"Yeah, maybe."

"Do you know anything about Gigi's family?"

"No. I left a message for Laura Murphy last night but she hasn't gotten back to me."

"What will you do now?"

I sighed and took a piece of bread and began to spread jam on it.

"First I'll try to get in to see Pierre Berger," I said. "Then I'll get a hold of any family Gigi has to see how supportive they intend on being."

"It is a terrible thing," Geneviève said.

I glanced at the TV set. "Is there more news?"

"Nothing we don't know," Geneviève said. "A young man was pushed to his death from the top of the Eiffel Tower."

"So they're saying he was pushed? They're not suggesting he jumped?"

"No, *chérie. Pushed.* And his girlfriend is in custody."

We were quiet for a moment.

"What now?" she pressed.

I wiped my fingers on the napkin on the table and gave her my most confident smile.

"First," I said. "I think Robbie and I need to make a visit to one of Paris's most famous landmarks."

8

The Eiffel Tower is 980 feet high and will always be the singular most historic punctuation that defines Paris. Visited by more than six million tourists a year, it is the quintessential symbol of the city's style, its strength, and its mystique.

Today it was lashed with spitting snow and an icy breeze and festooned by fluttering blue and white police crime tape on the second level, announcing to the world that something terrible had happened there.

In spite of the ongoing police presence I was able to buy a ticket and go to the top floor with Robbie in his stroller.

The view from the top was of course stunning, showing Quai Branly boulevard, the river, and an unimpeded view of the city of Paris itself. I couldn't help remembering the last time I'd stood here—with Bob—years before our last fateful visit to Paris together.

The few news reports that I'd read on the incident said that Jean-Bernard had fallen through a waist-high railing on the second level of the tower onto the roof of the Altitude 95 restaurant on the first tier.

I stood shivering and unprotected as the cold chill rolled off the river and the Avenue Gustave Eiffel and looked up on my phone the details of the recent work on the famous structure. A thirty-five million euro security upgrade had started in 2016 after the series of attacks by Islamic militants had left more than two hundred and forty people dead across the city.

The article I read reported that the bulletproof glass surrounding the tower was nearly three inches thick with metal barriers made up of curved prongs that protected the structure on the sides that faced the Seine. The three-meter-high glass and metal barriers added to the tower were said to be strong enough to stop a truck on a suicide mission.

I looked sadly at the fluttering crime scene tape.

But clearly not a young man in the prime of his life.

It was too cold to stay on the tower for long. Once I came down to the ground again, I went in search of the nearest café. As I walked away I noted that there seemed to be more guards than usual strolling the base of the tower. Interestingly, I didn't see a CSI team processing the scene. I was sure that if Adele had worked the scene last night she would be sleeping in this morning.

I hated to wake her but I needed answers.

I settled into a nearby café with a decent view of the tower and ordered a hot chocolate and unwrapped the cookie it came with for Robbie.

I called Adele.

"I thought I'd hear from you," she said groggily.

"You worked the Eiffel Tower scene last night, didn't you?" I asked.

She yawned. "*Oui*. And I'm working in the lab today so I can't meet with you."

"But you can tell me what you found out."

"I shouldn't."

"They arrested Gigi for his murder," I said.

"I know, Claire."

"Was he really pushed?"

"All we know at this point is that he fell," she said tiredly. "If you're asking if there were handprints on the back of his jacket—?"

I sighed heavily to indicate I didn't appreciate her sarcasm.

"The newspapers say he fell on top of the restaurant?" I prodded.

"*Oui.* Altitude 95. I heard the diners heard the loud crash, looked up at the ceiling, and continued to eat."

Well, this is France after all. Eating is important here.

"So is that where you examined the body?" I asked.

"My team didn't examine the body. At least not closely. That's the ME's job," she pointed out.

"What about the forensics?" I asked.

"Are you asking if we found Gigi's DNA on the body? I don't know since we only just bagged and collected it last night and nothing has been analyzed but Gigi and the victim were dating so he's probably covered in her DNA."

"Drugs? Alcohol?"

"I don't know, Claire. They're doing the autopsy today."

"You'll keep me informed?"

"You know I will," Adele said through another yawn.

After hanging up with her, I ordered a vanilla macaron for Robbie although I could see he was already nodding off in his stroller, and called Pierre Berger.

"Berger," he answered his voice sounding hurried and young.

I wasn't surprised that he answered his own phone. He was probably the lowest on the hierarchy totem pole in his practice of defense lawyers.

Unless worse, he was a one-man shop.

"Hello. My name is Claire Baskerville," I said. "I am Gigi Rozen's employer calling to talk to you about her case. Do you have time to meet with me today?"

"Who are you?"

I literally felt my blood pressure begin to jack up.

"I am someone interested in helping you defend Gigi Rozen," I said slowly and deliberately. "Is she your client? Did I get that wrong?"

"You are talking about the one who pushed the guy off the Eiffel Tower?"

"Has she confessed?" I asked coldly.

"No, she says she didn't push him. But five people say different."

"Can you tell me how it was physically possible for this to have happened? Because I just walked around the tower. There are thick protective walls up everywhere."

"They think it was a loose panel. A work order got misplaced."

At first I didn't think I heard him correctly. Was he telling me that Gigi and Jean-Bernard just happened to be standing by the one weak spot in the whole tower which allowed him to fall to his death?

"A loose panel," I clarified. "So it was an accident?"

"Well, no. Like I said, Mademoiselle Rozen was seen pushing him."

"But you just said the panel gave way! Wouldn't Gigi have had every reason to believe the panel would hold?"

"I don't know what she believed."

"But if it was an accident due to a loose panel that's not murder!"

"Frankly it's whatever the police say it is."

This I knew was unfortunately very true. The facts of any particular case often came down to case clearance rates—especially when that case involved something as iconically famous as the Eiffel Tower. News had already spread around the world about the murder—*the first ever at the Eiffel Tower!* I could see how Detective Muller would be under considerable pressure to wrap this case up as tightly and as quickly as possible.

"Were there any CCTV cameras near the incident?" I asked.

"No, but as I said *there were eyewitnesses*. The police report said there are five, plus two of them said they saw Mademoiselle Rozen and the victim arguing before she pushed him."

I heard paper rustling over the phone as Berger was obviously looking at a page of notes.

"They said the two—and I quote—'*were violently arguing moments before the assault.*' End Quote."

"How do they know they were arguing?" I said indignantly. "The French have conversations about where to go to lunch that to people from other cultures sounds like they're about to punch each other out. Was it tourists who said they were arguing?"

"The eyewitnesses also stated they saw the victim slap Mademoiselle Rozen," Berger said. "I think hitting someone pretty much says *argument* in any language."

"Jean-Bernard struck her?"

"*Oui*. At which point Gigi said something like '*the hell with you!*' And pushed him. And over he went. Listen, I must go but I will call you back about that meeting."

He hung up and I sat there staring at my phone and feeling like the world was rushing by me.

"Gaga?"

I looked up and saw Robbie watching me, wide awake now. "Gaga" was what he called Gigi. He looked around as if eager to see her any moment in the crowd inside the café and I felt a gut punch at the look on his face.

"No Gaga," I said to him, pushing another cookie toward him and trying to smile.

9

I took my time getting back home after that.

The sun came out briefly on our walk home and since Robbie was happily snoozing in his stroller and Izzy was now riding in it too, I decided to allow myself the respite of a walk through Parc Monceau.

One of the things I like best about Parc Monceau, aside from the fact that it's just a few convenient blocks from my apartment, is that it can literally be anything you're in the mood for.

Featuring all the manicured grace of a perfect French garden with green stretches of lawn and tumbling hedges of colorful flowers, it never fails to soothe or energize—depending on what you're in need of. Even on a frozen January day without its flowers, carousel, ice cream kiosks or frolicking children it's still a pleasure trove of arching bridges over ice-glazed ponds. Just magical.

I settled on a bench, made sure Robbie and Izzy were wrapped up snugly in the stroller and put another call into the police station to ask to see or at least be able to speak with Gigi.

I was told to leave a message and Capitaine Muller's administrative assistant would get back with me.

Then I called Pierre Berger back to set up a time for that meeting we'd talked about but I got his voice mail. I left a message telling him I'd really like to be able to see Gigi as soon as possible if he could help arrange it.

I tried to temper my inevitable disappointment. But right about when I realized that sitting in the park wasn't improving my mood after all, I got up and pushed the stroller toward the park exit and the direction of another Indian take-out place and home.

That night after dinner Geneviève popped upstairs to see how I was doing. I told her how I'd spent my day and what I'd learned, which wasn't much and she did her usual thing of acting like she knew me better than I know myself.

"You will feel better when you get some answers," she said.

"No one will talk to me," I said.

She patted my arm and smiled knowingly.

"You will not be able to rest until you find out the truth of what happened."

"Maybe," I said, feeling a creeping wave of frustration when I realized she was probably right.

"Just look into it a little bit more. People will open up. They always do. After all, Gigi says she didn't do it."

"They all say that."

"I'm sure they do. But you will not rest until you find out the truth."

After she left and after Robbie had finally gone down I settled onto the couch in my cashmere sweatpants and thick socks, with Izzy by my hip as usual. I intended to look up more financials on the husband of one of my clients or at least check out the new Netflix movie I'd been reading about on my Facebook feed when my phone rang. It was Laura finally calling me back.

"Hey Laura," I said, picking up.

"I am sorry it took me so long," she said, her voice sounding jagged like she'd been crying, something I found difficult to visualize. Laura Murphy was as tough as they come. She belonged back in the days when broads and dames wore red lipstick and spit bullets.

"Are you okay?" I asked her.

"Of course," she said tersely. "Have you been able to see Gigi?"

"No," I said. "Family only. I assume she has family somewhere?"

"She does. They're elderly and live in Bayeux. They don't drive and they have no money."

"So they can't help with hiring a decent lawyer?"

"No, but the Expat group has a fund that can help. It won't be enough to buy her an Allen Durshowitz, but it'll be better than whoever the court appoints. Do you know who that is?"

I filled her in on Berger's background.

"I'm not sure what else we can do for the girl," Laura said. "Did you know she was having problems with her boyfriend?"

There was more than a tinge of reproach in her voice as if I should have known my au pair was thinking about flinging someone off the Eiffel Tower.

"No," I said, my mouth set in a firm line against her accusation. It wouldn't help to bicker with Laura. If she wanted to blame me for this mess, so be it.

"It's a shame her folks are so far away," I said. "Because I'm pretty sure the cops aren't going to let me fill in for them."

"It is what it is," Laura said.

Don't you hate it when people say that? Or is it just me?

"In other news," Laura said, "I reached out to Haley's

parents and she's available to come by to meet Robbie tomorrow."

"Who?"

"As I said, she's a bit of an acquired taste but I haven't heard any complaints about how she is with the kids."

"Oh, right. Yes, fine."

After that we signed off. But before I could sink back into the couch and wonder if I had the energy to look up my client's husband's financials, my phone rang again. When I answered I heard a recorded voice.

"Will you accept a call from an inmate of the Paris detention center?"

I sat up straight.

"Yes, of course," I said. "Gigi? Is that you?"

After a moment there was a hissing sound on the line and then Gigi's voice.

"Claire? Are you there?"

"Oh, Gigi! I'm so glad to hear your voice!"

"Claire," she said, tearfully. "Do you know what is happening?"

"Have you talked to your lawyer yet?"

"I have not talked to anyone except a horrible detective." She broke down and began to cry in earnest.

"Gigi, listen to me," I said. "Please don't talk to anyone without your lawyer present."

"I am so afraid, Claire. What can I do? Jean-Bernard was a monster! I thought he was getting better, *mais non!*"

"Why didn't you tell someone?"

I felt a flash of fury that Gigi would allow Robbie to be anywhere near a man she knew was violent.

"How could I? It would be so embarrassing!" Gigi said.

"Eyewitnesses said you pushed him," I said.

"They're lying!"

"There's five of them, Gigi. They all say they saw you push

him."

"I don't care if all of Paris says so! They're lying!"

"Okay, okay. Calm down."

"You will help me, Claire? Please!"

"Of course, Gigi. I'll do whatever I can."

An hour later I finally went to bed, having accomplished exactly nothing. My call with Gigi only lasted a few seconds longer before we were cut off and after that I was in no mood for television or Internet research. I made myself a very small whiskey—something I rarely do. After checking on Robbie, I tucked myself up into bed, socks and all, with Izzy.

I think I knew before I took my first sip of whiskey that I was going to call him. Maybe I'd known all along, as the effects of the events of the day built up inside me one frustrating and debilitating disappointment after another, until I felt I *deserved* to pick up the phone and call him.

He answered on the second ring which made me think he wanted to hear from me. Surely he knew it was me when he picked up.

But that didn't mean he was happy about it.

"Why are you calling, Claire?"

His voice was so familiar, so dear, and so sad. I don't know what I was thinking, maybe that after seven months of mourning his dead wife and blaming me for it he'd be ready to renew his friendship with me. Maybe I thought we'd pick up again as if nothing had happened. Him in Nice, me in Paris. And a whole wide countryside of pain between us.

"My au pair is in trouble," I said. "The Eiffel Tower killing was her boyfriend."

There was a pause on the line and I tried to imagine Jean-Marc wrestling with himself. He would have to be interested in the case, surely. He would have to at least be curious.

All of a sudden it occurred to me that he might not be alone.

"I can't do anything from down here," he said finally. "You know that."

Maybe I just wanted to hear your voice. Maybe that's enough.

"I'm sorry," I said.

"Just...don't call again. Please."

He hung up.

I set my phone down on the nightstand and, fighting the excruciating throb of Jean-Marc's rejection, pulled Izzy into my arms.

Looks like I really am all on my own after all.

10

The next morning, I felt better. Because I'd slept so poorly the night before, I'd made up for it last night and had slept soundly in spite of my phone call with Jean-Marc.

I went through the motions of dressing Robbie and feeding him, and then making my coffee—*ever notice how as caretakers our needs are always pushed to the back of the queue?*—before plopping him in his playpen to await the arrival of Haley. I exchanged texts with Adele to arrange to meet at Café de Flore for lunch.

As I watched Robbie roam the parameter of his playpen before settling down to gnaw on some rubber blocks while Raffi music played on the HomePod, I made a list of everything I needed to do if I was truly going to try to help Gigi.

First and foremost, I needed to talk to her face to face. I needed to hear her version of what happened. Then I needed to reach out to Gigi's parents to get permission to work as proxy for them. I made a mental note to see if Berger could help me set that up.

I turned on the TV to see if there was any news coverage of

the Eiffel Tower accident and was surprised and little concerned to see that not only did Robbie turn his head in the direction of the TV, he stood up and pressed himself against the bars to see the screen better.

The blonde female anchor on the news program showed a picture of the Eiffel Tower and the restaurant Altitude 95 bedecked in blue and white crime scene tape.

"*...the victim was pushed over the top of the third platform to his death by his wife, a Madame Gigi Rozen...*" the cheerful newscaster said. "*The couple was witnessed arguing just seconds before Madame Rozen threw her husband off the side of our magnificent national treasure. Inside sources say the two had been going through fertility treatments and Madame Rozen had become discouraged at the lack of results in that regard.*"

Her fellow news anchor, a middle-aged man with a shaved head, piped up:

"Maybe it's a good thing some people can't become parents!"

His partner nodded. "*Exactement*, Ronald," she said solemnly.

I snapped off the set, so angry I felt like throwing the remote control across the room. Where do they get their information? Is it true that the media just makes things up if they can't get the facts? Jean-Bernard and Gigi weren't married! And it was ludicrous to believe they we're undergoing fertility treatments!

But it didn't matter if it was true or not. Here was a semi-respected news program stating that Gigi had killed Jean-Bernard and giving her motive for doing so! How was Gigi going to get a fair trial now? These people had publicly painted her as France's enemy and the desecrator of its most sacred national monument!

A tentative tap at the front door pulled me from my silent tirade and I realized it must be the babysitter Haley. Izzy ran to the door ahead of me, yipping helpfully in case I'd somehow gone deaf and wasn't aware there was someone at the door.

I gathered up my notes and turned them face down before going to Robbie and scooping him up for the formal meet and greet.

I have to say I'm not sure I knew what to expect with Haley, especially after Laura made such a fuss about what an odd duck she was and not to everyone's liking. When I opened the door, I found a slim, serious-faced girl-child with short black hair, kohl-rimmed eyes and a pierced nose. She didn't smile when I greeted her, but her eyes went right to Robbie and I have to say I thought that was a good sign.

"Come in," I said, stepping out of the way and setting Robbie down on his feet. "You must be Haley."

Haley stepped into the room and glanced around before turning to look at Robbie again.

"I'm Mrs. Baskerville," I said. "And this is Robbie."

Haley knelt by Robbie and touched him on the chest as if she was about to push him over.

"Hello, little man," she said in a husky voice.

Robbie grinned at her and pushed her with both his pudgy hands, which made Izzy bark and Haley laugh.

When the girl smiled I felt something in me relax. She wasn't pretty, but her smile opened up something agreeable in her face. Robbie must have thought so too, because when Haley held out her arms to him, he instantly went to her.

Haley patted him on the back and looked around the apartment again.

"Nice place," she said, that deep voice a surprise from someone so young.

"Thank you," I said as I turned to get Izzy's leash and the stroller I'd parked in the kitchen. "Why don't we go for a walk to get to know each other better?"

11

By the time I was watching Haley walk away from the park bench where we'd walked to from my apartment I felt like I'd found out the main things about her that I needed to know.

I learned that she liked dogs and perhaps more importantly they liked her. Or at least Izzy did. I learned that she had no brothers or sisters, she was a sophomore at the American School but hated school, she wasn't wild about the French and she missed her friends back in the States.

I asked her how long she'd been in France.

"Forever," she said as we sat on a park bench and watched some children play in a cold frosted field across from us. "But it's only been a couple months. Dad says we're here for at least three years."

"That must seem like a long time if you're not sure you like it here," I said.

She looked at me and made a face.

"Are you a psychologist?" she asked.

Her question made me wonder if she had had much personal experience with psychologists.

"No," I said. "I just know how it feels not to fit in."

She snorted but was either too polite or too disinterested to disagree with me.

In any case, the biggest question about Haley was how she got along with Robbie and that was answered immediately by Robbie's unadulterated acceptance of her. She wouldn't be his au pair. She wouldn't move in. She'd just be his on again off again babysitter. And for that she was fine.

After we agreed on a schedule and compensation she headed off. I was impressed that she took the time to say goodbye to both Robbie and Izzy before she left.

Yes, there was definitely something about her. I could see how she would set some people off. That nose ring for one thing. I couldn't see it lasting too long with Robbie's little grabby hands or even Izzy whose energetic kisses could get a little bitey.

I arrived early at the café where I was to meet Adele and found a good table where I positioned Robbie's stroller away from other diners so they weren't tripping over him. I ordered a hot mulled wine while I waited.

I hadn't gotten very far in my outline of Gigi's case this morning before Haley came but I decided it didn't matter. At this point I knew so much less than what I needed to know that I could just let Adele talk and fill in all the blanks later.

I put another call into Pierre Berger who still hadn't called me back after the two calls I'd made to him yesterday. That bothered me. It meant he wasn't taking me seriously. I hope that didn't mean he wasn't taking the case seriously.

"Hello," he said.

"Hello, Monsieur Berger," I said primly. "This is Claire Baskerville calling again. I was wondering if you'd had a chance to talk with Gigi yet?"

"Not yet, Madame," he said patiently. "My office is very busy."

"I'm sure it is," I said. "But I can't imagine too many other cases are as internationally distinguished as this one. It's being talked about all over the world."

Berger didn't seem swayed by my point.

"I have many other important cases," he said.

"Look," I said firmly. "I need you to get me in to see Gigi. Can you do that?"

"What is your relationship with her?"

"I'm her aunt on her mother's side," I said. "And I need the names of the five eyewitnesses who said they saw her push her boyfriend off the Eiffel Tower."

"What?"

"I know you heard me, Monsieur Berger. I too have a busy schedule but I do know that every defendant is entitled to face her accusers and since these people are accusing my niece of—"

"Yes, yes," he said. "I will text the names to you."

"I can wait if you like," I said, determined not to be put off.

He sighed and I heard him talk to someone on his end which frankly surprised me. I didn't think he was a big enough fish to rate an assistant.

"Anything else?" he said.

If he thought I was getting off the phone before I got those names, he didn't know me yet.

"I need to meet with you," I said.

"Yes, okay," he said. "How about...tomorrow at sixteen hundred hours?"

I frowned at Robbie who was already yawning. That was not a great time for me—or rather for Robbie. He would be in the process of trying to nap which would then impact his night-time sleep schedule. No, four o'clock any day was not good for me. At all.

"Fine," I said. "Sixteen-hundred hours. Your office? By the way, I'm still waiting on those names, Monsieur Berger. You wouldn't happen to have phone numbers to go with them, would you?"

Tracking down phone numbers and addresses was not a problem for me. In fact it was literally what I did for a living every single day of my life. But still, it never hurts to try to lighten the load.

By the time I saw Adele striding down the boulevard Saint-Germain toward our café I had all five names of the eyewitnesses and at least a vague sense that I was finally, possibly, *maybe* getting somewhere.

Adele was wearing jeans and a black leather jacket with Prada motorcycle boots that must have cost her a month's salary. Maybe more. She had dark hair and eyes which were fringed in thick lashes which hinted at a Middle Eastern background.

"Bonjour, Claire!" she said and kissed me on both cheeks before seating herself to address Robbie with a cuddle and another set of *baisers*. "Oh, he is growing so big! Soon he will be pushing *you* in the stroller!"

"Ha ha," I said. "Very funny. Let's order so we can talk." I handed her the menu.

I knew Adele. She was French and would need a moment to study the menu in order to give it exactly the right consideration she felt it deserved. To me it was all delicious. My palate hadn't yet developed to the point where I was very discerning. I remember many a meal when Jean-Marc had teased me about that.

The waiter came and took our orders for cheese and smoked ham in puff pastry and two glasses of Sauterne.

"You look good," I said.

"He wasn't worth the tears," Adele said with a shrug.

"Not if he cheated on you."

"I don't want to talk about Michel," she said, crossing her arms across her chest. "Have you spoken to Gigi?"

"Only briefly by phone. I'm still trying to get in to see her."

"What about her attorney? Is he any good?"

"I don't know. He's inexperienced. We're supposed to meet but he keeps putting me off."

"That's not good," she said frowning. "Gigi needs someone top drawer. The cops want to put this one to bed fast."

"What do you know about the new detective? Muller?"

"He's a swine. *Woman-hater* is the word around the *Préfecture*."

I had to admit that didn't surprise me. Not just because of the coarse way he'd treated me the one time I'd met him. But because the woman who'd had his position before Jean-Marc hadn't done much to encourage men to view women with respect. In fact, the exact opposite.

"What about Gigi's family? Can they help her?" she asked.

I shook my head. "As I understand it, they have no money. What about you? Do you have any information about the case you can share?"

"I shouldn't share any of what I know," Adele said as the waiter set down our plates of stuffed puff pastry. Like most French people, Adele instantly became fixated on her meal. I would have to wait until after at least the first few forkfuls before I could regain her attention.

"What did you learn from the autopsy?" I asked.

I knew of course that Adele wasn't anywhere near the medical examiner's office when the autopsy was being performed. But she was in the general vicinity and forensic techs tended to talk among themselves.

"He had drugs in his system," she said as she reached for a bottle of Badoit.

"What kind of drugs?"

"I don't have that information yet. But it explains why he

went over the edge so easily," she said. "It wouldn't have taken much. He was probably pretty unsteady on his feet by then."

"Why would he take drugs to spend the day sightseeing?" I asked.

"Maybe he didn't knowingly take the drugs," Adele said with a raised eyebrow.

My eyes widened in surprise.

"Does the ME think someone drugged him?" I asked.

"It's not his job to think that," Adele said. "He just knows what was in his system. It's up to the detectives to figure out why."

"Or not to even bother," I said with mounting frustrating. "They already have their suspect. Why should they investigate further?"

"*Exactement.*"

I thought about this for a moment and found myself feeling both better and worse with the information about the drugs. On the one hand, it made it easier to believe that Gigi had not meant to push Jean-Bernard over the side. On the other hand, of course she could have been the one who drugged him.

"Have you heard about the videos?" Adele asked, cutting into her pastry.

I frowned. "What videos?"

"Videos of the victim hitting Gigi."

"I thought there were no videos on the tower level that they were on."

"There aren't. These are from other days, other locations. One was taken in the hallway of Jean-Bernard's apartment building and the other was outside a bar."

Adele scrolled on her phone and handed it to me. I watched the videos, grainy and out of focus but undeniably Gigi and Jean-Bernard. I watched him grab her by the hair in one video and slap her and put his hands around her throat in the other.

My stomach twisted as I watched. "Bastard," I breathed.

"I'll send you the links," Adele said, taking her phone back. "But the prosecution has them and they intend to prove that these speak to Gigi's motive."

"Of course," I agreed dismally.

I glanced at Robbie as he slept in his stroller, the winter breeze gently ruffling the hair around his face.

Things were not looking good for his beloved Gaga.

Not at all.

12

That night I settled Robbie down earlier than usual so I could have some part of the evening to myself and get some work done. Until I could see Gigi or talk to her lawyer or interview the eyewitnesses to the crime, there wasn't really that much I could do. But I could at least try to clear my desk of my existing caseload.

I downloaded the photos I'd taken of my client's cheating spouse, added my own thoughts of what I thought I'd seen—pretty self-explanatory and not at all savory—and told her I would be happy to continue surveillance once my schedule opened back up. And then invoiced her.

Then I took a glass of Merlot to the couch and called Laura.

"I thought I'd hear from you today," she said.

"I've made arrangements with Haley for two afternoons a week after school," I said. "And three full days. She does some kind of independent study at school so she can do full days. She's starting tomorrow."

There was a pause on the line before Laura spoke again.

"Well, you do surprise me," she said. "I'll talk to her parents in case Haley hasn't shared the details with them."

After disconnecting with her I went through all my other open cases and either put them on hold or quickly wrapped them up.

I had the feeling that something was going to happen soon with Gigi's case and I would need every bit of my undivided concentration to deal with it.

I put another call in to Berger to confirm our four o'clock meeting tomorrow but my call went to his voicemail. I sat on the couch with my empty wine glass and a feeling of general failure, as if business was not at all finished but I didn't know what else to do.

When my phone rang, I was delighted to see that it was Catherine calling.

When my daughter had gone back to the States last August there had definitely been discord between us. It had been six months and we were just now beginning to mend the chilly breach that had been created.

"Hey, Mom," she said. "You busy?"

"Not particularly," I said. "I'm so glad you called. Everything okay there?"

"Yes, everything is fine. Cameron got an award in his science class. He'll be sending it to you via Facebook tomorrow."

"Tell him I'm proud of him. What about you? How's work?"

Catherine worked as a medical receptionist at a local clinic in Jacksonville, Florida. She had a degree in Library Science but because she wanted to stay in Jacksonville where Todd worked, she hadn't been able to find something in her field. I knew this was a cause of frustration for her. And I also know I was probably the last person she would ever admit that to.

"It's good," she said. "Monotonous but the money spends. How's Robbie?"

"He's trying to rush the developmental charts," I said. "Toddling, walking, falling, grabbing. I can't keep up with him."

"But Gigi is helping?"

I hesitated. I didn't want to get into a whole big discussion of what was happening with Gigi. This was shaky ground for me and Catherine since Catherine tended to feel guilty about not taking Robbie. Any childcare problem I related to her inevitably made her feel worse about her decision to return to the States without him.

"Gigi took another job," I said. "I've got a young American teenager now. Robbie likes her a lot."

"Oh. Well, that's good."

There was a hesitation on the line which made me wonder if there was a specific reason for why Catherine had called me tonight. If she was having trouble with Todd, she'd likely not share that with me. But I was her mother. If she had a problem, she would at least reach out to me like she had tonight. Even if she didn't truly believe she needed to.

Just before I was about to try to nudge her in the direction of opening up to me, there was a loud knock on my apartment door. Izzy barked and ran to the door. I froze, since with my building's security system people off the street shouldn't be able to get to my apartment door.

"Hey," I said, "I've got someone at the door. Can I call you back?"

"No need," she said. "I was just checking in."

"Okay, well, give Cam a kiss for me," I said. "And take care of yourself, sweetie."

"Will do, Mom."

The knock came again on the door, more insistent this time, and I felt a tremble of apprehension, again wondering who could possibly be at my door.

I kept my phone in my hand and joined Izzy at the door. I'd had a peep hole installed last fall and was grateful now that I had. A shadowy figure stood outside, his face hidden from me.

"Yes?" I said through the door. "Who is it?"

The face of the individual outside looked up. I could now see it was a young woman on my threshold.

"Misou Bordeaux," she said, "from Ajax delivery services." She held up a package.

I hesitated and then unlocked the deadbolt and opened the door.

Instantly, the girl took a step back with the parcel in one hand and thrust a large envelope at me instead with the other.

"*Merci*, Madame," she said cheerfully. "You have been served."

13

I sat at the dining room table with the letter open on the table and a glass of brandy beside it.

The document was very straightforward. I was being asked to attend a meeting with Joelle Lapin, my ex-sort-of step-mother and her lawyer on the subject of the legality of my having Robbie live with me. The way the "summons"—and I was under no illusion that this was anything else—was worded made it difficult to understand what my options were. Biting my lip I photographed the document and sent it to my lawyer.

I know that Joelle felt she had gotten cheated out of what she believed was rightfully hers. French inheritance law is very stringent about the rule that prioritizes *children* to inherit, not widows. The fact was, Joelle shouldn't have expected to inherit when my father died. She knew better.

But when she found out that I was not Claude's biological child, she'd made the somewhat logical leap to believing that that meant he was heirless, making her first in line for his money. And then Claude made it clear in his will that, biological child or not, he wanted me to inherit. So that was that.

Just not as far as Joelle was concerned.

The way I saw it, this latest gambit of hers couldn't really benefit her in any way financially. It was only a way to hurt me. The summons stated only that the child Robert Purdue was not believed to be my legal ward nor was I qualified to adopt him and unless a relative was found who could take him in the interim, he should be surrendered immediately to social services.

Pretty scary stuff and I had no idea how real the threat was. In my mind it was the sort of scheme you read about in fairy tales where the wicked witch conspires to take the hapless orphan away from his loving champion.

For no other reason than rancor and spite.

It's true I'd been having some trouble getting my guardianship of Robbie confirmed. I'm over sixty years old for one thing and I came to France chased by a significant number of creditors—thanks to my late husband's reckless spending. What responsible social services agency would hand over a baby to an elderly, non blood-related guardian?

So yes, there'd been some road bumps. And possibly because the whole process was so interminable I'd dragged my feet on getting all my i's properly dotted. I stared at the document in front of me, my vision momentarily blurred by tears.

But the worst of it? The worst of it was how well Joelle knew me. Even though I'd always believed she didn't know me at all. One thing she did know was how important Robbie was to me.

"Why does she hate you so, *chérie*?" Geneviève asked on the phone.

I'd called her as soon as I opened the envelope and realized what it was. I knew she couldn't really do anything to help but I felt better sharing the problem with her.

"I'm pretty sure she wasn't loved as a child," I said, trying to force myself not to overreact.

"What will you do?"

"I don't know. Talk to my lawyer, I guess."

"Joelle cannot take him from you, *chérie*. I'm sure the French courts would not allow it."

She had a lot more confidence in the French courts than I did.

"Anyone can see that Robbie belongs with you," she said. "We will fight to make them see it."

"Thanks, Geneviève. You're right. We'll make them see he needs to be with me."

"Were you able to talk to Gigi's lawyer?"

"No. I'm seeing him tomorrow."

"What about Adele? Did you talk with her?"

"I did but it wasn't very encouraging. There are videos out there showing that Gigi was abused by Jean-Bernard."

Geneviève sucked in a horrified breath.

"*Il etait un monstre!*" she said.

"I know," I said, rubbing a place between my eyes in an attempt to forestall the headache I could feel coming on.

"*Chérie*, will you not call Jean-Marc? I am sure he could give you good advice."

"I did call him, Geneviève," I said wearily. "He wants nothing to do with me."

"He is upset."

"Yeah, well, I'm a little upset too."

"Get some rest, *chérie*. Your plate has become too full. You need all your strength."

I felt a spasm of helplessness as I glanced at Robbie's bedroom door.

If I lose him, I don't know what I'll do.

"You have me," Geneviève said. "And Adele. And together we are *formidable, n'est-ce pas?*"

That made me smile. It was good to be reminded of how right she was.

～

The next morning Haley was over early to watch Robbie so I could head downtown for a meeting I'd been able to set up with Detective Muller.

Unlike last time where I waited two hours in the hallway only to have Capitaine Muller appear and talk to me briefly before asking me to leave, I arrived and was immediately taken down the hall to a small waiting room where an elderly couple waited, both of them staring at the floor in what looked like complete, undiluted misery.

I was reminded of how much unhappiness there was in the world—and most of it could be found in hospitals and police stations.

I had no sooner sat down when Muller came through the door and abruptly signaled for me to follow him. The fact that he hadn't bothered greeting me was a very big tell on his part. Personally, I don't like to reveal my hand so soon but I suppose Muller thought it expedient to let me know from the start what an ass he intended to be.

I followed him to a door with his name scrawled on a piece of paper and taped to it.

I stepped into his office, grateful that it wasn't the one that Jean-Marc had used when he was in Muller's position last year. But honestly all the offices looked very similar. Desk, visitors chair, dead plant.

"What can I do for you, Madame?"

You have to understand that in France, deliberately not using my last name is a message of extreme disrespect. The only people you would call *Madame* without a last name would be shopkeepers whose last names you would not be expected to know. He was telling me in sledgehammer shorthand that he did not intend to help me. I didn't know if he was anti-American or if he knew my background enough to know that I could be a pest within police ranks. Or if there was some other reason for his behavior.

"I am working with the court-assigned public defender," I said, "on Gigi Rozen's case. It's imperative that I get in to see Mademoiselle Rozen as soon as possible."

"No," he said, his eyes focused on my breasts.

"No one has yet seen Mademoiselle Rozen," I said, grinding my teeth in irritation. "Not her family, not her attorney—"

"Her attorney is welcome to see the suspect whenever he makes an appointment with us," he said. "Her family has not asked."

"Her family does not live in Paris," I said. "It is a hardship for them to come."

He shrugged, his eyes still boring holes into the front of my coat.

"That is not the problem or responsibility of the Paris Police department," he said and then stood up. The interview was over.

"She is entitled to see her family," I said.

"Again. Noone is stopping them."

He picked up the handset of the landline and barked into it before waving to the door. By the time I stood up, the door opened and a young policeman was ready to escort me back to the waiting room.

I don't know what I expected. Most police detectives didn't want to do anything to jeopardize the case they were building against a suspect they had. It would've been hard enough to get in to see her even if I had been related but it was completely impossible since I wasn't. My only hope was through Berger.

Speaking of the devil, as I stepped outside the *préfecture* building, I received a text and saw that it was Berger. He was begging off our four o'clock meeting but was available to meet in his office if I could come immediately. I glanced at my watch and saw it was noon.

Annoyed because of how it would rearrange my day, I quickly called an Uber and walked to a nearby cross street.

While I waited for my ride I put a call in to Laura but it went to her voicemail.

I sent her a text instead.

<How much $$ can the expat fund come up with for Gigi?>

By the time I was settled into the back of my Uber and on the way to Le Marais and Berger's office, Laura texted me back.

<15K euros>

I sighed. That wasn't near enough for a top tier defense attorney. I plugged in the phone number of the attorney I'd researched the night before and called it.

When the receptionist answered, it was clear she was screening my call.

"Could you please tell Monsieur Sonet that I am calling on behalf of Gigi Rozen," I said briskly. "That's the young woman accused of murder at the Eiffel Tower."

I waited for nearly two full minutes before the woman came back on the line—never a good sign.

"Monsieur Sonet regrets he is unable to speak with you."

""Wait a minute! This is an international news incident! The media coverage alone will be massive!"

"One moment, Madame."

The woman again put me on hold. She came back a few seconds later. "Monsieur Sonet's retainer is twenty thousand euros," she said. "And four hundred euros per hour."

"Please tell Monsieur that it is imperative I speak with him," I said, forcing my voice not to become shrill. "I believe this case is a matter of international diplomacy."

The next thing I heard was a man's voice.

"Bonjour, Madame," he said. "This is Albert Sonet. I understand you are looking for defense representative for Mademoiselle Rozen?"

"Yes, that's right," I said, a wave of relief sifting through me.

"May I assume you are able to pay my retainer?"

I took in a long breath.

"I was hoping," I said, "that considering the circumstances of the case, you would consider doing the case either probono or..."

"Madame, let me stop you right there. While your desire to help is commendable, Mademoiselle Rozen is not a celebrity or a political luminary. If anything, she has been villainized by the media. I would of course be happy to defend Mademoiselle Rozen for my full fee as my secretary as already outlined to you. But I'm afraid without financial compensation, representing her could only hurt my reputation."

I felt a headache begin at the base of my skull as he continued to speak.

"It is only business, Madame. You are American. Surely you of all people understand that."

14

I was of course discouraged after my phone call with Sonet, which was followed by two other phone calls where the lawyers didn't even bother talking to me. I suppose I shouldn't have been surprised. I'm not sure what I had to offer these defense attorneys if I couldn't offer them their full fees. Which of course I couldn't.

I was stuck with Pierre Berger.

I marched to the front desk of his office and gave my name to the receptionist who instructed me to wait in the sparse, unadorned waiting room. It appeared that most of the lawyers in this building were not in practice together but had pooled their money to afford a common receptionist and a basic, frill-less waiting room.

Berger was indeed a one-man shop.

I didn't wait long. Only moments after I'd sat down, a young woman who looked more like a Lancôme representative than a legal assistant came out and asked me to follow her.

She led me down a long dingy hallway and stopped outside a door with a half glass pane and the words *P Berger* painted on it. She opened the door to reveal one desk, two chairs and two men inside.

"Ah, Madame Baskerville," the young man at the desk said as he stood up.

Pierre Berger was balding, slim and pink-faced. He wore thick glasses but his suit was well-fitted and looked new.

We shook hands.

"Bonjour, Monsieur Berger," I said and then glanced at the other man in the room.

"May I introduce Paolo Rozen?" Berger said waving a hand to the man. "Gigi's brother."

Paolo didn't bother to stand. His broad face was frozen in a scowl. While he wasn't wearing a suit as Berger was, his clothes were stylish. He wore tight jeans and a pink cashmere sweater knotted around his neck. A black puffy jacket lay on the seat next to him.

"I am happy to meet you," I said. "Gigi was in my employ when...when this happened."

Paolo barely nodded at me before turning away.

I was just telling Monsieur Rozen," Berger said reseating himself, "that I have not had a chance to talk with his sister since the preliminary hearing and have very little information to share."

My mouth dropped open in disbelief.

"When was the hearing?" I choked out.

"It was held the day after she was charged," he said.

I was about to rant indignantly about the fast-tracked hearing when I realized it didn't matter. It was done. I needed to move forward.

"Monsieur Berger," I said, taking a long calming breath. "I need to see Gigi as soon as it can be arranged. I have no idea how she is being treated or how—"

"Oh, she is fine, Madame, trust me," Berger said loftily. "The

Paris police take particular pride in their detainees, especially the women."

"I want *Gigi* to tell me she's fine," I said. "I want to see with my own eyes that she's fine."

"Perhaps that is how things are done in the US but I fear that is not the case here," Berger said with a shrug. "And as I was just telling Monsieur Rozen I am afraid I have an appearance in court in less than fifteen minutes."

"But we were supposed to be meeting!"

"Yes, and we will. In the meantime, you should know that the department of race relations has already met with Gigi and they found that—"

My skin literally tingled with fury.

"Gigi isn't black!" I said.

Is he truly confusing Gigi with another of his clients? Her white brother is sitting right in front of him! Is he a total moron?

Berger frowned and glanced down at his notes before giving up.

"I am sorry, Madame," he said. "I might be thinking of someone else. In any event I'm afraid I cannot stay and talk longer. Perhaps you and Monsieur Rozen can meet instead? Yes, I think that is a good idea. Now if you will excuse me."

Berger gathered up his briefcase, along with a half-eaten sandwich and his cell phone and, smiling regretfully, hurried out the door, leaving me standing there staring after him.

15

Paolo and I decided to take Berger up on his suggestion that we have lunch. The restaurant, just around the corner from Berger's office, was a classic *brasserie* with deeply recessed paneling and moldings and the waiters moved around the tables in starched shirts and long white aprons.

While I'd already eaten today, I had no trouble ordering another meal with Paolo. Although I must say in any other circumstances he would not be my first choice of dining companion.

He was sullen, resistant and resentful.

But he was also Gigi's brother and stood an even better chance than I did of getting in to see her. I wasn't sure what help he might be but I had the time I'd set aside to meet with Berger so I figured I might as well get to know him better.

I ordered the *pot-au-feu* and a glass of Burgundy while Paolo ordered the rabbit with a Merlot.

"When did you and Gigi come to Paris?" I asked as I handed the menu back to the waiter.

He frowned as if thinking.

"I came first," he said finally. "Ten years ago when I finished school."

"Oh? Where did you go to school?"

He appeared reluctant to answer me which immediately made me realize I would have to go on the Internet and find out who he was—and if what he told me today was the truth.

"Université de Strasbourg," he said.

"And then Gigi followed you to Paris?"

"*Oui.* When she finished school."

"I can't imagine how upset you must be. Did you know Jean-Bernard?"

"*Oui.* I knew him."

His face was unreadable, neither accommodating, angry or even sad.

"I wasn't sure how long Gigi and Jean-Bernard had been dating," I prompted.

I was trying to find out not just how long Gigi and Jean-Bernard had been together but if they'd known each other *before* they'd started dating.

"Do you know how they met?"

"*Non.* I know he worked at a nonprofit doing case work for the indigent."

"And Gigi was an au pair," I said. "Not much chance of them crossing paths unless Jean-Bernard had kids which I don't believe he did."

Paolo snorted.

"You said you knew him," I pressed. "And obviously didn't like him."

He didn't answer. We waited for the waiter to finish setting down our lunch plates.

"Did you know he hit Gigi?" I asked once the waiter had left.

"I knew," he said, rubbing the back of his neck and then pushing his plate away.

"That must have been very upsetting for you."

He gave me a sharp look as if he'd suddenly twigged to what I must be thinking. Specifically, that he'd known that the victim abused his sister and now the victim was conveniently dead.

Just when I was trying to think of a way to ask him where he was during the critical time, he did me the favor of telling me without my having to ask him.

"I was with my partner at the time," he said. "Nowhere near the Eiffel Tower."

I nodded.

Except of course the real killer was whoever had drugged Jean-Bernard.

And that person didn't need to be anywhere near the Eiffel Tower.

16

fter my lunch with Paolo, which frankly yielded very little and was about as unpleasant a forty minutes as I've spent in a long time, I stayed at the table after he left and ordered a coffee and a chocolate éclair and checked in with Haley.

"He's napping," she said.

"Okay, that's good."

On the one hand I appreciated Haley's commitment to just-the-facts but a little embellishment might have gone a long way to soothe what I've already determined was a burgeoning pathology on my part.

"Is that all?" she asked when I didn't hang up.

"I was wondering if you were free to stay for dinner tonight," I said, just thinking of it. "I'll pay you for the time, of course."

"Sure. Okay."

"Great. I'll be home in a couple of hours."

She disconnected without saying goodbye, although, in her defense, it was clear we were winding up the conversation. But still, I was starting to see what Laura said about the girl being odd.

As I sipped my coffee I stared out onto a side street off the café. It looked like a Christmas postcard all coated with snow. For some reason it hadn't gotten muddy and ugly on this street. As I gazed out the window it occurred to me that the address for one set of eyewitnesses that Berger had given me wasn't too far away.

I called up their address on GoogleMaps to confirm. In fact, if I went by way of the Pont de Bir-Hakeim, it was even sort of on my way home.

Deciding that talking to the eyewitnesses would go a long way toward making me feel as if my day wasn't a total loss, I finished my pastry and signaled the waiter for the bill. While I waited for him to deign to recognize me, I saw I'd missed a call from my personal attorney, Sabine Garnier.

I called her back.

"Hey, Sabine," I said. "So what did you find out? Are things as bad as I thought?"

"Bonjour, Claire," Sabine said. "Possibly a little bit worse."

I swallowed hard and cursed myself for putting even the slightest positive spin on the situation.

"So what's going on?" I asked.

"It appears your stepmother has found a technicality in your quest to adopt Robbie."

"What does that mean?" I asked, feeling my blood pressure begin to ratchet up.

"It will take some research on my part—or rather my assistants'—but I fear this may be more involved than just a few papers that were not correctly filed."

"Okay. What does that mean for me?"

"I do not know yet but it may get expensive."

I stopped myself just in time from saying *I don't care what it costs*. I was talking to a lawyer after all.

"Well, keep me updated," I said.

We talked for a few seconds more and then I disconnected, paid my café bill and set out for the sixteenth arrondissement and the home of Miguel and Beatrice Zenn, all the while trying not to feel as discouraged as my afternoon was presently warranting.

The sixteenth arrondissement where the Zenns lived was an odd mixture of upscale homes and seedy domiciles. From one street to the next you never knew what you were going to get. The street where the Zenns lived was a mixture of the two, definitely not high end but this close to the Eiffel Tower, not cheap either.

As a private investigator I often find myself standing on the doorstep of someone's house—frankly half the time I'm hiding in the bushes or in a car—with people inside who, although they don't know it yet, probably do not want to talk to me.

Add to that the fact that I know for sure that Detective Muller was not likely to be amused by my ambushing his eyewitnesses and that my French language skills were middle school level at best and it was a wonder I had the nerve to do what I do.

But if I don't, who will?

The Zenn's apartment building was set up the same as mine. There was a big double door off the rue de Dernier that allowed entrance via the correct code punched into the security panel.

Failing that, since of course I did not know the security code, I would just have to wait for someone to come in or out so I could slip in behind them.

Being a somewhat reputable looking elderly woman, no one had ever given me a hard time for attempting this. I'm sure that's because most people can't imagine that a well-dressed "woman of a certain age" could be up to no good. Stereotypes have worked against me—and most women frankly—my whole life. I was fine with being in a situation to finally benefit from them.

Since it was closing in on the time of day when people would be coming home from jobs and shopping, I didn't have to wait long. A young woman with too much on her mind to worry about why an older woman was loitering about her apartment building kindly let me in after she punched in her security code. I smiled as if I was someone's dotty old granny who couldn't remember her online banking password or her building security code.

I went straight into the main apartment building and up the staircase, which was almost identical to the one in my own building, and found the apartment of Monsieur and Madame Zenn on the third floor.

I rapped on the door which was opened by a very short, sweet-faced older gentleman who cocked his head at me as if he had been expecting the Amazon delivery guy and was surprised to see me instead.

"Bonjour, Monsieur Zenn," I said brightly. "May I come in? I am here about the tragedy at the Eiffel Tower a few days ago."

His face softened at my words and he opened the door wider to allow me inside.

"Who is it, Miguel?" a woman's voice called from behind him.

"Come see, *cherie*," he said, ushering me into the living room.

Most apartments in Paris are small. I am always surprised when I visit someone else's apartment to see that it is even tinier than mine. I don't have a walk-in closet or room for my ironing board. My dryer is stacked on my washer and I have trouble squeezing more than three people around my dining table.

And yet days like today remind me of how lucky I am.

The Zenn's apartment was two rooms. A bedroom and one other room which was their kitchen, living room and dining area in one space. One very small space.

Madame Zenn stepped away from the kitchen sink, drying her hands and looking at me with open curiosity. She had bright red hair and was extremely small in stature. Both features meant, in spite of my neurological affliction, that if I ever saw her again, I would remember her.

"Bonjour, Madame Zenn," I said. "My name is Claire Baskerville. I am working with the police in connection to the accident at the Eiffel Tower two days ago."

"Oh zut!" she said, sucking in a sharp breath. "Yes, come in, come in."

We moved to their living area where they motioned for me to sit down. They sat opposite me and all our knees touched the narrow coffee table between us.

I pulled out a small notepad and a pen.

"Just a few more questions," I said. "I'm sorry for the inconvenience."

"The Paris police department has hired an American?" Monsieur Zenn asked.

"Canadian," I said, realizing that of course they could tell I wasn't a native speaker. I hoped the Canadian reference might make them think it was slightly more likely than the Paris police hiring an American which of course wasn't at all likely.

"First, did you know the victim, Jean-Bernard Simon?" I asked.

They both shook their heads.

"What about the woman with him, Gigi Rozen?"

Again they shook their heads.

"Could you possibly describe to me in your own words exactly what happened that day?"

"We have already given a statement," Madame Zenn said.

"I know, and thank you for that. This is just a follow-up confirmation and afterward we will not bother you again."

"Except for the trial, yes?" Monsieur Zenn said. "You will need us to testify, yes?"

"Yes, except for the trial," I said.

"I saw them start to quarrel," Madame Zenn said. "Didn't I, Miguel? And I said to Marguerite, '*Look at that couple!*'"

"Excuse me, who is Marguerite?" I asked.

"Marguerite Baldoche. We were there with her and her husband Herbert."

Baldoche was the name of the other two eyewitnesses.

"So you all knew each other?"

"Well, yes. We came together."

"Okay good. Please continue."

"I said, '*Marguerite, those two do not look happy!*' Didn't I say that, Miguel?"

Monsieur Zenn nodded solemnly.

"The young man grabbed the girl's arm and said something to her. Something nasty! I was so shocked! But it all happened so fast. And I get dizzy at heights. Don't I, Miguel? I was hanging onto the railing but not looking down."

"Were you able to see over the barriers?" I asked.

"Oh, yes. It's glass you see. Have you not been to the top of Eiffel Tower?"

"I have, yes. What happened then?"

"Well, he slapped her! I heard the sound and jerked my head. I got dizzy at the motion! I do that sometimes."

I turned to look at Monsieur Zenn.

"Did you see the slap?" I asked. Because it was very clear by what Madame Zenn just said that she wasn't looking when the slap happened. She hadn't seen it.

"Of course he saw it!" Madame Zenn said. "We all saw it! And then the young lady shouted something like '*I've had enough of this!*' Didn't she, Miguel? And she pushed him over the edge!"

"But how was that possible?" I asked. "You said yourself that there was glass there."

"I don't know how. I just know what I saw."

Madame Zenn crossed her arms and glared at me.

"She pushed him. There's no mistake about that. We all saw it."

17

B y the time I had picked up Indian food on the way home and trudged up the stairs to my apartment I'd found enough holes in the Zenn's eyewitness account to feel a tad more hopeful than I had beforehand.

First it was clear that neither of them had actually seen the slap and upon further questioning even the so-called push had been at least partly blocked from sight. Monsieur Zenn had been in the way of Madame Zenn getting a good visual and Monsieur Zenn himself had been standing with his back to Jean-Bernard and Gigi.

I was hopeful that a decent defense attorney—was that Berger?—would be able to demolish their testimony on the stand. I hated to have Berger dismantle that sweet couple in a public court of law but neither did I want Gigi to go to prison because someone *sort of* saw something.

When I got home I was immediately greeted by Izzy, who then turned back to the party that was happening on the floor of the living room where Haley and Robbie were playing a game. I could see that Robbie's books and his blocks were scattered about. Gigi had been fastidious about tidying up after

Robbie's playtime but I had to admit there might be an argument in favor of disheveled play.

It was clear that Haley had been reading to Robbie and perhaps showing him the letters on the blocks. Although he was too young to be able to make sense of them, I personally believe it's never too early to start at least exposing a child to reading.

"Hey, you two," I said as I unloaded the vindaloo curry in the kitchen.

"*Maman!*" Robbie called to me and began to toddle toward me.

I don't remember when he'd started calling me that but I was fine with it. When the time came I'd make sure he knew about Courtney—his real *maman*.

I dropped to one knee and intercepted him. He needed changing and he was still wearing his lunch on his chin but his eyes were bright and happy.

"How was your day, little man?" I said kissing his cheek.

"I think he knows that *cow* begins with a C," Haley said.

It occurred to me that in the country he would be raised in, Robbie might want to know that *cow* begins with a V. But it didn't matter. He'd end up learning the word in both languages somehow. Thinking Haley could probably use a break, I picked Robbie up and went into the guest room to change him.

"Do you like Indian food?" I asked over my shoulder.

"It's okay," she said as she followed me.

I changed him quickly and wiped down his chin while I was at it. I didn't want to make Haley feel I wasn't satisfied with what she was doing. For the most part I was satisfied, wet diapers or not.

"My friend Madame Rousseau will be having dinner with us," I said.

"I met her when I took Robbie down to the courtyard with Izzy," Haley said.

That didn't surprise me and once again I was reminded of what a strong support system I'd established for myself since I'd moved to France.

"So tell me about yourself, Haley," I said, knowing I probably sounded like every vacuous adult the girl had ever had to endure. "Do you like sports? Music? Movies?"

"Everyone likes movies," she said.

She had me there.

"Do you have a favorite subject at school?"

"Not really."

I turned to glance at her. She was dressed boyishly and her fingernails were bitten to the quick.

"No hobbies?"

"I like to read," she said. "In my other school I played field hockey."

"I guess it's pretty hard to play field hockey in Paris."

She snorted.

"He calls me *Gaga*," she said as I set Robbie back on his feet.

"That's what he called his au pair," I said as Robbie toddled away toward the living room with Haley and I behind him. "I imagine he'll come up with a name for you soon."

"He calls Izzy da-da."

"I think he's trying to say *dog*. He's just a baby still."

"Yeah, but he's really smart," Haley said. "He repeated a few of the letters."

"Did he?" I found that hard to believe, but if she enjoyed thinking so, I wouldn't ruin it for her.

A knock on the door told me that Geneviève had arrived.

"Why don't you two watch cartoons while I set the table?" I said, going to the door to let Geneviève in.

For someone who only thought Indian food was "okay," Haley did a fair impression of someone who really loved it. It occurred to me that perhaps she'd never had Indian food before. It pleased me to think I'd introduced her to it.

After dinner, she insisted on giving Robbie his bath and putting him to bed. I had to remind myself that she was thirteen years old—plenty old enough to give a baby a bath—and I was right in the adjacent room if she had a problem. Forbidding Geneviève to touch the dishes, I ushered her into the living room with coffees—decaf for me—and brandies.

"Thanks for keeping an eye on her today," I said.

"I didn't really," she said. "She is very good with him. I'm sure you can relax."

"I'm pretty sure I can never relax," I said with a laugh. "But it's a thought."

"How did your day go today?"

I sighed.

"I talked to Detective Muller who is as big an ass as I was afraid he was. And then I talked to Gigi's lawyer, Pierre Berger, who basically did a bait and switch on me."

Geneviève frowned at the American phrase.

"It means he made an appointment with me and then when I got there he handed me off to Gigi's brother."

"Gigi has a brother?"

"Yes. A very weird, very suspicious brother."

"Meaning what, *chérie*?"

"Meaning he clearly hated Jean-Bernard. For good reason of course but he basically had a motive for wanting him dead."

"Ah."

"He also seemed to act like he was holding something back."

It wasn't until I was relating my lunch with Paolo to Geneviève that I realized that I'd been thinking this about him all afternoon long without putting it into so many words. All through lunch he'd acted like he had a secret—a not very nice secret.

"Anyway, after I had lunch with him, I tracked down two of the eyewitnesses. They are a very nice older couple who insisted they saw what they saw—Jean-Bernard hitting Gigi and Gigi pushing him off the side. And yet I'm not at all convinced they really saw that."

"Why would they say they did?"

"Maybe they thought they did because they were right there."

"But why do you think they didn't see it? If they say they did?"

"I don't know. It just sounded...dubious."

"That is good for Gigi, surely."

"Yes. *If* her attorney is able to believably show to a jury what I saw today. But that's a big if."

A burst of laughter from both Robbie and Haley came to us from the other room where they were playing on the floor.

"She likes him," Geneviève said.

"Yeah. She's good with him."

"Did you find out any more about what Joelle wants from you?"

"I talked to my lawyer. She seems to think it's going to be expensive and that Joelle is trying to cause trouble by having Robbie taken away from me."

"As we feared. Does your lawyer have any idea why?"

"No but I already know it's for spite," I said. "Joelle wants to hurt me because she thinks that's all that's left to her now—hurting me."

"And after you proved her innocent of murder six months ago!"

"I'm pretty sure she doesn't even see that connection. People like Joelle are too self-absorbed to see anything except the thing that hurt them."

"She is a woman obsessed."

"It gives her something to focus on besides her pain. Like with a lot of people, hating gives her something to live for."

"You are not worried, *chérie?*"

The sounds of Robbie's sleepy laugh came to us from the other room.

"Of course I'm worried," I said. "Joelle literally could not threaten me with something that terrifies me more."

18

The next morning, I was up and moving around a good thirty minutes after Robbie. Because the night had gone later than I expected I'd called Haley's folks to ask if she could stay the night. They were happy to let her. I spoke with her father who seemed nice enough but I couldn't help wondering what kind of people they were.

Was he just so busy with his career that he didn't realize that Haley was having trouble fitting in at school? Because I'd deduced that much after two days of talking to her.

If Gigi had still been with us, my coffee would have been ready and waiting for me when I came into the kitchen finally dressed. But I was happy enough to see that Haley had made herself a Pop-Tart and Robbie was already in his highchair with applesauce and oatmeal. He clapped his hands when he saw me.

"Good morning, you two," I said. "A good night's sleep, I hope?"

"Why do adults always ask that?" Haley asked and then blushed as if she hadn't meant to say it out loud.

I grinned at her.

"I think it's because as you get older," I said, "it's not always a guarantee. Do you need to run home to get a change of clothing?"

"No, I'm good," she said. "I think I'm taking Robbie to the park today. Can I take Izzy too?"

As soon as she spoke, I felt the familiar needle of disquiet drill into me. I knew I couldn't go on living like this. Robbie needed to be able to go off with other people besides me. I was even apprehensive when he was with Geneviève now. Not just because of her age, but also because he'd been with her that terrible day in the park when he'd been snatched.

Joelle's threats weren't making it any easier for me to gain confidence in handing off his childcare.

"Sure," I said, forcing myself to sound cheerful because every warning bell in my body was ringing like mad.

Izzy yipped with excitement and she ran to the door as if she knew what we were talking about.

"I'll just run her downstairs to wet the pavement," I said, reaching for my coat, "while you get the stroller."

Thirty minutes later I was striding down rue Gager-Gabillot. The clouds overhead looked bone white but still ominous as if they were about to dump snow any minute. I normally love snow—especially in Paris—because now that I don't have to worry about driving in it and I have a cozy warm place to hole up in, it's all just magical ambience like a Parisienne Instagram post come to life.

But for some reason this morning, I wanted it to hold off on the magical fluff falling from the sky. As an image of Haley pushing Robbie's stroller through a snowbank formed in my mind, I once more scolded myself over my destructive imagination.

Let her do her job, so you can do yours.

With Sabine up at bat on the whole Joelle debacle, there was nothing more I could do. My goal today was to try to interview the people at Jean-Bernard's office. So far I had a very sketchy view of the man himself. The Jean-Bernard that I had met was friendly, warm and cordial. The Jean-Bernard who had emerged from CCTV videos and eyewitness testimonies was violent and erratic.

His office building was a nondescript brick structure on a nondescript street, which is saying something for Paris. But I could see how a nonprofit wouldn't want to look too glitzy for the sake of its donors.

Mission accomplished, I thought, as I hurried up the smooth stone steps and walked into the cramped waiting room.

Mieux Faire, which literally translated means "*Make Better,*" was a social services nonprofit with satellite offices in Kenya, Greece, Turkey and the UK. The website I'd found last night was very basic. But a little more digging determined that the organization enjoyed tax-free status from the French government as well as private donations through the company's international developmental arm.

From what I could see, if their Paris office was any indication of how they were doing, I'd say most of their donors were focused globally on the homeless and downtrodden.

I stepped across the waiting room to a young woman who sat behind a basic Ikea desk. She looked up and immediately scanned me head to toe before asking if she could help me.

"I have an appointment with Madame Delacroix," I said.

I'd found the personal phone number for the Paris office director through my people-finding sites and had texted her last night asking to talk with her about Jean-Bernard. She'd texted me back immediately in the affirmative. But I could see how the receptionist might not believe that, since I hadn't made the appointment through her.

"I do not have you on her calendar," she said glancing at my corduroy coat as if not entirely sure I didn't steal it.

I pulled out my cell phone.

"Please let Madame Delacroix know I am here," I said. "Unless you want me to call her personal number."

Her eyes widened at that and she seemed to quickly calculate her win-loss ratio as she reached for her phone and spoke into it. Within seconds, she smiled at me.

"Marie-France will be right with you," she said. "If you would care to take a seat."

I turned to look at the grimy seating area. As it happened, I didn't need to try to figure out which one would not give me syphilis or typhus because the door beside the receptionist opened and a tall, dowdily dressed woman stepped into the room.

"Madame Baskerville?" she said.

After shaking hands, I followed her back through the door and down an even shabbier hallway to her office. On the way, we passed a storeroom with boxes, a broom closet, an office with a man working at it, his back to the door, and a door marked *Toilette*.

Marie-France's office was tidy nearly to the point of austere. There was a credenza behind her desk displaying several awards and certifications. A large photo showed Marie-France with Emmanuel Macron holding a shovel in what looked like a groundbreaking ceremony for a project in the Paris suburbs.

Marie-France sat down behind her desk and gestured me to sit in the metal chair in front of it.

"How can I help you, Madame Baskerville?"

"I'm hoping you can tell me more about the kind of person Jean-Bernard was," I said.

"I will try."

"How long did you know him?"

"Three years. He came to work for me after a job in civil law."

"He was a lawyer?"

"Yes. His work at *Mieux Faire* was a combination of working to solicit more donations for the work we do here and hands-on fieldwork."

"Fieldwork? What does that mean?"

"We are not just academic here, Madame Baskerville. Our mission at *Mieux Faire* is to provide positive ways within the community for under-represented people to better face the challenges in their lives. We do that by getting to know them and their obstacles."

"So Jean-Bernard was a social worker?"

"He was very much a social worker in all the ways that counted. With his law background he was driven by principles that naturally challenged inequalities and discrimination and worked to empower people to be in charge of their lives."

"Okay, it's just that nonprofit fundraising and challenging inequalities is not the first thing one thinks of when someone has a background in law."

"But that was what drove Jean-Bernard! He worked to guide and aid the people in the community who needed his help."

"Did he have any other qualifications to do this?"

"If you are asking if he was licensed to treat the mentally ill in our community, then no. But he had something even more valuable. He had empathy and cultural competence. That is what his clients reacted to."

"Only I would have thought a code of ethics was integral to the kind of work you do."

"Of course it is."

"Jean-Bernard was known to physically abuse his girlfriend."

"Abuse her?" She looked at me as if I'd suddenly lapsed into Urdu.

"He hit her," I clarified.

Marie-France went white.

"I find that difficult to believe. Are you sure about your sources, Madame?

"I've seen the videos. So yes, pretty sure."

I could see she was shaken so I had to believe that what I was telling her was news to her. If so, it meant that Jean-Bernard had kept his mask on pretty tightly at the office. It wasn't unusual for people who lived next door to deviants and murderers to be shocked at what their friendly mild-mannered neighbors had been doing in their basements when everyone else had gone to bed.

After that I was getting one and two word answers from Marie-France. She was clearly upset and I had probably gotten all I was going to get out of her until she processed this new view of a man she obviously respected and cared about.

I stood up.

"I'd like to look at Jean-Bernard's office, if that's okay," I inquired.

She stood too.

"Yes, of course," she said as she moved around her desk in the cramped room.

She led me down the hall to a door beside the toilet. The office she opened the door onto was even more unadorned than hers, made doubly so by the fact that it was now uninhabited. The bare desk was shoved up against the wall under a window frosted with ice and dirt that masked a view of an alley outside.

"Great," I said. "Thank you. Also, I was wondering if there were any other workmates of Jean-Bernard's I could talk to."

"There is Julien," she said rubbing the wrists of both hands and clenching her jaw.

"Julien?" I asked.

She tried to snap out of her daze.

"Yes, he is also an ex-lawyer. In fact, Jean-Bernard is the one who recommended Julien to us. I will thank him for that for the rest of my days. Julien could work anywhere but he chooses to help the disenfranchised."

Part of her spiel was starting to sound repetitive, even rehearsed. I tried to give her the benefit of the doubt. Maybe she spoke at a lot of fundraisers around town about *Mieux Faire.* Inevitably, catch phrases would quickly become rote.

"I will send Julien in to speak with you," she said, her voice flat.

"Thanks," I said with a big smile. But she didn't see it as she turned back to her office.

It was just as well. I'd obviously seriously upset her world with my revelation about Jean-Bernard's violence.

And all the smiling in the world was not going to make that go away.

19

I t's very strange going through the belongings of a stranger, let alone a dead one.

I suppose I've been doing it for so long that it no longer gives me the creeps. But there's always a patina of discomfort attached to it.

I sat at Jean-Bernard's desk—facing a framed photo of him and Gigi from what looked like a vacation on the Calanques in the South of France. They both looked so happy that it was hard to look at that photo and remember how their story had ended.

With Jean-Bernard dead from a fall from the Eiffel Tower and Gigi in jail for his murder.

I rubbed away the shiver that thought gave me and proceeded to search Jean-Bernard's desk drawers. I found nothing of any interest beyond the usual office stationery. I wasn't surprised to see that there was no office computer to search.

The office was a serious bare-bones operation. But when the receptionist came in to give me a cappuccino and a small plate of *chouquettes*, I asked her about the absence of a computer. She said all the workers were required to use their own laptops since the company couldn't afford to buy them. She also told me that the police had not visited their offices.

I wondered what the police had found on Jean-Bernard's laptop. Surely it had been found at his apartment. I made a mental note to ask either Berger or Adele about it.

After getting no luck from Jean-Bernard's desk drawers, I stepped across the room to the two filing cabinets against the wall and went through everything in them.

Mostly the cabinets held corporate literature about *Mieux Faire* itself, and since the Turkey and Kenya offices appeared to do more far-reaching social work, the emphasis was on them. I found very little about the Paris office itself.

Just as I was about to pack it in, I noticed a notebook that had slipped in between two of the hanging files in the file cabinet. I pulled it out and saw it was Jean-Bernard's work diary. Feeling a burst of excitement, I took it back to his desk and looked through it.

Unfortunately, since it was almost February, there were just a few weeks of notes in the book to review. There were also two names with notations beside them that seemed to indicate visits Jean-Bernard had made.

Beside the name of Evelyn Couture, Jean-Bernard had written, *76 years, crippled R leg, trouble getting basic repairs from her landlord, evidence of malnutrition.*

I flipped to the next week and saw that he'd planned on visiting her. Beside her name he'd written, *Buy her a meal? Ask Marie-France.*

I assumed he wanted to make sure that Marie-France thought it was okay if he bought Evelyn a meal. I made a note of Evelyn's address and then pulled it up on my phone. It was in the seventeenth arrondissement.

I'd never been in that part of town before but I do know it's considered generally not one where tourists are encouraged to go. I moved on to the next name.

Zéro Petit. Age 28.

That was all Jean-Bernard had written. Zéro also showed up as an appointment Jean-Bernard had been expecting to keep next week although there was no suggestion he intended to buy him a meal.

Two case studies.

I looked at the file cabinet. There were no files on either of them. Were they on Jean-Bernard's laptop?

I texted Adele.

<Can you help me get Jean-Bernard's laptop?>

I waited for her response for a moment and then texted Haley.

<Everything okay? Having fun?>

She probably thought I was a clingy over-attentive mom.

<Are you serious?> Adele texted me back. *<No.>*

No from Adele didn't necessarily mean *No*. In my experience it meant *not right now*. I'd try again in a little bit. Meanwhile, Haley had yet to text me back.

It occurred to me that I needed to make clear to her that the last time a babysitter didn't text me back she ended up in jail for murder. I didn't mean for that to sound as threatening as it did. I just needed to let her know I needed to hear back from her when I reached out.

"Madame Baskerville?"

I looked up from my phone to see a tall young man standing in the doorway.

"Bonjour," I said, standing to shake hands with him. "You must be Julien."

He had cropped chestnut-colored hair that framed his face and accentuated his full lips and dark brown eyes. Handsome. And he knew it.

"Marie-France suggested you might want to talk to me about Jean-Bernard," he said.

"I do," I said, turning away to slip the work diary into my purse. "But can we do it somewhere else? It's nearly lunch time. Would you mind?"

"*Pas du tout*," he said turning and sweeping his hand out to indicate I should walk before him.

20

The restaurant was small and utterly charming. Antique and mismatched candlesticks sat on white starched tablecloths on tables that lined both sides of the small space with leather banquettes for seating. I sat on the banquette facing the window onto the street and watched the snow slowly drift down outside.

Julien sat opposite me, his legs outstretched, his arms crossed. Typically I see that sort of body language as an indication of resistance and it made me wonder why. Before I could try to assess Julien, however, I received a text from Haley.

<*All good*> she texted and included a photo of Robbie and Izzy both in the stroller together eating an ice cream cone while the snow came down.

I can't tell you how much that photo made me want to hug all three of them. Even though I was horrified that Haley was letting Robbie eat an ice cream cone in the snow! But his face was so jubilant with the joy of his afternoon that my first response was that Haley was hitting all the right notes.

I must have been smiling because when I looked up Julien had his head cocked at me in curiosity.

"Good news?" he asked.

I put my phone down on the café table.

"Not particularly," I said. "So, Marie-France told me that Jean-Bernard recommended you for the job at *Mieux Faire.*"

"Is that a question?"

This is the point when you know if someone is going to be an ass or not and it seemed that Julien had decided to be just that.

"Are you confused as to what I want from you, Julien?" I asked sharply. "I'm sorry I don't know your surname so I can't be as formal with you as perhaps you would like."

He grimaced as if he'd over played his hand which of course he had. I guess he saw my age and had made a knee-jerk assessment about my mental abilities. Normally, I like to encourage that sort of arrogance. It makes it much easier to catch people with their pants down. But today I wanted Julien firmly trousered and paying attention.

"Jean-Bernard recommended me for the job, yes," he said.

"How did you know him so well that he felt comfortable doing that?"

"We were roommates at one point."

"When?"

"Last year."

"Why did it end?"

"It was time."

"Why was it time?"

He huffed out a breath of annoyance and then sat up straighter as the waiter came back with our drinks. I'd ordered mulled wine. He'd ordered a coffee.

"He wanted to ask his girlfriend to move in," Julien said.

"So it was Jean-Bernard's decision not to live together anymore?"

"That's what I just said."

"Was that upsetting to you?"

"No. I was ready also."

"Oh?"

"Again. Not a question."

I studied him for a moment. The fact was he could've stayed in his office and waited for me to either leave or track him down. But he'd come looking for me. There was something he wanted to tell me but he didn't want to be seen wanting to.

"How did you and Jean-Bernard become roommates in the first place?"

"I found his name on an online ad service."

"Which one?"

"*Comment*?"

"There are many such ad services on the Internet. Which one did you find his ad for a roommate?"

"It was through my last job," he said.

"Which was?"

"*CDB et Associés.*"

To give you an idea of how famous and prestigious CDB is as a law firm, I instantly recognized the name. At Julien's age, he'd probably had a relatively low-level position. Even so, it was an enviable start for any brand new lawyer.

"That's impressive," I commented.

He looked around for the waiter. Either he was suddenly very hungry or he didn't like talking about his old job.

"Why did Jean-Bernard advertise on your firm's personal ad site?" I asked.

"He used to work there too."

"So he advertised for a roommate on his old firm's site, presumably because he wanted someone who was a lawyer?"

"I guess so."

"Then during the months you lived together he convinced you to consider working as a social worker?"

"He knew I was unhappy at CDB."

"There must be at least one or two other law firms in Paris besides CDB."

"Jean-Bernard knew I was uncomfortable billing hours to make the partners rich. He knew I wanted to help build something meaningful."

"Commendable."

He looked at me as if trying to decide if I were being sarcastic or not, but the moment was interrupted by the arrival of our food.

I waited a few moments for both of us to enjoy a few moments with our respective dishes, for me *soupe au vin blanc* accompanied by a steady assault on the breadbasket, and cassoulet for him.

"So did you know his girlfriend Gigi?" I asked.

If he tells me no, I'll know he's lying.

He hunched over his meal, focused on shoveling it in as quickly as possible.

"I knew her."

"How well?"

He looked at me and then dropped his fork on the table with a clatter. It bounced and fell to the tile floor. I have to say I thought that was a pretty significant reaction unless it was because he was in love with Gigi—and since my observation of Julien was that he was most likely gay, it could only mean that he was in love with Jean-Bernard.

Turned out I was wrong on both counts.

"I am dating Gigi's brother," he said, then signalled to the waiter that he needed new cutlery.

My eyes widened in surprise.

"Paolo?" I asked.

It was his turn to be surprised. He snapped his head around to look at me.

"You know him?"

"I had lunch with him yesterday," I said.

Julien leaned back in his chair as he tried to process this information.

"Have you not spoken to him since his sister was arrested?" I asked.

The waiter returned, set a fork and knife beside Julien's place and then retreated.

"*Non*," he said. "We...had a quarrel last weekend."

I let him eat without interruption for a few seconds. It shouldn't have surprised me that there were connections within connections with the people I was speaking to. After all, that's where most murders came from—a friend, a family member or someone who was the friend of either.

So Julien was Jean-Bernard's roommate and the partner of the brother of Jean-Bernard's girlfriend. It was a little convoluted but nothing I couldn't keep straight as long as there weren't love children to sort out as well.

"Paolo said he hated Jean-Bernard," I said, testing the waters since technically Paolo had admitted no such thing.

"That's a little extreme."

"Why would he lie?"

He narrowed his eyes at me.

"I am not saying he didn't have his issues with Jean-Bernard. But if you knew Paolo, you'd know he could never have hurt him."

"Paolo's alibi is that he was with you at the time of Jean-Bernard's murder," I said.

The look Julien gave me then, if you'd forced me to swear on a stack of Bibles and put money on the table, I would have said was authentic.

"Was Paolo *not* with you that day?" I pressed.

Julien shoved his plate away and dragged a hand across his face.

"*Non*," he said finally. "He wasn't."

21

After our lunch I watched Julien leave the restaurant to head back to his office. There were still several questions I had for him. But after realizing that his boyfriend had given him as an alibi which he couldn't confirm I think he was feeling a little vulnerable.

Still, before he left he'd made a valid point that, wherever Paolo was that day—or with whom—as long as he could prove he was nowhere near the Eiffel Tower, he was in the clear.

I wasn't about to tell Julien that being at the tower might well not mean anything as far as corroborating Paolo's innocence. Since I knew—and assumed Julien didn't—that drugs had disabled Jean-Bernard and made his death inevitable—anyone who had access to Jean-Bernard in the hour or so *before* he went to the Eiffel Tower could have been his killer.

I was pretty sure that Julien's next move would be to contact Paolo and demand to know why he'd given him as an alibi. Then the two of them would comfort themselves with the idea that since Paolo hadn't been at the tower he was in the clear.

Far from it.

As was becoming my habit, I ordered a cup of coffee from

the waiter and texted Haley again. She responded fairly quickly that she and Robbie were now back at the apartment. Feeling relieved, I called the number I had for the Baldoches. I wasn't too far from where they lived and was hoping to question them before I called this day done.

The line rang and was answered quickly by a gruff elderly-sounding male.

"*Allo?*" he said.

"Hello, Monsieur Baldoche? My name is Claire Baskerville. I'm working with the police to fine tune some of the statements collected over the recent incident at the Eiffel Tower."

"*Non,*" he said and hung up.

I sat for a moment holding the phone, wondering what to make of it. I decided, as unpleasant as it now promised to be, that I would actually have to go and knock on their door at some point. I sipped my coffee and felt a wave of exhaustion filter through me.

At least the snow appeared to have stopped. I paid my bill, anchoring the euro notes under an ashtray that nobody was legally allowed to use. Then, using the GPS function on my phone, I headed down the sidewalk toward the section of Paris with the ominous sounding name of Stalingrad.

Let me just say that Stalingrad is not the area of Paris that most tourists see.

The streets were more like alleyways, narrow and trash-filled and lined with stores that had been boarded up a long time ago. Graffiti and curse words were scrawled across the store fronts and garbage blew in the streets. The odor of mildew, marijuana and excrement was pervasive.

It was pretty clear from what I saw all around me that the inhabitants of Stalingrad would absolutely qualify for the services of *Mieux Faire*. On the other hand, if there were just three social workers, including Marie-France, working to help the people in this community it was hardly likely any real change could be achieved. There were just too many needy people.

I was again reminded of how odd it was that there were no case notes for Evelyn or Zéro, or at least none that I could find. That was another thing I'd meant to ask Julien about but hadn't. It didn't matter. He and Marie-France were only a phone call away and Marie-France looked only too eager to sit down with me to tell me all about the mission of *Mieux Faire*.

Stalingrad appeared to be largely populated by African and Arab immigrants. Young men stood on street corners, smoking and talking, many of them looking unhappy if not downright angry. They looked at me with distrust and curiosity. If I'd been younger, they might have been emboldened to ask why I was in their neighborhood. But my advanced age—good for very little in most instances—worked to my advantage here. No one cared to question an elderly woman.

I'd deliberately dressed down today—part of the reason why the receptionist at *Mieux Faire* had given me the once-over that she did—but I was still too fashionable to belong here. Honestly, my hair alone was a giveaway. I have shoulder length brown hair with honey blonde highlights.

There was no way, casual trousers and worn corduroy raincoat or not, that I looked like I belonged here.

I followed directions to the apartment where, according to his diary, Jean-Bernard had met Evelyn. I'd checked her and Zéro out on my French people-finding site *Cherchez-Moi* after Julien left our lunch table.

I use the site when I need to do more than just find evidence of the last time someone used their ATM card and where. During the early years of my marriage before Bob had become uncomfortable with me doing it and before I'd had

Catherine, I'd made my living as a skip tracer back in Atlanta. I didn't see it as a sleazy way to make a living, as Bob did. I found it interesting and exciting.

The address I uncovered led me to a building that looked like it was built in the nineteen seventies, totally utilitarian and devoid of architectural enhancement.

I knocked on the door. There was no security system, in spite of the fact that danger was literally everywhere. I tried to imagine how these people lived like this. Did you ever get used to it? Did you never really relax?

"I'm coming!" a voice yelled from inside.

I waited another full minute on the threshold, fielding several unfriendly looks from men as they passed. I felt my hands become damp in my coat pocket and wished I'd thought to pack my pepper spray this morning.

Finally the door inched open as far as the security chain would let it. The stench of stale cigarettes seeped out of the crack as the old woman glared at me.

Evelyn Couture was hawk-nosed with sharp eyes and carefully styled gray hair that was clearly a wig. I wondered if she'd lost her hair to illness.

"Who are you?"

"I'm a friend of Jean-Bernard's," I said.

Her face showed distrust and surprise and she raked my appearance from top to toe with her eyes. Then without a word she closed the door and unhooked the chain. When she opened the door wider I could see she was leaning on a cane. Behind her was a wheelchair and the sounds of a daytime television game show in French.

"I heard he was dead," she said sourly, still not inviting me in.

Jean-Bernard's notes had said she was seventy-six and she looked every bit of that. Her shoulders were rounded and her posture stooped—maybe from years of leaning on the cane.

The lines around her mouth revealed decades of heavy smoking and the creases across her forehead were deep.

"Madame Couture," I said, "may I come in?"

"Jean-Bernard always brought me *croquembouche*," she said glancing at my empty hands.

"I'm sorry," I said. "I didn't know that."

"Are you his replacement? From the place?"

"From *Mieux Faire*? No. I'm just a friend."

She snorted then and stepped away from the door to allow me inside.

The place smelled of fried food and cigarettes. I followed her to the living room. She motioned for me to sit on the sofa. It was shabby but clean. The room contained an odd mix of ceramic and glass curiosities and other flea market junk.

On the side table was a photo of a young man in a faux-silver frame with his arm around a younger version of Evelyn. I wondered if it was her son. I wondered if she ever heard from him.

She saw me looking at the photo and placed it face down on the table before turning back to me.

"I'm sorry he's dead," she said, lighting a cigarette off one she had smoldering in the ashtray. "But I hope this means they'll assign me someone who knows what the hell they're doing."

"What do you mean?"

"Jean-Bernard never did any of the things I asked him to do! He never made my complaints to the people he was supposed to make them! He never got my landlord to fix the toilet! Nothing! He was the worst."

"But you liked him personally?"

She snorted again. "What does that matter?"

At that moment a heavyset gray cat lumbered into the room and stopped when it saw me. Evelyn used her cigarette to wave in his direction.

"I like the stupid cat too but that doesn't help anything!"

"I have to ask you, Madame Couture, was Jean-Bernard ever violent with you?"

I was sure she would say no. Most abusers were cowards who only lashed out at the ones closest to them—and counted on their affection and care not to report them.

She looked at me as if I'd grown a second head.

"Are you mad?" she asked incredulously. "Jean-Bernard?"

"So, that's a no?"

"He was a bigger pussy cat than Neige there." She waved again in the direction of the cat who had now come closer but seemed no less ready to accept that I was really there.

"How so?" I asked, frowning. The Jean-Bernard I'd met, as affable and charming as he'd been, I wouldn't have gone so far as to call him a pussy cat.

"He thought I didn't know," she said nodding her head with a knowing smile and jabbing the air with her lit cigarette.

"Didn't know what?" I asked, wondering if I was going to get any useable information out of this woman or if she was just dotty?

"Can't let that kind of thing get around, you know? Can't let the big wigs find out. Could do serious damage to his career."

"You mean his career as a social worker?"

She snorted again.

"I told you he was a crap social worker. That was just a temporary gig."

"So what big wigs are you referring to?"

"At the big firm he was hoping to get hired at."

I pulled out my notebook and poised a pen over it.

"Any chance you have a name for this firm?"

"CDB," she said.

I hesitated, surprised. I seriously doubted that Jean-Bernard would be telling Evelyn Couture that he was hoping to get a job at Julien's old firm. On the other hand, he'd clearly mentioned it to her or else how did she know the name?

"When was the last time you saw Jean-Bernard?"

"Two weeks ago. He brought me *croquembouche*."

"That's nice. So what was the thing that you know all about that he couldn't let become common knowledge?"

"That he was gay, of course."

22

I received this information with a patient smile.

I'm not saying Jean-Bernard *wasn't* gay. I had only met him for the briefest of moments but I would have been very surprised to learn that this was true. Not to brag, but my gay-dar is nearly infallible.

Just because Jean-Bernard had a gay roommate at one time, didn't mean he was thinking of switching sides himself.

"Today's companies no longer care about the sexual preferences of their employees," I said. Even I could hear the patronizing tone in my voice and Evelyn certainly could.

Her face flushed with anger.

"That's what you know," she said hotly.

It was time to leave. With the possible exception of the fact that Jean-Bernard may or may not have been trying to find a job at Julien's old firm—and I would definitely dig more into that when I got home to see if there was any truth to it—I'd gotten no real information from Evelyn except that Jean-Bernard wasn't a good social worker.

I found myself wondering how Marie-France checked up on her employees. How did she evaluate their effectiveness?

Did they just sit around the table drinking cappuccinos after hours complaining about how difficult it was to implement social responsibility for the poor?

I stood up.

"Well, thank you, Madame Couture," I said, turning toward the door. "I'll definitely talk to the people at *Mieux Faire* to see about that toilet. And thank you for answering my questions."

"I'm sorry I did!" she shouted at me as she struggled to stand up from her chair, grabbing her cane to support herself.

I was pretty sure that an elderly crippled woman screaming at me as I left her apartment was not going to go down well with the neighbors so I hurried down the hall toward the front door, hoping to get out and down the street before she got any louder.

Foolish hope.

"Don't come back here again!" she shouted, now hobbling surprisingly quickly behind me down the hall.

I reached the door and was out and on her doorstep when I nearly bumped into a thin man in rags standing on the sidewalk as if waiting for me.

"Jean-Bernard never did nothing for me! None of them did!" Evelyn shrieked from behind me. "Hey! This woman is American! She's here snooping around where she doesn't belong!"

I felt a stab of fear at her words. I was nearly across the sidewalk when the thin man grabbed my arm and pulled me roughly to a stop.

"Let go of me," I wheezed, all of my senses on full alert as I felt his fingers tighten on my arm through my coat.

"What are you selling?" he snarled. "Haven't you people done enough?"

"She was asking about Jean-Bernard," Evelyn said from the doorway of her apartment.

"Jean-Bernard?" The man instantly dropped his hand and I staggered a few steps away and turned to look at him.

I'd been expecting to see someone who looked like they fit in this neighborhood but this man was clearly not of Middle Eastern or North African descent. He was thin but muscular, with blond hair and blue eyes.

It was cold out but he wore only a t-shirt. When I stepped away from him I saw the hypodermic needle tracks on his arm.

"Do you know him?" I couldn't help but ask.

The look on his face was a combination of fury and disgust as he regarded me. A long scar stitched up from his chin to his cheek and reminded me of the threat of violence that these people lived with.

"Tell her, Zéro!" Evelyn shouted. "Tell her how Jean-Bernard helped *you*!"

"Shut up, Evelyn," he said tightly.

"Wait, you're Zéro?" I asked him.

"What is it to you?"

"Nothing," I said and then taking a chance, I addressed him earnestly. "Except there is a young woman who is being held for Jean-Bernard's death. A young woman who—"

"Are you talking about the girl who pushed him?" Zéro said, grinning and revealing several missing teeth.

I don't know why I assumed Jean-Bernard's clients would like him. Maybe because I figured that if Jean-Bernard had been seeing them and doing what he could to help them, there was a positive relationship between them. But that wasn't the case.

"We don't believe she killed him," I said.

"*We*? Who is *we*? Because the police believe it," Zéro said, taking a step away from me as if about to leave.

"I know they do," I said. "Which is why I am doing everything I can to find out whatever I can to help her."

"And so you came here?" He snorted and turned to look at

Evelyn who spat on the ground and slammed her front door shut.

"I was hoping to find someone who knew Jean-Bernard," I said. "Someone who might be able to shed more light on what happened to him."

"What happened to him," Zéro said, jutting his chin out angrily, "was that someone who knew him killed him. The only mystery is that it didn't happen sooner."

23

I was able to hit Monoprix that evening before it got dark and before the snow started up again. I'd invited Adele and Geneviève over for dinner. I picked up a chicken and leek potpie at the supermarket that was honestly better than anything I could make from scratch, plus all the ingredients for a salad. I knew either Adele or Geneviève would probably bring dessert but I picked up more cheese just in case.

By the time I got home and got dinner going—and by that I mean heated up—Geneviève was already at my apartment setting the table and Adele was interrogating Haley about what she wanted to do with her life.

"Evening, all!" I called out as Izzy greeted me in her pathologically enthusiastic manner that made me glad to be a dog owner. "*Je suis ici!*"

"You are just in time, *chérie*," Geneviève said as she adjusted the tablecloth. "Adele has nearly decapitated herself in your toilet."

"That sounds interesting," I said as I began to unload my bag of groceries.

Adele joined me in the kitchen to top off her glass of wine.

"You have a four-foot metal towel bar leaning against the wall behind the toilet door," she said accusatory. "I closed the door and it nearly impaled me!"

"Sorry," I said. "With no man around the place, chores tend to go undone."

"Don't use that as an excuse!" Adele said, aghast. "We are independent women, *non*? Do you want the name of my parents' handyman? When he shows up, he is excellent."

I laughed and slipped the potpie onto a cookie sheet and then into the oven.

"No. I promise I'll get the towel rod up before the next time you come over," I said.

Haley stood in the doorway with Robbie on her hip.

"Can you stay for dinner, Haley?" I asked.

She shrugged. "I guess so."

"Call your folks and tell them."

She shrugged again and left the room.

"So what's new with the investigation?" Adele asked as Geneviève came into the kitchen and I poured us all wine.

"I went to Jean-Bernard's office," I said. "And I talked to one of his officemates, including his boss. They both liked him a lot. I even talked to two of his clients."

"*Sérieusement?*" Geneviève said, clearly impressed.

"Yeah, although I wouldn't recommend a tour of the neighborhood. It was rougher than I expected."

"You should be more careful, Claire," Adele said. "Not everyone in Paris loves Americans."

"Ha ha. Love your sense of humor, Adele."

"What did you find out?" Geneviève asked.

"Not much. One client said Jean-Bernard was a crap social worker but I got the idea she'd say that about anyone. She probably complains about the mail carrier too."

"And the other one?"

"The other one was a pretty rough character. He suggested that anyone who knew Jean-Bernard would want to kill him."

"Goodness, " Geneviève said.

"Yeah. Plus I saw tracks on his arms and his eyes were dilated."

"Promise me you won't go back there again," Geneviève said.

"There's no need anyway."

"Where did he work?" Adele asked.

"A place called *Mieux Faire*. And here's something interesting. Jean-Bernard worked with this one guy who was his ex-roommate who just happens to be in a relationship with, wait for it, Gigi's brother."

Adele and Geneviève both frowned.

"Don't you think that's a lot of people *coincidentally* connected to a lot of other people?" I asked. "Jean-Bernard's workmate, Julien—the one who used to room with him—is romantically involved with Gigi's brother Paolo who hated Jean-Bernard."

"Naturally he would," Adele said.

"But listen to this. When I asked Paolo where he was when Jean-Bernard was getting pushed off the Eiffel Tower, he said he was with Julien. Except Julien said he wasn't."

Adele frowned. "Why would Paolo lie about that?"

"Isn't that a good question?"

"That reminds me," Adele said. "The toxicology report came back on Jean-Bernard and it confirmed that the drugs in his system would've killed him if he hadn't fallen to his death."

My face broke into a smile, but Adele quickly attempted to quell my jubilance.

"That doesn't let Gigi off the hook," she said.

"Doesn't it? You're essentially saying Jean-Bernard was already on his way to being dead *before* Gigi pushed him."

She waggled her hand.

"Gray area there," she said.

"Even if Gigi *had* shoved him *without intending to toss him over the edge*, he was probably weak enough from the drugs in his system to have fallen through the bad panel all on his own. That's not murder, that's an accident."

"Maybe," Adele said. "But the prosecution is going to say it wasn't the drugs that killed him, which is technically true— even though they *would've*. It was the fall that killed him."

"Does Berger know this?"

"I'm sure he does."

"I'm going to call him to see about possibly having the charge reduced to manslaughter or even death by misadventure."

"I'm sure he's already thought of that if it were a possibility."

"You have more confidence in him than I do."

～

After Geneviève and Adele left and I'd called Haley's folks again to see if she could spend another night, Haley got Robbie ready for bed and I settled down with my laptop at the dining room table to do some of the Internet research that the day had prompted.

The first thing I did was look up the law firm *CDB et Associés*. It was one of the biggest in Paris. Its website looked like it had cost a fortune, its mission statement packed with all the latest politically-correct phrases, the photographs of the firm's partners looking like mannikins. Plus they were all men. I thought that was odd since I was pretty sure there were now more female lawyers in the world than male.

While I listened to the sounds of Robbie in his bath, I went back to the *Mieux Faire* website. Since I'd been there yesterday someone had added an *In Memoriam* page with a head and shoulders shot of Jean-Bernard. I looked at the picture and something stirred in me.

While my inability to remember faces was pretty nearly complete it didn't mean that some vestige of recognition didn't occasionally flicker around the back chambers of my brain. It was possible that I was remembering vestiges of Jean-Bernard's face from the single time I'd met him at the café with Gigi.

The caption under the photo talked about how much Jean-Bernard would be missed by everyone at *Mieux Faire*. I went to the pulldown menu under *Our People* and found the biographies for Marie-France, Julien and Jean-Bernard. I skimmed them but learned nothing new. I already knew that Julien and Jean-Bernard had backgrounds in law. Marie-France's resume was solidly immersed in social work and activism.

Izzy made a low-throated growl to remind me that she hadn't had her last visit to the courtyard outside so I got up and slipped into my mid-length cashmere coat. I tiptoed to the guest room, careful not to show myself in case that derailed Haley's efforts to get Robbie to fall sleep. I saw that they were lying together on the guest bed with a book.

I snapped Izzy's leash on her and went downstairs, mindful not to hurry on the slick stairs. Opening the main building door off the lobby, there was a blast of cold that seemed to shoot under my coat. I shivered and stepped out into the courtyard which displayed a fine dusting of snow. I could only imagine how beautiful and sparkling white the Latin Quarter must look tonight.

I let Izzy do her thing but recognized that I felt an uncomfortable sensation as I waited—as if someone were watching me. I shook off the feeling and hurried back upstairs, grateful for the sound of the heavy front door slamming shut behind me.

Upstairs, I dried the snow off Izzy's feet and went once more to check on Haley and Robbie. He was in his crib now and

Haley was a blanket-covered lump on the bed, her Doc Martens on the floor.

I'd need to encourage Haley to go home tomorrow and get some clean clothes. I was all for her spending the night here. But she needed to let her jeans find a washing machine once in a while.

Was it weird that she didn't want to go home? Was it weird that her parents didn't seem to care if she didn't? I tried to think back to when Catherine was this age but she'd been a compliant, accommodating teen with lots of friends and outside activities. Haley couldn't have been further from my experience of raising a daughter.

Just the thought of that reminded me that Haley wasn't my job to raise. I could be a friend to her, in fact I found myself wanting to be a part of her life. But she had parents. It occurred to me that I should probably meet these parents. No judgement, I warned myself. Just because they're not raising her the way I would doesn't mean they're doing it wrong.

But it might be wrong for Haley, a small voice said.

Shutting out all voices small or otherwise, I opened up my laptop and went to Facebook to see Catherine's post that mentioned Cam. At the same time I saw the flag that indicated I had a private message. When I clicked on it I saw a picture of my grandson with a wide smile across his face and the science award trophy in his hands.

Tears pricked my eyes because the first thing I thought of was how proud Bob would have been. There was no use in wishing away these kinds of thoughts when they came. Probably I'd wrestle with them my whole life long.

I typed in my gushing congratulations and then right-clicked on the image so I could use it as the desktop photo on my laptop and be able to look at Cam's happy, proud face every time I opened up my computer.

I checked my email to see if I'd gotten anything from

Sabine. She was supposed to be fashioning a letter to Joelle's lawyer. But there was nothing.

A chime on my phone heralded the fact that a text message had come in and I saw it was from Paolo. My first thought was that he must have talked to Julien and was trying to do damage control with me. But that was because I didn't trust Paolo. Perhaps he was only hoping to get information on Gigi.

His text asked if we could meet for coffee tomorrow. I sent him a time and a place. I was a little surprised that he'd contacted me after our lunch where he'd seemed in such a hurry to escape. Also, I didn't remember giving him my phone number, but I assumed he got it from Berger.

Speaking of Berger, I texted him and reminded him that I still needed to see Gigi and that he still owed me a real meeting. I saw that my message had been received and read. But nothing happened after that.

I was beginning to feel tired. It had been a busy day and—especially with the moment when I hadn't been at all sure Zéro wasn't going to assault me in the street—an emotionally trying one too. But I still needed to track down the fifth eyewitness from the Eiffel Tower, Eloise Caron. I wanted to interview her tomorrow but I needed a little background so I didn't go in cold as I had with the Zenns.

I went back to Facebook and typed in *Eloise Caron* in the search window. Her Facebook page came up immediately. From her homepage I saw that Eloise Caron was young, probably mid-twenties, and pretty. She had a tattoo on her arm, and in some of the photos I scrolled through, she was wearing a Chanel jacket with jeans.

Her information on Facebook said she worked as a graphic designer at Jean-Delmas Studios and was not currently in a relationship. There were several photos of her in cafés and *brasseries* eating, drinking, laughing and generally enjoying being twenty-five-ish.

Since she was so active on Facebook I thought it was weird that she hadn't written a post referring to what had happened at the Eiffel Tower. I get that she'd probably been warned by the police not to mention publicly what she'd seen in detail, but why wouldn't she have at least mentioned the tragedy?

I kept scrolling down her timeline because so far I wasn't finding anything unusual about her to suggest she was anything special. Just a young woman with all of Paris at her feet and a whole exciting life ahead of her.

And then I saw it.

Because of my face blindness, at first I didn't know what I was seeing. All I knew was that the photo I was looking at—with Eloise sitting at a restaurant table with a New Year's crown on her head and a man's arm around her, his lips firmly planted to her cheek—was vaguely familiar. I studied the photo but it was no use. I couldn't remember if I'd ever seen him before.

I opened up a new browser on my laptop and went back to the *Mieux Faire* website where I pulled out my phone and took a photo of the *In Memoriam* picture of Jean-Bernard and also the bio photo of Julien. Then I went back to Eloise's Facebook page on my laptop and held the photo of Jean-Bernard on my phone beside the Facebook photo of Eloise on New Year's Eve.

My mouth fell open.

Two years ago on New Year's Eve, Eloise was being kissed by none other than Jean-Bernard Simon.

24

The next morning, I could barely contain my excitement as I raced through breakfast, kissing Robbie goodbye and agreeing to allow Haley to walk Izzy because I was in such a hurry.

After my blockbuster discovery last night about the fifth eyewitness, I'd spent another hour drilling down into Eloise's Facebook history and discovered that not only did Eloise know Jean-Bernard, she'd been his girlfriend two years ago!

Did the police know about Jean-Bernard's relationship with Eloise? They must not! Why was she at the Eiffel Tower that day? Had she been stalking Jean-Bernard and Gigi?

I was so excited about what I'd discovered—and so sure that it would be a game changer in what the cops had on Gigi— that I put a call in to Berger as I hurried down the sidewalk to my meeting with Paolo. When my call went to voicemail I left a long message telling him what I'd found out the night before.

I was glad I was meeting up with Paolo this morning. At first I was glad because I actually had something positive to tell him. But as soon as that thought came into my head I immediately began to reconsider. I didn't know how Paolo found my phone number. He probably did get it from Berger, but just in case he was better at tracking people than most people were, I decided not to share with him what I'd learned about Eloise lest he tried to go after her too.

The bottom line was that Paolo didn't seem altogether normal or balanced to me. I only had a gut feeling to base that on, but I've based opinions on much less and been right. The last thing anyone needed at this point was for Paolo to somehow be able to track Eloise down and perhaps hurt or frighten her before things could be put right with the cops.

I hated not thinking I could treat Paolo as an ally. But the fact was, this was way too important to rush and make assumptions that might blow up in my face later.

I'd had plenty of experience with that too.

Paolo was already seated by the time I arrived at the café and by the looks of the three empty coffee cups he'd been there at least a good hour before my arrival. He looked agitated as if he hadn't slept.

We shook hands and I gave my order for coffee to the waiter. It was too cold to sit on the terrace of the café, so we were seated inside in front of a huge plate glass window. Even on a cold day like today, any sun at all it would have warmed us through the glass. But there was no sun today.

Paolo's hands shook as he tore open a sugar packet and sprinkled it into his espresso cup.

"Everything okay?" I asked him as the waiter deposited my own espresso in front of me.

"Not really," he said. "I talked with my parents last night. They're very upset that I haven't been able to get in to see Gigi."

Have you tried? I wanted to ask but didn't.

"Is Berger helping you get in to see her?" I asked.

He shrugged and I got the distinct impression that he hadn't been in contact with Berger since he left the lawyer's office yesterday with me.

He brought his coffee to his lips and I saw the cup shake.

"What's going on, Paolo?"

"I talked to Julien," he said, putting his cup down with a clatter that I don't think he intended.

"You should have told me you were romantic with Jean-Bernard's roommate," I said.

"*Ex*-roommate. I didn't mention it because it wasn't relevant."

"Everything in a murder investigation is relevant. Did Julien tell you he won't confirm your alibi?"

He wiped a hand across his face.

"It doesn't matter. I didn't push Jean-Bernard. I wasn't even there. There's nobody who can say I was."

I thought it was about time to pull the plug on that particular fantasy.

"The cops know that Jean-Bernard was drugged prior to his visit to the Eiffel Tower," I said.

He covered his mouth with his hands. "Drugged?" he said, blinking in shock.

"They even know that the drugs would've killed him if he hadn't fallen first. So not being at the Eiffel Tower may not be as much a free pass as it sounds."

Paolo stared at his cup as if lost in thought. Either he was a very good actor or he hadn't known about the drugs.

"What did you want to see me about?" I asked.

He looked at me as if suddenly realizing I was still sitting there. He flushed and signaled to the waiter.

"I shouldn't...it doesn't matter," he said. "This was a mistake. *L'addition, s'il vous plait*," he said to the waiter.

This was interesting, I thought as I scrutinized him. He asked to see me and came looking like he'd had a very bad night. Then, when I told him his alibi about not being at the Eiffel Tower the moment Jean-Bernard died was irrelevant because of the drugs, he immediately started doing everything he can to get rid of me.

What does that mean?

"Someone who knows Jean-Bernard has suggested he might have been gay," I said.

Paolo stopped in the act of pulling a couple of euros out of his wallet.

"Well, he wasn't," he said.

"You knew him that well?"

"Well enough. If nothing else, I know the type."

"Are you saying he was homophobic?"

"Are you saying that because he had a gay roommate he couldn't be?"

Okay this was getting us nowhere.

"Fine," I said. "Let's table the question of Jean-Bernard's sexuality for now."

I still had to seriously consider the possibility that Paolo was actually in love with Jean-Bernard and that Paulo's so-called hatred of him was just a cover to mislead me.

He stood up.

"I'm sorry to have wasted your time, Madame Baskerville," he said before turning and hurrying out of the café.

I watched him go and wondered not for the first time what it was he was hiding.

As was becoming my habit, I leaned back in my chair, ordered another espresso—this time with a lusciously gooey *kouign-amann*—and called Eloise Caron. It had been easy to find her number of course. I even discovered that she was a finished artist of dolphins and was attempting to sell her work through various social media platforms.

"*Allo?*" Eloise answered the phone.

"Yes, hello, Miss Caron? My name is Claire Robinson. I found your name on Facebook and absolutely fell in love with your work. You are still painting, aren't you?"

After the briefest of pauses, Eloise answered.

"Yes! Yes, I am," she said, her voice bright with excitement.

"Oh, how lovely, because I think your work is exactly what I'm looking for. I'm the curator for a series of very tasteful bed and breakfast establishments in California. They are looking for artwork—original artwork—in just the style I saw online in your work. Would it be possible to meet and discuss this more?"

"Yes! Absolutely. Are you in Paris?"

"I am, as it happens. When and where would be a good time to meet?"

We arranged to meet at Ladurée at four o'clock. This would qualify as a full-on ambush. The girl expected one thing from the meeting and was going to be shocked to realize it wasn't that at all. But I wasn't fooling around anymore. I was determined to get my questions answered.

I paid my bill and left the café heading toward the slightly more fashionable neighborhood of L'Opera where the oblivious and completely unsuspecting Monsieur and Madame Baldoches lived.

The neighborhood was not a bad one but not upscale either. The streets were lined with Haussmann style buildings but looked a little worn. The wrought iron Juliette balconies could use a paint job and the cream-colored base stone could also stand a scrubbing.

Like with the Zenn's building, I had to once more go through the charade of pretending to have forgotten my code so I could slip in with one of the building's residents. I checked the mailboxes in the lobby to see which apartment belonged to the Baldoches, then went upstairs to put a bell on the damn cat.

I rapped on the door and when it opened, I received the

look from Madame Baldoche that I'm sure I get on my own face when someone from inside my building knocks on my door and I'm wondering how they got in. But while I'd taken a softer approach with the Zenns, I'd already decided not to take any prisoners with the Baldoches.

For one thing, hanging up on me the other day told me that they were, if not exactly combative, then mildly obstreperous.

And either of those two attitudes was best dealt with from a position of strength.

If not downright bullying.

"Madame Baldoche?" I said, pushing past her and entering her apartment. "Is Monsieur Baldoche here?"

I nearly faltered when I saw her frail husband as he came tottering out to see who was bulldozing his elderly wife. But I squared my shoulders. The sooner I got through this, the sooner they could go back to their hot water bottles and cross-word puzzles.

I whipped out my prop notepad and marched into their tiny living room.

"I am here to confirm what you saw on the twentieth of this month at the Eiffel Tower," I said in my most commanding voice.

When I turned to look at them, they were standing side by side staring at me with the most confused looks on their faces. I wasn't about to explain why my French accent was awkward. I didn't want to distract them. I would be as bombastic as I could and pray for forgiveness later for terrorizing a couple of old sweeties.

"The day the man Jean-Bernard Simon fell to his death," I prompted ruthlessly as if to jog their memory of what had to be one of the most horrific afternoons of their lives.

"I didn't see it," Monsieur Baldoche blurted out.

I fought to hide the surprise on my face. I had actually been coming closer to the theory that these two hadn't really seen anything but had merely succumbed to the peer pressure of their good friends the Zenns to corroborate the Zenn's story.

But even I hadn't expected them to fold so quickly.

"I see," I said, officiously, jotting down nonsense scribbles on my pad. "And you, Madame Baldoche? Did *you* see anything?"

Madame Baldoche looked at her husband and then at me and blushed. I think now that her husband had come clean, she was afraid to agree with him lest it appeared she'd either been lying all along or was just plain a dotty old lady.

Trust me, I know the temptation to do whatever was necessary to avoid appearing as the later.

"I saw him slap her," she said.

"Did you," I said, making it more a statement of doubt than a question.

"Well, I heard it at least!" she amended, although her choice of words had just eviscerated her credibility.

"Did you see her push him?" I asked carefully, measuring out every word.

She took a step back. "Yes! I saw him fall!" she said, her voice quavering.

I was really going to hate myself after this.

"No one is questioning if he fell," I said. "Did you *see* her push him?"

"I'm sure I did," she said, looking at her husband as if she would find the answer in his face. "I'm almost positive. Beatrice was talking about it and it was so real. Yes, I'm sure I did."

"Beatrice is Madame Zenn?"

She nodded and licked her lips.

I raised my voice. "Are you seriously willing to testify in a court of law before a jury of your peers that you saw a woman push a man to his death?"

Madame Baldoche looked at her husband, her eyebrows drawn together worriedly.

"Actually, Beatrice was closer to them than we were."

"Is it possible you didn't see anything?" I asked. "Is it possible you *didn't* see a woman push a man over the railing to his death? Think carefully, Madame Baldoche."

Again, Madame Baldoche looked at her husband.

"Well, *I* never saw any of it," her husband said to her. "You know that."

"Oh, dear," Madame Baldoche said, turning to me. "I'm not sure I did either."

That was all I needed to hear. I snapped my notebook shut and thanked them for their time and quickly left their apartment.

Pierre Berger would have to do the work necessary to discredit the old couple from this point on. But if we were lucky the Baldoches would retract their statements entirely and save everyone the pain and inconvenience—them most of all.

As I walked down the flight of stairs to the lobby, I felt buoyed by what I'd done. I'd discredited two of the five eyewitnesses. Three, if you counted Miguel Zenn, who'd essentially backed out of his testimony when I talked with him yesterday.

That just left Beatrice Zenn.

Whether I could get her to admit she hadn't really seen anything I would soon see. In any case she definitely merited another visit.

25

L adurée, the famous luxury bakery and sweets store on the Champs-Élysées also happens to be extremely convenient to my apartment. I try to arrange a meeting there at least once a week.

My basic strategy for today's meeting was to spend a few minutes winning Eloise Caron's trust before swooping in and destroying it completely, but hopefully not before she told me what I needed to know.

I arrived first and commandeered a table by the window so I could see her coming. When she arrived I saw that she was exactly what I expected. She was French so she was slim, and young so she was wearing clunky black boots, cropped jeans and a coat that looked like it was two sizes too big for her. I'm sorry, but give me the days of Chanel jackets and cinched belts any day.

Although I'm pretty sure Chanel makes oversized coats and cropped jeans now too.

We greeted each other cordially and ordered macarons and coffees while I gushed praise over her terrible aqua acrylic dolphin paintings that I'd seen online, wondering what parent thought they were doing their child a favor by encouraging such hideous art? I was glad the girl had a day job.

"Do you sell quite a few?" I asked as I sugared my coffee. "I imagine you do a brisk business."

"You will be surprised to learn that no, I don't," she said.

"I am shocked."

"I know."

"Have you lived in Paris long?"

"I came here right after art school."

Dear Lord, your parents paid for art school?

"Have you ever done any painting of the architectural wonders of Paris itself? You know, the Haussmann buildings, the Latin Quarter..."

"Oh, there are so many artists doing that! I would just be one of many."

But she frowned as she spoke as inevitably she must be thinking of one Paris wonder in particular—as was my intention.

"I would imagine," I said, "that the Eiffel Tower would be an irresistible subject for an artist."

She nodded and pushed her dessert plate away, clearly no longer hungry.

"I was there the other day when the guy...when the man..." she started and then stopped.

I studied her closely. Jean-Bernard had been her boyfriend. If she'd truly seen him fall to his death, that had to be the dictionary definition of traumatic.

I chose my words carefully.

"Oh, my goodness," I said. "You were there? Did you see it?"

Her eyes filled with tears. "Yes. I did. He was my boyfriend," she said in a shaky voice.

I gasped on cue.

"Oh, my dear," I said. "How ghastly! I am so sorry to hear it! But..." I frowned as if hesitant to approach such a delicate subject. "I mean, I thought the woman they are holding in the incident was his wife?"

She shook her head. "No, the media got that wrong. Jean-Bernard wasn't married."

"But if you were his girlfriend..." I said letting the implication hang.

"We...we were dating other people," she said.

"I see. So he was at the Eiffel Tower with someone else?"

"With the woman who killed him! Yes!"

"But then why were *you* there?"

She looked at me with a look of trepidation.

"It's not how it looks," she said. "I'm glad I was there so I could help bring the woman who murdered him to justice."

"So you saw what happened?"

"Yes."

"Did he know you were there?"

"What?"

"Did your ex-boyfriend know you were there at the Eiffel Tower?"

"No. I don't think so." She put her fingers in her mouth and began to chew on them. "I wasn't following them. It was just a coincidence."

"Were you there alone?"

She blushed darkly. It was highly unlikely that anyone, especially someone who lived in Paris, would go to the Eiffel Tower all by themselves. After a while it was all you could do to make yourself go when you had visitors from out of town.

Eloise didn't answer me and began to glance toward the exit so I decided to pull back a tad if I didn't want to lose her altogether. I was already feeling confident her testimony would fall apart as soon as Berger got her on the stand.

Hoping to distract her from what had probably started to feel like an attack, I tried to go down a different path.

"How did you and...what was his name?"

"Jean-Bernard."

"How did you and Jean-Bernard meet?"

"We knew each other from school. That's how we *all* met and eventually that's how Jean-Bernard met the woman who killed him."

"How do you mean?"

"Before Jean-Bernard went off to law school and me to art school, we were all at Université de Strasbourg together. I only went for a year but that's where the whole gang got started."

"Gang?"

"We originally started hanging out together because we were all interested in birding, if you can believe it. Or rather Jean-Bernard and Paolo were interested in birding. I just joined because I wanted to get closer to Jean-Bernard."

I stared at her.

"Jean-Bernard and Paolo went to school together?"

"Yes. We all did. Eventually I dropped out and another guy joined their group. They really were the three musketeers until Jean-Bernard started dating Paolo's sister."

"Who was the other guy?"

"I didn't know him. He joined after I left."

"It's important that you remember his name. Please try."

She gave me a very strange look since I'm sure she was starting to think by this time that I wasn't someone interested in buying her dolphin paintings at all.

"Zebra?" she said.

I felt a punch of surprise.

"Do you mean Zéro?" I asked.

"That's it."

I tried to understand what this meant. Zéro the drug addict who Jean-Bernard had as a client had once been a close friend of his?—and Paolo's—from school?

I needed to talk to Paolo again. And also Zéro.

"You're not really interested in my art, are you?" Eloise asked.

"No, sorry, but I think the police will be very interested in how you ended up at the Eiffel Tower that day with Jean-Bernard and Gigi. Were you following them?"

"No!"

"Because that's what it looks like."

"That wasn't the...it wasn't true! Jean-Bernard and I were still seeing each other."

My eyebrows raised.

"In fact he spent the night with me. I made him breakfast that morning."

"So you got back together with him?"

It was incredible to me that this young woman was telling me so many intimate details of her life. But sometimes when you find yourself believing a lie, it helps to say the lie out loud with hopes that if you can get someone else to believe it too it'll feel more real to you.

"Not really," she said, her shoulders collapsing in defeat. "It was more like goodbye sex. He told me he only wanted to date *her* now."

"That must have been painful."

"I wasn't expecting it," she admitted as she wiped away a tear.

"But still, how dreadful that must have been," I said, "to leave the bed you shared with him hours earlier only to witness him being shoved off the Eiffel Tower! You should be in counseling."

"I didn't really see it," she said in a quiet voice.

"I'm sorry?"

She shook her head sadly.

"There was an old lady there shouting that Gigi had pushed Jean-Bernard and so when the police came and asked everyone what we saw, I just..."

"You just lied."

Eloise looked at me. "I was confused."

"Perhaps you should contact the police and let them know you were confused," I said firmly.

"I will," she said, sniffling. "I just got caught up in all the drama."

I signaled to the waiter to bring the bill and brought my wallet out onto the table.

"I'm happy to get this, my dear," I said to her. "So, tell me, this *goodbye sex* you had with Jean-Bernard...it took place at your apartment?"

"*Oui.* I wanted to make him breakfast. He always loved my *crêpes aux fraises*," she said wistfully.

I'm sure he did, I thought grimly.

And I'm equally sure he'd never have noticed a little odorless liquid opioid slipped into the batter among the strawberries.

26

After leaving the restaurant with Eloise, who by the time she left didn't even look angry that I'd lured her there under false pretenses, I went to Monoprix to shop for dinner and pick up a few staples.

As I waited in line at Monoprix, I put a call in to her father. His secretary answered and, when he wasn't available to talk, gave me Haley's mother Mindy's number.

"Hi there!" Mindy answered brightly. "Is this Claire?"

"Yes," I said, thinking Haley's mother sounded very normal if somewhat young. "I thought we should connect since we seem to be sharing time with your daughter."

"I hope she's doing a good job for you?" Mindy said.

"Very good," I said. "I'm really enjoying getting to know her."

Mindy laughed loudly and then said, "Oh, I thought that was a joke."

"Not at all."

"Well, Haley is a good girl and I'm glad she's working out for you. She needed something to keep her busy since the drugs weren't working."

Drugs?

"Oh, sorry, I have to run! I'm substitute teaching a yoga class at the Paris American Club. But thank you for calling and again I'm glad you weren't calling to fire her or anything. Bye!"

I disconnected and tossed my phone in my bag. Poor Haley. I couldn't think of two people who were as completely different as the vapid insensitive woman I'd just talked to on the phone and the intense Goth-girl who lumbered through my apartment making Robbie's life and my daily round a little bit better.

I hope her father at least saw Haley for who she was.

What drugs, I wondered?

That night, Haley went home on time for a change. I got the impression that she had actually something to do. I came right out and asked her what her evening plans were but she managed to avoid actually answering.

Maybe she was meeting some friends at a café? Or working with other students on a mutual study project? Maybe her parents just missed her and wanted to see her smiling face at their dinner table for a change?

Whatever it was, I didn't know because Haley wasn't sharing. I'd assumed that having her watch Robbie by day would give me all the break I needed to handle him in the evening. But I was wrong. I don't know whether he's getting in the habit of being more active with Haley, but I literally didn't have a moment to myself from the minute I got home and took over from Haley to the minute I attempted to put him down to sleep —which took no less than two hours to accomplish, after which I just wanted to go to bed myself.

However, I refused to waste an entire evening by crashing after chasing a baby around the living room and picking up the mess that chasing created. I settled on the living room couch with my laptop, my dog, a large glass of white Bordeaux, and the baby monitor on the coffee table in front of me.

I was keenly aware that the dinner dishes were still sitting in the sink in the kitchen, but tried to find some sort of peace or calmness before digging into more Internet research. I heard the clock on the mantel ticking loudly, the sound of Izzy chewing and licking her feet for some God-only-knows-why reason, and of course the constant hum of the traffic outside my window.

Because I still had a few loose-ends questions for Julien that I didn't want to ask over the phone, I texted him and invited him to meet me for drinks tomorrow.

He answered in the affirmative. I wondered if Paolo was with him. We set the time for three o'clock at BiBoViNo, a popular wine bar in Le Marais.

Something about my brief text interaction with Julien left me feeling unsettled for a reason I could not put my finger on. I'm not sure some of it didn't have to do with the fact that I was fairly confident he was lying to me. Or maybe because I just didn't like him. I like most people. But Julien felt off to me. I can't describe it but I definitely wouldn't ignore it.

As a result of my uncharitable and totally unfounded thoughts about Julien, my nerves felt taut and jangly. All the effort of willing myself to feel peace or to relax was not working. I took a swig of wine and that helped a bit. My phone rang and I picked it up, noting first that it was Adele.

"Hey," I said. "I was hoping you'd call."

"Today any better?" she asked.

"Maybe," I said. "I have now met with all five eyewitnesses, four of whom have basically said they didn't see Gigi push Jean-Bernard at all."

"Well done, Claire! How did you do that?"

"By asking each of them, making them walk me through it and then listening to what they said."

"You said four. What about the fifth?"

"The fifth is one Beatrice Zenn who is the only one who still thinks she saw something."

"But you don't think she did?"

"She said she saw the slap too, but then she admitted she only turned her head *after* the sound of the slap."

"Meaning she didn't see it."

"Right. And as far as witnessing the so-called *push*, it sounded as if she *wanted* to see it but I'm not at all convinced she really did."

"How will you find out the truth?"

"I don't know. Plus her pals the Baldoches will have called her by now to tell her about my visit. So it'll be even trickier."

I saw I was getting a text from Pierre Berger.

<Set up for you to see Gigi tomorrow morning. Ok?>

"Berger has arranged for me to see Gigi tomorrow," I said to Adele as I quickly typed back a positive text response to the lawyer.

"Finally!" Adele said. "Now let's just hope she doesn't start things off by confessing that she killed him."

27

I was at the *Préfecture* early the next morning. I expected to see Muller. He would have been the one to approve my seeing Gigi regardless of whatever strings Berger had pulled. I also expected my visit with Gigi to be recorded and wondered if I should tell Gigi that.

My visit with her was scheduled for ten in the morning but I was at the police station by nine-thirty, just in case. It was ten-thirty before the door to the waiting room opened and a policewoman stepped through and called my name.

She led me down a hall to what looked like an ordinary interview room. I'd been in no fewer than three of them at this very *Préfecture*—each time on the ugly end of being interviewed—but I couldn't say for sure if this was one of the rooms I'd been in.

They searched my clothes and gave me a ticket for my purse which they took from me. Then they led me back into the hallway and to another room.

Gigi was already there, sitting at a long metal table in one of three chairs, all riveted to the floor. A pair of handcuffs hung on a chain from the table. There was a large two-way mirror on one wall.

As I entered, Gigi stood up and I got the idea that she wanted to run to me but the nearby policewoman stopped her. Just the look on Gigi's face when she realized she wasn't going to be able to hug me nearly broke my heart.

The policewomen told me to sit at the table opposite Gigi and then left. I was glad to see that Gigi wasn't handcuffed. I leaned over and held her hands.

The gesture depleted her. She hung her head and sobbed. I couldn't help but think of all the times she'd given Robbie his bath, fed him, sung to him, or walked to the park with him in his stroller. She'd always been a basically cheerful girl and I hated that this was happening to her now.

"I'm innocent, Claire," she said, her voice muffled by the curtain of hair which hung in her face.

"I know, sweetie," I said.

I didn't want to rush her. As far as I knew, I was the first and only friendly face she'd seen since she'd been arrested. But I also knew our time was limited. I waited as long as I could.

"Can we talk?" I said gently.

She nodded and pushed her long hair from her tear-streaked face.

"I'm innocent, Claire."

I looked around the room. There were no obvious cameras but that didn't mean the cops weren't listening.

"Tell me what happened," I said.

"We got in a fight, me and Jean-Bernard. I don't even know what it was about."

She shivered as if cold and I waited patiently for her to begin.

"I thought he was drunk," she said finally, after taking a tissue from the box on the table. "I said to him *How could you get drunk? I'm in charge of a baby!*"

"Why did you think he was drunk?"

"He was slurring his words and he kept stumbling. It wasn't even midday! I thought he must have a flask, because we'd been together all morning. How could he be drunk?"

I thought everything she was saying was very good for her defense. It showed that she didn't know he'd been drugged. Of course the cops probably wouldn't believe her. But still, it couldn't hurt.

"He got so mad! He just lashed out at me!"

"In words or for real?" I asked.

"Both," she said miserably. "I was just about to lift Robbie up to let him look over the railing."

My stomach churned when I realized how close Robbie had come to possibly going over the side himself.

"He...he slapped me." She looked stunned as she said it as if even she couldn't believe it. "I mean he'd done stuff like before but never in public."

"Did you push him?" I asked in a low voice.

She hesitated.

"I think I was so horrified that he'd do it in front of people —in front of Robbie—that I might have...maybe...pushed him a little, just to get him away from me."

Her eyes held the horror in them as she relived the moment when she saw Jean-Bernard go through the panel.

"One minute he was there," she said. "I don't know how it happened."

"There was a loose panel," I said. "And because of Jean-Bernard's height and his compromised state, he lost his balance and hit the side. It gave way and he went over."

She blinked at me. "That's how it happened?"

"Nobody told you?"

She shook her head. "The panel was loose?"

"It was supposed to be repaired but the work order got lost

and the person who'd put it in, as I understand it, had gone on holiday."

She looked around her in bewilderment.

"So why am I in jail?" she asked, her voice rising with building hysteria.

"I don't know, dear. Gigi, can I ask you a few questions?" I knew I didn't have long.

She nodded as if in a trance.

"When did you meet Jean-Bernard?"

"My brother was friends with him in college. I met him one time when they came home on summer break."

"But you didn't start dating then?"

"No, I was too young. We didn't start dating until I was out of school and had moved to Paris."

"Do you know a man named Zéro?"

"The name sounds familiar. Wasn't he the other one with Jean-Bernard and Paolo? They were inseparable at school. Some kind of club."

"Do you know what happened to him?"

"I'm sorry, no."

"That's all right. So you're telling me that your brother and Jean-Bernard were close once. Can you tell me why they fell out?"

"I'm not sure. Maybe when Paolo came out? Maybe when Jean-Bernard asked me out? Those two things probably didn't help."

"Was Jean-Bernard homophobic?"

"No, not at all! I swear it! It's just that he and Paolo were so close at school and maybe for just a minute Jean-Bernard worried about what people might think about him when they found out Paolo was gay."

"Do you think he was afraid people might think he was gay too?"

"No way. You saw Jean-Bernard. He didn't have a gay bone in his body."

"Okay," Claire said. "I believe you."

"It's just that Jean-Bernard and Paolo didn't always hate each other, you know? And when they did, well, that's on me." She stared down at her hands.

"Except it's not, of course," I said. "Wait. Do you mean Jean-Bernard hated Paolo?"

"Well, yes."

"Why?"

"What do you mean why?"

"I can see why Paolo hated Jean-Bernard. After all, your boyfriend was abusive to you. But why did Jean-Bernard hate Paolo? What was *that* about?"

"I never really thought about it. I just know he did."

28

When I think of how long I've lived in Paris—just shy of two years now—I'm amazed that my language skills have improved as much as they have. Adele and Geneviève both tend to use me to practice their English which leaves me having to practice my French on surly bakery shop cashiers and dentist receptionists and of course the ever-patient waiters. Although since I spend no less than a third of my days sitting in cafés and *brasseries* I pretty much have my script down pat with waiters.

The wine bar in Le Marais was trendy, elegant and stuffed with wealthy tourists—mostly Japanese. I was surprised that Julien would suggest it. But the tasting menu was extensive and the view of the busy street outside the huge plate glass window made me feel cozy and cosseted. I ordered a kir and a plate of smoked salmon canapés to wait for him.

After the waiter brought my kir, I pulled out Jean-Bernard's work diary and flipped through it. I'd already noticed that he'd written Evelyn's name down for next week with the question about whether he should buy her a meal. But when I flipped to the previous week, I saw he'd written her name two days before he was killed.

There was a check mark next to her name. Did the checkmark mean he'd seen her? Because didn't Evelyn say she hadn't seen him in weeks? I pondered this and sipped my drink. I found myself thinking how odd it was that Paolo never mentioned he'd once been close to Jean-Bernard but had a falling out. Was that pertinent? Wasn't it?

And then it turned out that Paolo was the partner of Jean-Bernard's workmate Julien? Was that relevant? Was that a problem for Jean-Bernard? Did he resent it?

I looked at my watch. Julien was due to show up in a few minutes and depending on how long that meeting went, I'd swing by the Thai restaurant a few blocks from my apartment and pick up dinner. I texted Haley to see if she could stay late.

I turned my attention back to Jean-Bernard's work diary.

And what about Zéro? What was his deal? He clearly resented Jean-Bernard. How often did Jean-Bernard see him? I really needed to get my hands on Jean-Bernard's case notes for these two in order to rule them out. I wondered if there was some kind of company-wide Cloud reservoir for *Mieux Faire* client notes.

Again, something I could ask Julien when he came.

My phone rang and I saw it was Sabine. We were meeting with Joelle and her lawyer tomorrow to see if there was some way to handle this without going to court. I couldn't imagine, unless Joelle was just hoping to make me jump through hoops, that there was anything Joelle would be happy with short of making me as miserable as possible. But Sabine was an optimistic sort of lawyer and insisted we go through this step before completely impoverishing me with her legal fees.

"Hey, Sabine," I said.

"The meeting is set for tomorrow at sixteen hundred hours," she said briskly.

It's not true what they say about lawyers being socially cold and reserved. At least not in France. It was highly unusual for Sabine to get to the point like that instead of greeting me and asking after my health and the health of Robbie and so on.

I felt an empty feeling in the pit of my stomach.

"Is everything okay?" I asked.

"I guess we'll see," she said. "Dress up."

"Sure."

While dressing to impress the jury might be something that was expected in the US, here in Paris, how you presented yourself—even in a private confab with two lawyers and the woman trying to destroy you—was considered basically essential.

I didn't mind. What I minded was that my lawyer seemed unnerved.

"No problem," I said. "Anything I should bring?"

For one mad moment I thought she was going to say, "just your checkbook," but most lawyers I know are not very humorous and Sabine was even less so.

"Just be on time," is all she said before hanging up.

This wasn't good. Sabine clearly knew something I didn't and it had thrown her. On the one hand, I thought she should have let me know what it was she knew. But on the other hand, she probably didn't want to do that because she didn't want me to act all squirrelly and hysterical tomorrow.

I took a long sip of my kir and felt it burn comfortably all the way down.

Chill out and focus on work, I told myself. *That's always the best answer to things you have no control over anyway.*

I turned back to Jean-Bernard's work diary although I'd practically memorized every entry in it anyway when my phone rang again. Thinking it might be Sabine deciding after all to ruin my day with the details of why she was so agitated, I picked it up with hope and expectation in my heart.

But it was Adele.

"Hey," I said. "I'm having drinks in Le Marais if you're anywhere near."

"Sorry, no," she said in a low voice which told me she was trying to hide what she was about to tell me. "I'm on a cigarette break but I thought you'd want to know something I just found out."

"I absolutely do," I said, picking up my pen in order to jot down any and all vitals that she might relate to me.

"The drug cocktail that was in Jean-Bernard's system was released this afternoon."

"To the press?"

"No, no, just internally."

"Let's hear it."

"It was a combination of codeine and paint thinner."

I stopped writing. "That's not a prescription opioid," I said.

"No, not prescription but technically still an opioid," Adele said grimly "The cocktail is a lethal street drug called *krokodil*."

I sat back in my chair digesting what she'd just told me. I don't know why I thought that the drugs found in Jean-Bernard would've been prescription drugs. Maybe because I thought Eloise was my best bet as his poisoner. And she doesn't look like the kind of person who could easily get her hands on something called *krokodil*.

In my mind, the fact that the drug that was used to kill Jean-Bernard was a street drug didn't mean Eloise *hadn't* drugged him. It was entirely possible she could've gotten the cocktail somewhere.

But it wasn't as likely as, say, a known drug addict who lived on the streets.

29

Julien showed up seconds after I hung up with Adele. He was wearing a well-cut blazer that accentuated his slim form and a Hermès scarf draped casually around his neck.

He greeted me brusquely and ordered a glass of champagne before glancing around at the clientele in the bar as if looking for someone he might know. As of course I suppose he might.

Le Marais was a popular tourist area but it also had a high gay population. I'd found Julien's address online days ago. He didn't live in Le Marais, but that didn't mean he didn't come here often or didn't have lots of friends in the neighborhood.

"Thank you for meeting me," I said.

The waiter deposited his drink in front of him and Julien took a sip, giving me a noncommittal shrug in response to my statement.

"I suppose you and Paolo have talked since I saw you last," I said.

"If you're hoping I'll share that conversation, I'm sorry to disappoint you," he said.

I cocked my head as I looked at him as if to study him better.

"You know Julien, my purpose in talking with you—and Paolo too for that matter—is only to find a way that Gigi might be released from police custody. All of my questions—annoying as I am sure they are—are to that end and that end only. I'm not here to make you miserable or because I want to pry into your personal life."

He seemed to soften a bit at that.

"I know," he said. "I am sorry. I guess Jean-Bernard dying and then you coming along and digging into...things...has just made other things which had been fine suddenly seem not so fine."

Was he talking about his relationship with Paolo?

"I'm sure Paolo is pretty stressed out right now," I prompted.

But he didn't take the bait.

"He is, of course."

"Okay," I said. "Again, please remember that the questions I ask are only to help Gigi."

"I have a feeling you said that because you are about to ask an incredibly invasive question," he said, taking another sip of champagne.

"Is there any way that Jean-Bernard might have been gay?"

He coughed into his drink and quickly dabbed at the spill on the table. He shook his head ruefully.

"Of all the things you might have asked me," he said, "that is the last thing I expected. No. Jean-Bernard was not gay."

"And he was not homophobic?"

"No more than most straight men."

"So is that a yes?"

He shrugged. "I don't want to speak ill of the dead."

"And I'm trying to get to the truth to *protect* one of the living," I said firmly.

"Look, Jean-Bernard was a friend of mine. He treated me as

a friend. If he didn't always hit the mark as far as being...sensitive to who I am, well, I forgave him that. That's what friends do."

I studied him for a moment. His face was closed and uncommunicative. He was done on this subject.

"Where are Jean-Bernard's case notes?"

"Those would be on his laptop," he said. "We don't use office computers."

I needed to make a more aggressive effort to get Jean-Bernard's laptop or push Berger to make sure *he* at least got his hands on it.

"You roomed with Jean-Bernard," I said. "And then he found you the job at *Mieux Faire*. Why?"

"You'll have to ask him."

"Is that supposed to be funny?"

He blushed when I called him on that. Even he knew he'd gone too far.

"Jean-Bernard and I were friends up to a point. We had our emotional compartments and we stayed in them. We were friends within our compartments."

"Did you know he hit Gigi?"

"I would have difficulty believing that about him."

"There are videos."

"Look, I'm not saying Jean-Bernard was a saint. But I never saw that side of him. If he hurt Gigi, that's on him and I'm ashamed of him."

"Paolo knew about the abuse. He never mentioned it to you?"

"We have a rule where we do not speak of Jean-Bernard when we're together."

"Is that because Paolo hated him?"

"He didn't hate him. That was all noise."

"If you say so. Because it would have been understandable. Jean-Bernard was hitting his sister."

"That's not why Paolo was upset."

I sat up straight.

"Yes? Really? Why else?"

"Never mind. Nothing."

"No. You said Jean-Bernard hitting Gigi wouldn't have been the reason Paolo was angry with him. What would have been the reason?"

"Maybe you should ask Paolo."

It was clear I would get no more out of him on that subject but it didn't mean the wheels in my head would stop turning.

What else was Paolo upset about with regards to Jean-Bernard?

"I did a little research on you online," I said. "You have an impressive CV, Julien. Marie-France said she was over the moon to have gotten you."

"Is that a question?"

Are we back to this again?

"I'm just wondering what someone like you with your credentials is doing working at a nonprofit."

"Providing empathy in order to challenge the inherent inequalities in our communities."

"That sounds memorized."

"Doesn't mean it's not the truth."

"Had you known Marie-France before you came to work for her?"

"I had not."

"And do you like her?"

"I respect and admire her."

I stared at him. He was here, ostensibly to be helpful but he was definitely stonewalling me.

There is a popular technique in questioning suspects that the police and psychiatrists use all the time. It's a method of staying silent after a session of rapid fire back and forth questioning—just like what Julien and I had just engaged in.

Silence can have a dramatic effect on even the most stubborn people.

That's because most people abhor a vacuum. Especially when it comes to speaking. Years of conversation and interacting with others have taught us that talking, smoothing things over, elucidating, will erase the discomfort that silence creates.

Stare at someone blankly or better yet slightly indictingly and it is the rare individual who doesn't start to feel self-conscious.

And start talking.

It was the last trick in my bag and with someone like Julien who was smooth, and always in control, I didn't have a lot of hope it would work.

But it did.

I stared at him as if I'd suddenly made up my mind about him, as if I had no more questions because I now knew the one thing he'd wanted to keep secret.

"Look," he said reaching for the peanuts on the table and then pushing them away, "I might have met Marie-France at a party the year before I went to work for her. I mean, she and Gigi were once together—before Gigi and Jean-Bernard got together."

My eyes lit up. "Together how?"

"It was just now and then—and mostly on Marie-France's side."

I felt a fluttering in my belly at his words.

Talk about everyone being interconnected! I was furious that Gigi had never mentioned that she'd had a fling with Marie-France—if that was in fact what she'd had.

"So is Gigi gay?" I asked.

"Just very *free*, I would say," Julien said with a laugh. "I mean, she was happy enough to hook up with Jean-Bernard later on."

"So did Gigi dump Marie-France for Jean-Bernard?"

"You could say so."

"How did Marie-France take that? No tension in the office afterwards?"

"Well, Gigi never visited the office. But I can't imagine there would have been even if she had. We all take the job very seriously. Plus Marie-France had enormous respect for Jean-Bernard."

I tried to digest what Julien had just told me. And while I appreciated his loyalty to Marie-France, I have to say my gut feeling was I don't care how much she loved her job. Continuing to work day in and day out with the person who'd stolen away your girlfriend would be tough for most people.

Maybe even impossible.

30

A s I walked home after my drinks with Julien I stopped at my favorite Thai place to pick up supper. While I waited in line at the cashier I put in a call in to Pierre Berger. Miraculously, he actually answered.

"I need to see Jean-Bernard's laptop," I said. "I need to see his case notes which are on his laptop. There's a guy from his past who was a client of his who could easily have gotten the drugs that were found in Jean-Bernard's system."

"Name?"

"Zéro Petit."

"Never heard of him."

I clenched my jaw and spoke through my teeth with forced restraint.

"Jean-Bernard, Zéro and Gigi's brother Paolo were a tight gang of three in college," I said. "For some reason, later on Zéro fell in with a bad crowd. He's into drugs and living rough. Not only would he have access to these particular drugs, he hated Jean-Bernard."

"I'll see if the cops have anything on him."

That comment only increased my frustration because even

if Zéro had a record it didn't contribute any evidence connecting him to Jean-Bernard's death. I needed Zéro brought in and questioned about where he was during the hours just before Jean-Bernard went to the Eiffel Tower.

"While you're at it," I said, "check out Marie-France Delacroix. She was Jean-Bernard's boss but she seemed to have had a romantic connection with Gigi. There might be a motive there."

"Might be? How about actual evidence?"

"How about if you go and talk to her and see if there's anything there?" I said raising my voice.

Do I have to do everything?

"There's no way I have time to go out in the field," Berger said with exasperation. "I barely have time to take this call!"

"Fine. I'll go back and talk with her."

"You're saying the victim's boss was sleeping with his girl-friend? With Gigi?"

"It happened a while ago," I said. "But if the boss held a grudge, that's motive, right?"

"But it makes no sense," Berger said. "If she held a grudge wouldn't it make more sense to kill Gigi? And if she was going to do it wouldn't she have done it years ago?"

I know positioning Marie-France as a possible suspect didn't sound very solid. Framing someone for murder wasn't as satisfying as killing them. If Marie-France had done it because of getting dumped, that's a classic crime of passion. So killing Jean-Bernard made no sense. As I saw my theory collapse around me, I grabbed for something more substantial.

"Did you get my message about the fact that Eloise Caron was Jean-Bernard's ex-girlfriend?" I asked.

"*Mon Dieu*, if I accused every ex-girlfriend of every murder victim I knew, I'd be pointing the finger at half the Paris phone book."

"She was there, Monsieur Berger," I said, attempting to

tamp down my frustration with his obstinacy. "At the Eiffel Tower. At the time of Jean-Bernard's death. You don't think that's suspicious?"

"Was she seen pushing him?"

"Well, no, but she admitted she was with him that morning! If she drugged him prior to his going to the Eiffel Tower, she might've shown up to see if the drugs had done the job."

"It sounds circumstantial at best," Berger said, "or the stuff of a Netflix cop drama at worst."

"Fine. Whatever. Just know that I'm doing my best to discredit all five of the eyewitnesses and I believe the fact that Eloise Caron was still in love with Jean-Bernard *and* followed him that day to the Eiffel Tower makes her an unreliable witness. If not in fact his killer."

"I have to go, Madame Baskerville," Berger said. "I will note all that you have told me."

I clenched my fists in frustration and felt my blood pressure inch upward. That's the only reason I can give for why I got my next idea and did something that I can only imagine someone might do who felt frustrated and a little bit desperate.

I called Detective Muller and asked him for a date.

Much like the other wine bar where I'd earlier spent forty minutes with Julien, Le Garde Robe near the Louvre was elegant, lush and crammed with people. But this time there were fewer tourists and more business people.

Muller sat at a small table in the middle of the room drinking a beer, his beady little eyes scanning the restaurant, the other diners, and the entrance to the bar. For me.

Of course it wasn't really a date-date but naturally I couldn't make that distinction clear when I called Muller, because there was no way he would agree to meet me if I did. I had to believe that if I could just lay all that I'd learned before him, it would at least set up some warning signs for him, a few red flags that he might actually give some credence to.

It was better than doing nothing.

Or so I thought.

Muller stood up as I approached his table, which surprised me. My initial take on him was that he was a sexist pig and showing a woman any kind of respect whatsoever would have not been worth his effort.

But of course, thanks to my invitation, he had an agenda tonight and not immediately pissing me off was probably step one on that agenda.

"*Bonsoir*, Madame Baskerville," he said as I seated myself across from him. "I have ordered for you." He signaled to the waiter.

"Thank you for meeting me tonight, Detective Muller."

He nodded and smiled and for just a split second I thought that perhaps getting out of the police station and allowing himself to relax a bit might actually serve the purpose of engaging with me as a human being.

I must have been mad.

The waiter returned with an ice bucket and a bottle of champagne and filled both our glasses.

This was worse than I thought. In any case, I drank down the first glass of champagne, needing it for fortitude, and was aghast when Muller leaned across the table and promptly refilled my glass.

"I like to see a woman your age wearing something that shows her figure," he said to me, his eyes dropping to my chest as soon as I let my coat fall behind me onto the back of the chair.

What a jackass, I thought as I smiled politely.

"I am wondering if the revelation about the drugs found in Jean-Bernard Simon's system will expedite the release of Gigi

Rozen," I said lifting my champagne glass up as if about to make a toast.

He behaved as if he hadn't heard me.

"Is that *Joy* you are wearing?" he asked. "Or *La Vie Est Belle*?"

He leaned toward me as if to smell me better and I fought the natural impulse to recoil. His mustache twitched as he hung his face over the center of our small table as if attempting to reach me with his nostrils.

"Since the cause of death has changed," I said. "I am hoping this means your suspect must inevitably change too."

He filled his own glass back up and frowned as if he'd just ran his memory tapes back in his head and heard what I'd said.

"What do you mean?" he asked.

"Well," I said reasonably, "surely the new fact that drugs killed Jean-Bernard changes things?"

He opened the menu and signaled to the waiter.

"I'm not sure if you are aware that one of the women who was at the Eiffel Tower that day was an ex-girlfriend of the victim," I said with mounting frustration.

Muller turned to the waiter and ordered a double serving of fries cooked in duck fat, snapped the menu shut and handed it to the waiter.

"Of course I am aware," he said. "That is one of the reasons I am holding her."

"Wait. No. I'm talking about Eloise Caron, not Gigi. Eloise Caron is one of the eyewitnesses."

He frowned an intensely ugly scowl.

"One of the people who claimed they saw Gigi push Jean-Bernard was actually an ex-girlfriend of his," I said. "She and Jean-Bernard had just spent the night together."

"So?"

I gave him a patient smile and opened my hands to him as if presenting my case.

"So she could have drugged him," I said.

"For what possible reason?"

Was this guy for real?

"In order to kill him," I said carefully. "Because he dumped her. Like in a crime of passion."

He made a disgusting sound in the back of his throat.

"Taking several hours to kill someone is not a crime of passion," he said.

"Fine, then. So we won't call it a crime of passion," I said through gritted teeth. "But it is still a motive. I had coffee with Eloise Caron and she confessed that she didn't see Gigi push Jean-Bernard. But she told the police she had—which of course has to be against the law, not to mention very suspicious. Did you hear the part where she spent the night with him? With plenty of time to drug him—and then she followed him and his current girlfriend to the Eiffel Tower where he fell? Then she lies and tells the police she saw Gigi push him! Don't you see?"

"You had coffee with her?" he said, his mouth agape in surprise.

I was really hoping he wasn't going to focus on that part of my story.

"She told me she didn't see anything," I said firmly. "She *lied* to your officers. She made a false statement. But more importantly, she was with him beforehand! She could've drugged him."

"No, she couldn't have," he said. "There wasn't enough time. I could arrest you for interfering in an ongoing investigation," he said, a small smile twitching on his lips. "I could take you right now, cuff your hands behind your back and put you in my cruiser."

Dear God, he is getting off on the idea of handcuffing me!

"Have you heard anything I said?" I asked peevishly, pushing my glass of champagne away from me.

"I have watched your lips with interest," he said, licking his own. "I have found myself imagining what else those lips might be capable of."

I fought a sick roiling in my stomach. I'd had too much to drink today and not enough to eat. The vegetable tempura that I'd bought for tonight's dinner was sitting in a bag at my feet. Just as I was contemplating perhaps stealing one or two out of the bag to prevent myself from fainting from hunger or revulsion when the waiter returned with the plate of fries.

"I was very surprised to get your invitation today," Muller said as I reached for the fries. "Surprised but pleased."

"Look, Detective Muller," I said, wiping the grease from my fingers on my napkin. "All I want to do is confirm with you that you registered that the autopsy showed the victim was drugged with enough sedatives to have killed him."

"Except the drugs did not kill him," he said as he helped himself to the fries. As he ate there was a glistening shine of fat on his upper lip. "It was the fall that killed him."

"Yes, but the drugs *would've* killed him!"

"I do not deal in *would'ves*, Madame. I deal in facts."

"I don't think that's true, Capitaine," I said, feeling my temper about to get the best of me. "I'm sure when you investigate any case you have to consider multiple possibilities."

He reached across the table and grabbed my hand, his eyes on mine, his expression wolfish.

"The drugs are irrelevant," he said.

I tried to tug my hand out of his grip as I felt my fury begin to build.

"How can you say that?" I asked and then yelped as I felt his other hand which had been under the table slip between my knees.

It's entirely possible that what happened next was a bit of an overreaction.

I jerked away from him, my knee banging loudly and painfully into the table which knocked both champagne flutes to the floor with a crash. I jumped to my feet and snatched up my purse and coat.

Just as I was forming a scorching exit line—and it was going to be a doozy—Muller did something that I never in a million years would have imagined he'd do.

He beat me to it.

He stood up and faced me, his face red with embarrassment as the other diners around us stopped talking and turned to stare.

"I was made to believe by the detective before me that you would be a little more accommodating," he said as he peeled off two euro bills and tossed them onto our table.

Then he left the bar, leaving me to stare after him, my whole body humming with revulsion and outrage.

31

I was relieved that I'd asked Haley to stay the night. She was able to distract and play with both Izzy and Robbie, allowing me to fume quietly as I heated up the *panang* and tempura and served them with a salad. I added a big glass of Merlot—although you would've thought I'd had plenty to drink today—and none of it improved things. At all.

I'd spent most of the walk home berating myself for thinking even for an instant that I would get a fair hearing from Capitaine Muller or that I could handle him when he realized my ruse.

I knew very well that he thought it was a date. The sheer blinding hubris and lack of self-awareness on my part to lure him there under false pretenses and then expect I could manage the fallout made me cringe. Maybe on some level the detective heard some of the things I told him. But after the disastrous way our meeting had ended, I'm pretty sure he would never again be receptive to anything I said.

In fact, it's a pretty safe bet that if someone were to mention my name in the future—let alone any views espoused by me—I imagine Muller would exhibit a classic Pavlovian reaction of snarling resistance, and antipathy to both me and those ideas.

The walk home had been cold and dispiriting. At least, during my rehash of the evening's disaster I'd succeeded in blocking out Muller's shocking exit line, which I suppose had to do with Jean-Marc. I'm a little vulnerable when it comes to Jean-Marc these days. The thought that he or anyone in his old department had talked about us was humiliating at best.

And just really depressing at worst.

In any case, I'd made an enemy of the detective on Gigi's case and that was a shame because, given my line of work, this was not the last time I'd be forced to work with him. Now he would shut down as soon as he set eyes on me.

Unless of course I was willing to sleep with him at some point in the future.

No, it was too soon to joke about it. Come to think of it, there was nothing about that thought that was remotely funny. Nor could I imagine ever would be.

Compared to my day, dinner that night—which was solemn and spiritless—was practically a party. Haley picked up the carrot bits that Robbie gleefully lobbed at both of us to Izzy's delight. Haley seemed not only to not mind the extra work this involved but to even be impressed with Robbie's antics.

"He's invented a game," she said as she popped another carrot piece onto the tray of his highchair. I bit my lip to prevent myself from asking her to stop doing that somewhere around the fifth time I watched Robbie gnaw on a carrot stick that had been rolling around the carpeted floor just seconds earlier.

She turned to me and frowned.

"So Robbie's not your grandson?" she asked.

I was surprised that she was only now just becoming curious about the setup I had with Robbie. On the other hand, most teenagers I knew were remarkably incurious about anything having to do with the adults around them.

"No," I said. "He's the orphaned child of a good friend of mine."

That of course was not at all true, since as much as I struggled with forgiving my husband after his death, even now I couldn't accurately call him a friend—good or otherwise.

At one point, Haley held up a finger to Robbie and he froze, his eyes watching her intently until she snapped her fingers. Since it really seemed more like a trick you'd teach to a dog, I glanced at Izzy to see if she played this game too, but she was too busy watching for falling French fries.

As Robbie and Haley played their little game, I felt a flinch in my heart and realized it was because I was sorry that Bob would never get to know Robbie. I know I've come a long circuitous route since learning of Bob's infidelity and indeed Robbie's existence, too. But the fact is, he's an amazing little boy and I have no doubt he'll grow into a special and unique young man.

And it's just a shame that his father will never know him.

"How did they die?" Haley asked. "His parents. Was it a car accident?"

I sighed and wondered if I should just make something up. In the end I didn't have the energy either for the truth or for the fabrication.

"No, they died separately," I said. "It was just bad luck for Robbie."

She turned to look at him. "I'll say," she said softly.

"But he has me," I said brightly and then hesitated. "And you."

I swear I literally saw her shoulders lift as if whatever burden or weight had been pushing her down was suddenly removed by my words. I didn't know how long the effect would last, but the split-second transformation—for however brief—

was dramatic and told me that Haley was struggling to find her place in the world.

She reached out and touched Robbie's hand. He instantly grabbed hers and held on tight.

"He's so smart," she murmured.

"Mart!" Robbie parroted back at her, making us both laugh.

Later after Haley had taken Robbie away for his bath, I realized that much more than when Gigi lived with us, life was tranquil and less complicated with Haley in the house. For one thing, I didn't feel as if I had to entertain her or make conversation. She was like a ghost who flitted around in the background, perfectly happy to be tending to the baby and doing her thing and not needing anything from me.

It wasn't until Haley came to be a part of my life that I realized that, with Gigi, I always felt as if I had a guest in the house. For some reason I didn't feel that way with Haley for some reason.

I sat down on the couch with my laptop and a glass of wine when I saw I had an email from Sabine. The subject line read: *Tomorrow's meeting with Joelle and her attorney.*

I groaned. I had totally forgotten that the meeting was tomorrow. I opened the email where Sabine again reminded me to dress up and to please let her do the talking. While this wasn't a mediation meeting per se, it might become one if I didn't ruin all chances by saying the wrong thing at the wrong time. Typical encouraging lawyer pep talk stuff.

I wrote back saying I'd be there with bells on, but she should be sure and tell me if bells were inappropriate dress. Then I sat back in the couch and let the feeling of dread course through me.

Just what I need. A midweek meeting with the one person in the world who truly hates my guts.

I closed out of my email and opened the Excel file I'd

created to help me sort through what I knew at this point about Gigi's case.

Very quickly I discovered that what little I knew wasn't going to help Gigi.

In combination with the fact that I'd made an enemy of the detective on the case—super bad move—was the fact that Gigi's lawyer didn't have the experience or time to build a winnable case for her. Plus, I couldn't afford to hire anyone better.

I opened up a new document on my laptop and typed three names into three columns.

Under the column with Eloise's name I wrote *motive and opportunity.*

Under Zéro's name I typed *opportunity and means.*

And in the last column I wrote Paolo's name and wrote *motive and opportunity.*

I felt mildly guilty about putting Paolo's name into a column but, brother or no brother, he had acted suspiciously and he had both motive and opportunity.

Plus he had something else. Something undefinable but still very real.

Passion.

When I thought back to what I'd told Muller—when I had the stomach at all to think back to our meeting this evening—I reminded myself that even if the murder had been set in motion hours before it actually happened, it could still be considered a crime of passion.

That thought reminded me of something he'd said that bothered me. He said Eloise Caron couldn't have drugged Jean-Bernard because "there wasn't enough time." What did he mean by that? What don't I know?

I forcibly put both Detective Muller and Eloise Caron from of my mind. The fact was, I had two prime suspects I was staring right in the face. Two men who had motive, opportunity and means to kill Jean-Bernard.

And something more.

Passion.

In fact, the more I thought about it, the more sure I was that the anger that both Zéro and Paolo revealed would have given either of them the drive and passion necessary to do the job.

32

I must have fallen asleep on the couch because all of a sudden I was jerked awake by the sound of a ringing phone. I picked up my cell phone and saw that it was after midnight and that my caller was Paolo.

"Hello?" I answered, looking around the room to see that Izzy was now standing at the front door to deliver her time-honored signal that she needed to go out.

"I am sorry to call you so late," Paolo said, his voice brittle and hesitant.

I stood up and slipped on my shoes.

"I was still up," I said as I went to the coat rack to get my coat and Izzy's leash. "Is there something you forgot to tell me?"

He let out an agonized breath.

"I don't know what is happening," he said. "Julien and I broke up tonight."

"I'm sorry to hear that," I said as I connected Izzy to the leash and stepped outside into the hall. Instantly the hall lights came on. Gripping the bannister against the ever-present danger of slipping on the slick steps, I began the careful walk downstairs.

"He said I was too clingy," Paolo said, his voice thick with tears.

"The breakup didn't have anything to do with Gigi, did it?" I asked.

"Gigi? No. Why do you ask?"

Is it possible the man was really this self-absorbed?

"No reason," I said. "But I'm curious: Why did you run away the other day?"

"What are you talking about?"

I pushed open the heavy front door off the lobby.

"You asked to see me and then once we got talking you bolted."

"No, I didn't."

I felt a headache coming on.

"What is the point of this, Paolo? Do you have something to tell me or not? Is any of this about Gigi?"

"How dare you insinuate I don't care about what's happening to my sister!"

"Then tell me why you're calling," I said, walking Izzy to the far side of the courtyard where she quickly squatted on the stones. The framing walls of the building opposite the courtyard blocked the breeze that I was sure was whistling down rue de Laborde outside my apartment building. But it was still very cold.

"I wanted to know…if you'd heard anything from, you know, her lawyer," he said unconvincingly.

"You're still lying to me," I said.

"I am not!"

"You never mentioned to me how close you were to Jean-Bernard in school," I said. "That's lying."

"What are you talking about? Jean-Bernard and I drifted apart. People do. It was no big deal."

"Except you hated him then so it *was* a big deal. Why did you drift apart?"

"If I told you...if you knew..."

I hurried Izzy back through the big double doors and into the warmth of the ground floor foyer or *rez-de-chaussée* as the French call it.

"Tell me, Paolo. Tell me what happened."

"It was stupid. Nothing." He paused. "We had a thing. It was just the one time. We were both drunk. But then when he started dating my sister, he became more and more insistent that it had never happened. He was furious at the thought I might tell Gigi."

"Would you have?"

I hesitated at the elevator. I was tired and tempted to take it. But I didn't trust it. Even if it didn't plunge me to my death—always a possibility—the thought of getting trapped in it for the night made me turn to the stairs to begin the trudge up the staircase.

"I don't know," he said. "Honestly, I was so screwed up by then and so angry. I couldn't tell what part of me was angry and what part of me was just hurt."

"Was Jean-Bernard angry with you, too?"

"He was," he said. "He said I was holding that one night over his head."

"Did you threaten to tell Gigi?"

"I told him I would never tell her unless he..."

I stopped in front of my door, my actions frozen by his words.

"Unless he what?" I said.

"It doesn't matter."

Blackmail is a gold standard motive for murder. So yes, it mattered. But I didn't push him. He would either tell me or he wouldn't.

Unfortunately, it turned out he wouldn't.

It seemed he'd made a confession to me that he hadn't

expected to make and now he was clearly feeling a little vulnerable.

"Paolo, I know you care about your sister," I said, trying to get him back on track as I opened the door and reentered the apartment, shrugging out of my coat. "And I can only imagine how horrifying it must have been knowing your ex-best friend was hurting her."

"You know nothing!" he said heatedly.

"Look, calm down," I said. "Have you talked to Julien about all this?"

"I told you! He broke up with me!"

"Yes, but he still cares about you, right? Surely you two talked?"

"I don't know," he said sadly, a little calmer. "Julien's going through some things right now too."

"Like what?"

"You know he never should have taken that job at *Mieux Faire*. I told him so."

"Why not?"

"You've met him! He's amazing. He could work anywhere. He could do great things. I'll never understand why he went there."

This was definitely sounding like it was devolving into someone who needed to talk about why his ex was now his ex. While I felt for Paolo, I was tired and it was late. Surely he had friends he could process his break-up with?

"I need to go," I said. "I'm sorry about you and Julien."

"Thanks," he said, totally dispirited.

I checked in on Haley and Robbie and then began my nighttime ablutions of flossing, washing my face and, though it was late, even doing a few yoga poses. It had been weeks since I'd made time for the yoga class I normally attended. I of all people know how important stretching and balancing is—especially at my age. There was really no excuse for skipping the class and I made a stern mental note to myself to start going back this week.

After Izzy and I curled up in bed, I decided I was too tired to read even a few pages of the novel I'd started so I snapped off the light and fell quickly to sleep.

I don't know how long I slept when I realized I was being rudely pulled out of my dreams by the sound of a ringing phone. I fumbled for it on my nightstand and looked at the screen for the caller ID.

UNKNOWN.

Suddenly the phone stopped ringing. Whoever it was had thought better of it. My mind raced with the possibilities, not least of which were my father or even Jean-Marc. Whoever it was had used a burner phone or had deliberately blocked his number.

Besides my creepy crazy father, who would do that?

There was no sense in wracking my brain. I wasn't going to found out who it was unless they called back.

Now fully awake, I decided to get up and make myself a rum toddy. Izzy followed me into the kitchen as I pulled out a mug from the cabinet and then extricated a bottle of rum from under the sink. As I put a little pan on the stove and added in a pat of butter, Izzy began to growl low and steadily.

My breath caught in my throat as I turned to look at her. She was standing rigidly on all fours, her eyes drilling into the front door. I snapped my fingers and she turned her head toward me and stopped growling long enough for me to listen.

That was when I heard the creaking floorboard outside my front door.

Someone was outside.

33

I signaled for Izzy to hush and crept to the door where I put my ear against it and listened. At first I couldn't hear anything but I *felt* someone on the other side. And then I heard breathing, faint at first but definite.

"Who's out there?" I said in as normal a voice as I could manage.

The breathing seemed to stop abruptly as if whoever was out there had begun to hold his breath.

I inched up to look out the peep hole that I'd had installed but it was totally dark. Darker than it should've been.

Whoever it was had their hand over the peep hole.

"Paolo? Is that you? Do you want to talk?"

And then I heard the footsteps walking away. I strained to hear if they would take the elevator but I didn't hear sounds of that. Pretty soon I heard nothing whatsoever.

I stood up and turned to look at Izzy who was sitting on the carpet, her head cocked as if trying to figure me out. I moved back to the kitchen and my hot toddy but decided I was no longer in the mood for it.

I don't know why I thought it might be Paolo in my hallway. It could just as easily have been Zéro or even Julien.

Or, God knows, Muller.

It wasn't easy to get into my apartment building. But somebody with Zéro's skills or Muller's access could probably have managed it.

Whoever it was, if they'd wanted to see me or talk to me why hadn't they answered when I'd spoken? What made them change their mind?

It was too much for me to figure out, especially at three in the morning. I motioned for Izzy to follow me back to the bedroom but I could've saved myself the effort. She would go where I went in any case.

In spite of the mysterious phone call and the middle-of-the-night visitor, in spite of Paolo's upsetting phone call and everything I'd learned today and in spite of the memory of Detective Muller's new-found enmity of me—in spite of all of that, I do believe I was asleep as soon as my head hit the pillow.

The next morning I was awakened by the sound of someone pounding on my front door. I grabbed my robe and raced to the door, looked out the peephole. I opened the door. Adele stood in the hall holding two coffees and a box of *pain d'épices, pain au chocolat* and croissants from Eric Kayser's. She stepped inside.

"Get dressed," she said. "I'll take Mademoiselle Izzy out."

"What's up?" I asked, feeling as if I hadn't slept a wink last night. I felt a wave of confusion as I stared into the hallway. It had only been four hours since my late-night visitor.

I closed the door and turned to Adele who had set down the pastry box and was already snapping Izzy's leash on her.

"I'm pretty sure the police are going to want to talk to you," she said. "Better hurry."

I felt my throat start to close up.

"Me? Why do they want to talk to me?"

Adele grabbed a croissant from the box and stepped back into the hallway.

"Hurry, Claire. Get dressed." And then she disappeared down the stairs.

"What's going on?" Haley asked.

I turned to see her standing in the doorway of the guest room, a sleepy Robbie on her hip.

"I'm not sure," I said walking toward my bedroom. "But Adele's brought *pain au chocolat*."

I jumped in the shower and dressed for the day in my typical winter uniform—wool slacks, and cashmere crewneck sweater. By the time I came back out of my bedroom, Adele and Haley were eating sweet rolls at the dining room table. Robbie was dressed and sitting in his highchair with a croissant. Adele had poured half her coffee into a ceramic mug to share with Haley. I didn't even know the girl drank coffee.

I picked up the remaining carton of coffee and took a sip. It was still hot.

"So what's going on?" I asked Adele. "Why will the police want to speak to me?"

"They'll want to speak to you because they cracked his phone and, lo and behold, there was a thirty-minute call made to your number last night."

The blood drained from my face, I sat down hard on one of the dining room chairs, my eyes on Robbie as he began to drop pieces of pastry to Izzy. Chills raced up and down my arms.

"No," I said. "Tell me it's not true."

"Sorry," Adele said. "Paolo was found dead this morning on his balcony."

34

For a moment I was having trouble breathing. I looked at Haley but she only shrugged.

"She already told me," she said.

"He killed himself?" I asked.

"Maybe," Adele said.

I licked my lips, trying to wrap my brain around what had happened and when. So was that *not* Paolo in my hallway last night? And if not him, then who was it?

"How?" I asked and then glanced at Haley.

"It's okay," she said. "I can handle it and Robbie can't understand."

"A friend of mine called me last night," Adele said. "He worked the scene and heard the detective when he picked up Paolo's phone and saw you were his last call. The detective didn't know you. It's because you have an unusual last name that he even said it out loud and my friend was able to over-hear. The detective thought it was a joke."

I swallowed hard.

What does this mean? Is Paolo's death somehow connected to Jean-Bernard's murder? Did this mean that Paolo didn't kill Jean-Bernard? Or he did and killed himself out of guilt?

Haley got up and went into the kitchen to get a washcloth for Robbie's sticky fingers. Adele turned to me.

"So you did speak to Paolo last night?"

"I did."

"Well, they're going to want to talk to you about it."

My stomach wrenched and I put the coffee down thinking I might throw up. I picked up a piece of croissant to settle my stomach.

"I can't believe he would kill himself," I said.

All of a sudden I remembered Paolo telling me his big secret—his one-night stand with Jean-Bernard—and how afraid Jean-Bernard was that Gigi would find out. Had Paolo been afraid that Gigi would find out too?

"Are you okay, Claire? You look green."

"I'm fine," I said, not feeling at all fine.

When Haley came back to the dining room she looked at me and frowned.

"You don't look too good," she said.

"Can you stay the day?" I asked her. "In case...in case I have to go down to the police station?"

She shrugged and turned to feed a piece of croissant to Izzy.

"Sure," she said.

I turned to Adele. The remark by Muller had bothered me on and off all morning.

"I need to know something, Adele," I said. "The drug cocktail that killed Jean-Bernard—how long after taking it would it have taken effect?"

"He would have had to ingest it thirty minutes beforehand," Adele said.

My stomach dropped.

Thirty minutes?

No wonder Muller didn't think Eloise Caron could have

done it. Even if she'd poisoned him the moment he walked out her door, it was still too much time before he collapsed.

Thirty minutes put the likely cause of death firmly back in Gigi's time frame. Eloise was in the clear. So was Zéro too.

The only person who could have poisoned Jean-Bernard was Gigi.

All of a sudden Izzy bounded to the door, barking maniacally.

"Uh oh," Adele said. "I'll bet that's them."

I felt a sheen of sweat develop on my forehead.

"Haley, if you need anything, you know Geneviève is right downstairs," I said.

"We'll be fine, Missus B," Haley said, completely nonplussed by anything that was happening. "Won't we, Sport?" She tickled Robbie under his chin and I felt a twinge of relief as I heard the sound of multiple heavy footsteps assembling in the hall outside my door.

At least I wouldn't have to worry about Robbie today.

Once more I found myself sitting in the cold and grim interview room of the Paris police department. Same metal table with the same handcuffs hanging from the underside. Same windowless approach.

The people who'd come to escort me downtown were not anybody I recognized. Often I can tell if people know me—even though I don't know them—because they tend to hold my gaze a second too long, or generally act put out with me when there's no obvious reason for it. Now, granted, cops generally tend to manifest both those aspects but even so, I had the feeling I'd not met any of these police before.

And the detective on the case was not Vincent Muller, thank God.

Detective Monet was a young woman. Not surprisingly, she was not at all friendly but neither was she staring at my breasts.

"How did you know Paolo Rozen?" she asked from where she sat across from me at the table.

"He's the brother of my au pair, Gigi Rozen," I said, my hands wrapped around a bottle of water they'd given me.

"The one who is a suspect in the Eiffel Tower murder?"

I licked my lips. I hated that she put it that way. But it was the truth.

"That's right."

"Why were you in contact with her brother?"

"We were discussing the case against his sister," I said although Paolo and I had actually spent very little time doing that.

"Were you romantically involved with the victim?"

My eyebrows must have shot up at that question.

"No," I said. "Paolo Rozen was gay."

The detective flipped through a file folder on the desk in front of her.

"How did Paolo kill himself?" I asked but she ignored my question.

"Where were you from twenty hundred hours until four this morning?"

Seriously? Because I had a phone conversation with him, I'm a suspect?

"I was at my apartment."

"Can anyone verify that?"

"I have an eighteen-month-old baby," I said, feeling my ire return. "Do you really think I would leave him alone in the middle of the night?"

Stupid question. I'm sure she's known people who would do much crazier things.

"So you have no one who can verify your whereabouts?"

"My babysitter spent the night with me last night," I said.

"Was she not asleep?"

I tossed my hands up in the air in a signal of capitulation.

"Yes, of course she was asleep."

"So in fact you were never in any danger of leaving an eighteen-month-old baby alone in the apartment and you do not have someone who can verify you were there all night." She looked at me and narrowed her eyes.

"You must really be desperate if you're trying to pin this on me," I said.

Suddenly the interview room door swung open and Detective Muller appeared. He didn't look at me but spoke in rapid fire French to Monet who got to her feet, the folder under her arm, and left the room with him.

I had a sour taste in my mouth.

What was that all about? Was Muller her boss? Was he attached to this case? Come to think of it, that would actually make sense since Paolo was related to his prime suspect. Could I even imagine a worse situation where a detective who now had a personal grudge against me was put in the position of considering me as a suspect for murder? I chased the negative thought from my mind. It wouldn't help to scare myself unnecessarily.

I tried to think of something else—anything else—other than the fact that poor Paolo was dead and for some reason the cops thought I knew more than I did.

It took nearly thirty minutes before the door opened again and when it did, my worst fear walked through it. Detective Muller now held the same file folder that Monet had held before. Without looking at me, he sat down in the chair opposite me.

"Where is Detective Monet?" I asked.

Muller ignored my question and opened the file folder. Looking at the photograph upside down, I could see it was a blurry photo taken from a CCTV camera.

"Detective Muller," I said. "I have been here for nearly two hours and I have not been apprised of my rights."

He looked at me and for the first time his eyes found my eyes.

I'm not sure that was exactly a step forward for us.

"French law does not require I read you your rights," he said. "I may keep you for whatever reason I like for seventy-two hours."

I knew that, of course, and I could have bitten my tongue for starting back in on him in a combative way. He clearly had a major problem with me.

And he held all the cards. The only thing I could do was make everything worse by talking.

Seventy-two hours is a long, long time when it's spent inside a jail cell.

"Surely you have no reason to hold me in connection with this suicide," I said, clearly not able to take my own advice to keep my mouth shut.

"Suicide?" Muller said with feigned surprise. "*Non.* The ME has just updated his findings. It is now a homicide."

My stomach roiled.

"No," I said. "How? I thought he...he..."

But the fact was nobody had yet told me *how* Paolo had died. Adele had only said *maybe* suicide. That was all.

"You thought what, Madame Baskerville? You thought it would appear that the victim would look to have taken his own life?"

"No, that's not what I meant."

"Paolo Rozen left no suicide note. The drugs that killed him were not recreational drugs. He had made an appointment with his hairdresser for eight this morning."

"You clearly know more than I do," I said. "So why are you questioning me? Why am I even here?"

He slowly and dramatically turned the folder around so I

could see the screen grab from the CCTV camera which revealed a woman in a raincoat, her face turned toward the camera but obscured by the shadows of the streetlamp outside an apartment building. The address was labeled on the photo. It was Paolo's apartment.

"We are questioning you, Madame," Muller said, his lip twisted in a curl, "because we have video footage that shows you leaving the victim's apartment at three o'clock this morning."

35

I stared at the photo in front of me. I could see how he might think it was me. But aside from general body type and clothing, there was no way he or anyone could say for sure that it was in fact me.

I kept saying that over and over in my head.

He can't prove it's me he can't prove its me he can't prove it's me

I pushed the photo away.

"This isn't me," I said as firmly as I could, locking eyes with him.

We stared at each other for a moment and I knew he was rerunning in his mind the tape of our last encounter where I'd humiliated him in front of a restaurant full of people. I held his gaze, thinking that breaking away first was somehow an admission of guilt or weakness. That's ridiculous, I know. There was no way this guy was ever going to respect me or see me as anything but the woman who embarrassed him and insulted his manhood. No matter how long I could hold his gaze without blinking.

But even knowing that, I couldn't look away.

"There's a CCTV camera outside my apartment building," I said. "It will prove I didn't leave my apartment last night."

I might as well have been talking to a wall. If I thought the CCTV camera would show anything except what Muller wanted to see, I was naïve. I put my hands in my lap because I could feel them shaking.

In the end, he stood up and gave instructions for the police-woman standing by the door to walk me out. Before he left the room, he came over to me and put his hand on my shoulder, gripping me so painfully I nearly cried out.

"We are not finished yet, you and I," he said before releasing me and stalking out of the room.

I felt a shakiness in my legs and even when the police-woman walked over to me, I stayed seated, only moving to wrap my hands around the water bottle on the table and drink. I took in a few long breaths but even then I needed more time to get myself together before I felt strong enough to get up and walk out of the room on my own.

I called Haley as soon as I was outside the police station to check on her and Robbie.

It was lunch time and I was astonished to realize I was starving. After Haley assured me that all was well on her end, I called Adele and we arranged to meet at Les Deux Magots which was far enough away from the police station to make me feel as if I'd put it in my rear view mirror but not too far that it was a challenge for me to walk the distance, shaken and hungry as I was.

Adele and I arrived at the famous café at almost the exact same time and snagged a table on the corner of the terrace. Even though it was outdoors and freezing, I preferred it to being inside. I didn't feel like being penned up today—possibly as a result of the scare that Muller had thrown into me when he made me believe I was his prime suspect for Paolo's murder.

After we ordered *croque tartine Parisienne* for her and *quiche Lorraine* for me, I snuggled deep into the comfort of my down parka and waited impatiently for my hot mulled wine to arrive.

"Muller told me that Paolo was murdered," I said. "Was it the same cocktail that killed Jean-Bernard?"

"As it happens, it was."

"I can see that that seems like too much of a coincidence," I said. "But was there another reason besides the CCTV video at Paolo's apartment that made them believe it was murder?"

"Honestly, Claire, they always thought it was murder."

"Really?"

"There were signs of a struggle, for one thing. And no note. Is there any chance your DNA will match anything we find there?"

"I can't imagine it will. I was never at Paolo's apartment."

"Good."

"Did you see the CCTV video?"

"Yes," she said, suddenly focused on the waiter who came over to us with our meals.

"Do you think it looks like me?"

"It's fuzzy but yes, it does appear to resemble you."

The waiter set our dishes down and peppered Adele's plate. Then he agreed to bring me another mulled wine even though he'd only now delivered my first.

"The police need more than a fuzzy CCTV video to hold you," Adele said. "If there's no trace of you at his place, you've got nothing to worry about."

"Are you sure?"

She shrugged. "Muller will attempt to make your life miserable, that's all."

Oh great. That's all.

I drank down my mulled wine and felt a little better.

I found myself swamped with questions about who would want to kill Paolo.

Who was the woman in the CCTV video? Was it Eloise? Marie-France? Someone I hadn't met yet in connection with Jean-Bernard's murder?

For one mad moment, I even thought it might be Joelle dressed up to try to implicate me. I totally wouldn't put it past her.

Midway into my meal, my phone rang and I saw it was Julien.

"I have to take this," I told Adele, turning in my chair and dropping my voice as I took the call. "Julien?"

"I need to see you," Julien said, his voice strained.

"Yes, of course," I said. "When and where?"

"I'm at work. Can you meet me here? In an hour?"

I glanced at my watch. "One hour." I hung up and turned back to Adele.

"Was that the victim's boyfriend?" she asked.

"It was. Do you think the cops questioned him?"

She shrugged. "They might not know he was connected to the victim. Is it possible *he* killed Paolo?"

Until she said it, that thought had not occurred to me.

"Anything's possible," I said. I took a bite of my *quiche* before pushing it away, suddenly no longer hungry. "But a motive for him doesn't immediately jump out at me."

"Perhaps it will after you talk with him."

I gulped down half of my wine and tossed a twenty-euro note onto the table before gathering up my purse.

"I'm sorry, Adele, but I'm meeting him at his office and it occurs to me that this would be a good time to question Marie-France again."

"Jean-Bernard's boss?"

"Yes. I found out that she had a fling with Gigi at one point."

"Goodness. All your friends are sluts."

"They're not my friends."

My phone pinged and I looked down to see a text from Sabine.

<Are you ready for today? 16 hrs?>

I had totally forgotten about the meeting with Joelle and her lawyer.

"Bad news?" Adele asked.

I glanced down at the slacks and baggy sweater I was wearing and imagined the horrified look on Sabine's face when I waltzed into the meeting at the high end attorney's address on the Champs-Élysee looking like I'd just come from working in my garden.

"It doesn't matter," I said as I doubled-kissed Adele goodbye and turned to hurry down the sidewalk.

Except I knew it absolutely did.

36

I t was a little after one o'clock when I arrived at *Mieux Faire*. I decided that if I bumped into Julien I would just ask him to wait until I finished talking to Marie-France. The receptionist took me down the hall to Marie-France's office past the closed door of Julien's office.

Marie-France stood up as I entered, her expression difficult to read but hardly welcoming.

"I'm sorry to barge in on you a second time in a week," I said. "But I have a few more questions if you would be so kind."

Her hesitation would have been barely perceptible if you hadn't been looking for it, which of course I was. She thought she was done with me and at least on some level she was resisting the thought of being questioned further. I would have to find out why.

As I sat down in the chair opposite her desk, she restlessly picked up and repositioned both the stapler and a paperweight on her desk.

"The police led me to believe they were through with their investigation," she said.

"I think they are," I said.

She raised an eyebrow.

"I guess by now you've heard about what happened to Paolo Rozen," I said.

"Of course I'm sorry he is dead but I didn't know him," she said glibly, her expression not at all mournful.

"But you knew his sister?" I said.

Might as well get right to it.

Her face tightened visibly as if she'd been ready for this question but didn't think it would come so soon.

"Yes," she said slowly.

"Could you please expand on that?" I asked pleasantly. "I am trying to find Gigi innocent of a crime I don't believe she committed."

"What do you want to know?"

"How well did you know Gigi?"

"I only saw her the few times she came into the office with Jean-Bernard."

"That's not what I heard. I heard Gigi was your girlfriend at one point."

Now of course that is an exaggeration but I have found in my experience in private investigation that if you take a fact and exaggerate it, one of two things will happen. Either the person who knows it's an exaggeration—but basically the truth—will deny the exaggeration—which of course means they confirm the basic truth, or they will *ignore* the exaggeration and deny the core fact. In that case, it's possible you got your facts wrong.

Marie-France went after the exaggeration.

"She was not my girlfriend! It was one night!"

"Why did you lie about not knowing her?"

"I don't have to answer these questions! The police have their killer! Gigi killed Jean-Bernard!"

That statement got the wheels in my brain turning. I hadn't seriously considered Marie-France as Jean-Bernard's murderer until that moment, but it did make sense that, for Marie-

France, killing Jean-Bernard and then framing Gigi for it had a very tidy *two birds with one stone* vibe to it.

Unfortunately I had very little time to consider that hypothesis at all, since Marie-France was now on her feet and her receptionist was at the door with a look of horror and consternation on her face. Standing beside her was Julien.

"You are early for our appointment, Madame Baskerville," Julien said to me.

"Get out!" Marie-France screamed at me as Julien put his hand on my elbow and firmly guided me out of her office.

The park we walked to was just around the corner from *Mieux Faire*. It was empty on this cold gray day. No children playing, no businessmen eating late lunches, no dog walkers or exercise enthusiasts trying to get their steps in.

Just me and Julien sitting on a bench that took both of us a full five minutes to brush clean of snow before we could sit down.

"I think you can forget about ever being allowed back in *Mieux Faire*," he said. "If I'd known you were going to confront her with what I told you about Gigi I never would have told you."

"You have to admit she acted pretty nuts back there. Violent even."

"If you're suggesting Marie-France killed Jean-Bernard, you can stop right there," Julien said. "Marie-France is a warm-hearted, passionate woman. It's a trait I personally admire her for."

His eyes seemed to mist and he turned his face away. I wished I had the chance to study his face to see if his tears were fake but he kept his face turned away until he composed himself. If that was what he was doing.

"Paolo didn't kill himself," I said bluntly.

He stared at me, blinking slowly. "Of course he did. What are you talking about?"

"The police believe it to be a suspicious death."

I watched him closely to see if he could be faking his astonishment. I honestly couldn't tell.

"Who would kill him?" he asked finally, looking away to stare forlornly at the frozen park landscape.

"I don't know, but there is CCTV footage that shows a woman leaving Paolo's apartment last night during the critical time."

"So you think Marie-France had something to do with Paolo's death?"

"Someone did. Why not her?"

I gave him a minute to digest that before I hit him with my second attack.

"Paolo called me last night."

A veil seemed to come down over Julien's face at my words. His eyes were instantly hooded and unreadable.

"Why would he do that?" he asked.

"He wanted to get some things off his chest," I said. "He told me he was encouraging you to leave *Mieux Faire*."

He gave me an incredulous look. "He told you that?"

"He said he thought you could do so much better. And that you never should have taken the job at *Mieux Faire* in the first place. He said he never understood why you did. Did Marie-France know Paolo was trying to get you to leave?"

"Stop trying to find a motive for Marie-France! She would never hurt Paolo. She knew how much he meant to me."

The big question of course was *how much exactly was that*? It took a lot of self-control on my part to bite back the question that would surely only trigger a series of impassioned denials from Julien.

We sat for a little bit longer in the cold. I saw by my watch that it was a little after three in the afternoon. My meeting with

Sabine and Joelle's lawyer was in less than an hour. But Julien still hadn't brought up the reason why he wanted to see me today. So far he hadn't mentioned what I would have thought was the very relevant fact that he and Paolo had broken up yesterday.

I watched him as he continued to stare out at the park grounds. Our puffs of cold breath were visible as we exhaled in the frigid air. Julien rubbed his nose and brushed a few unmelted snowflakes off his slacks.

I have to say that even before I moved to France, waiting had been a big part of my life. Mostly because I was a private investigator, it was at least ninety percent of what I did daily: waiting for the cheating spouse to show up with his girlfriend so I could take their picture, waiting to gather all my facts so I could invoice my clients, waiting for a suspect or interested party to tell me what I wanted to know. And in Paris the waiting is even worse.

Here the waiting is actually cultural, which means it's at every level of life.

I spend half my life waiting for waiters to recognize my existence and take my order, then wait again for them to show up with my bill. I stand in line forever—waiting for greengrocers to finish advising the shopper in front of me on how to stew the cut of lamb they're selling or what to serve with the cheese.

With all the waiting I'm forced to do, you'd think I'd be better at it.

"The last time I spoke with Paolo," Julien said, turning to me, his eyes damp with unshed tears, "he told me he felt responsible for Jean-Bernard's death."

"Responsible how?"

"He didn't go into detail. But I got the impression that he...that he..."

"Are you saying he confessed to killing him?"

He stared at his gloved hands.

"Are you saying Paolo confessed to killing Jean-Bernard?" I repeated more firmly.

"Not in so many words."

"It's not much of a confession if you're not sure he confessed," I pointed out.

"I'm sorry I got you out here in the cold," Julien said, clearing his throat and suddenly standing up. "But I felt I had to tell someone."

There was no way I believed Paolo killed Jean-Bernard. For some undefinable, probably emotional, reason, just hearing Julien accuse him of it made me all the more convinced of that.

Paolo didn't kill Jean-Bernard.

But Julien wanted me to think he did.

As I watched him walk away, his steps becoming quicker the further he walked from me, I found myself wondering what he would look like in a woman's wig and overcoat.

Could he pass for the person I'd seen in the CCTV video?

37

When it comes to mediation in a legal dispute there are a couple of obvious tenets recognized the world over.

If you are the one being sued *and* you are the one with the most to lose, you will go into the meeting on the defensive, bewildered, afraid and vulnerable.

I sat at that mediation table, less prepared for what was coming than I had ever been for anything in my life. And that's saying something, because I have been arrested for murder and spent two long hours waiting for a French medical examiner to tell me my husband had been murdered.

Joelle's lawyer, Mireille Absalom, smiled mechanically— she clearly knew Sabine—and nodded a curt greeting at me. The age-old French handshake was not in evidence here. Just as well. There was no way I was going to shake Joelle's hand.

"*Okay*," Absalom said. "We are here today to present the facts regarding a possible custody hearing for Robert Purdue."

As soon as she said Robbie's last name I cursed the fact that I hadn't moved faster on changing his name to Baskerville. Not that it would've made a difference today but it might've.

"My client and I are under the assumption that this case will be presented before a family judge," Sabine said with more confidence than I'd heard her demonstrate in a week.

"Yes, of course," Absalom said, "although after today you might agree that isn't necessary."

I felt a pinch of terror. What in the world did their side have that might make me not interested in bringing this mess before a judge? I may not have dotted my last i's on Robbie's adoption papers but there was no way I wasn't a fit guardian for him. Just the fact that I'd been caring for him for the last year surely gave me a serious leg up in that regard.

"As requested," Sabine said, "here are my client's petition-to-adopt papers."

Absalom glanced at the papers that Sabine pushed across the table to her but didn't touch them. I thought that was a bad sign.

I was right.

"I have seen them already," Absalom said. "They are a matter of public record."

Sabine frowned. "Since they are unfinished, they are not accessible publicly."

Absalom shrugged. "I think you'll find that they are. Shall I send you the link?"

Why was I starting to wish that Absalom was my attorney?

I glanced at Joelle who was watching me intently, a smile playing on her tight little pursed lips.

Petite, with auburn hair and a masterful plastic surgeon, Joelle was probably beautiful twenty years ago. Today, she just looked like a caricature of the perennially stylish French woman.

I'm honestly astonished that Joelle would be willing to spend what little money she had to go through this farce. Why was she even here? If she was hoping to take Robbie from me, that was a matter between me and child services. Where did she figure in?

That was the question that kept me up nights.

Was she hoping to make money somehow? Sabine told me that Joelle was asking to have all her attorney's fees covered by me if I lost the case. But even then, even if she "won," she could only get her money back. Her only real benefit was watching me lose. I guess that was a good enough gamble for her?

Maybe that's what someone feels when they have nothing really to lose.

Me, I have Robbie to lose. So I can't play games. I can't bluff. I can't take chances. If it comes down to it, I'll give Joelle back her apartment.

As I looked at her today across the table something told me that that wouldn't be enough.

"May I ask why it is you believe the court's input might not be relevant?" Sabine asked.

"We have found evidence that makes the question of your client as a suitable guardian for the child a moot point."

My stomach clenched.

What had they found out? I'd committed no crimes. True, I'd been accused of murder a couple of times but in every case I'd been exonerated.

Absalom reached into the file folder in front of her and pulled out two sheets of paper. This time she pushed one to me and the other to Sabine.

It was a statement of the adoption procedures in France and one I'd seen before. I'd confidently ticked all the boxes but I reread it quickly to try to see how in the world this could be something used against me.

In France I was able to adopt if I was married and had my spouse's signature, or if I was unmarried and over twenty five; if I was able to establish that I could provide proper parental care for the child; if I was able to establish that the child was an orphan as defined by French law; and finally if I could establish that I had personally observed the child before or even during the adoption proceedings.

Check and double check.

And yet. Joelle was using this seeming benefit against me somehow. I glanced at Sabine and she looked as confused as I felt.

"We are aware of the regulations for French adoption," Sabine said in that haughty tone that I'd missed so much. "As I said, we intend to adopt under American tenets. Both my client and the child are American citizens. Frankly, I am perplexed as to why your client has even contacted us on what is a personal family matter."

"Adoption under American law is not a given," Absalom said, ignoring Sabine's unspoken question as to why Joelle was involved. "My preliminary inquiries have suggested the case will be settled under French adoption jurisdictions. That is, unless your client intends to relocate back to the US?"

I forced myself not to look at Joelle. She knew I couldn't go back to the States. Not with all of Bob's creditors still lined up to intercept me the moment I got off the plane.

"We are petitioning the French courts to consider the matter," Absalom said.

"In what possible capacity do you petition the French courts?" Sabine asked testily. "It is a matter between my client and whichever country's adoption laws are petitioned."

"My client is serving as proxy for an interested party."

"What the hell does that mean?" I asked in bewilderment. I felt Sabine stiffen next to me. I knew she wanted me to keep my mouth shut.

With one ruby red talon Absalom tapped a paragraph on the sheet she'd just presented to us. When I leaned closer, I saw that the paragraph referenced that "the child was an orphan as defined by French law."

"Robbie has no relatives," I said and as soon as I did I saw what Joelle was up to.

She is going to prove that Robbie isn't an orphan.

My mouth was dry and I felt a roiling nausea begin in the pit of my stomach.

"We have found a relative of Courtney Purdue's," Absalom said, "who is willing to take the child."

"You're lying," I said before I could stop myself.

"Claire," Sabine said, putting a hand on my wrist in an effort to calm me.

"She's lying," I said, more heatedly. "Robbie has no next of kin. Both Bob and Courtney were only children. Both outlived their parents."

My heart began to beat faster. Saying the words out loud made me realize how weak that argument sounded. Could an aunt or cousin somehow be scraped up?

If someone really put her mind to it?

I turned to look at Joelle. She smiled evilly.

Her lawyer pulled another piece of paper out of her file folder and pushed it across the table to Sabine.

"Her name is Emily Bickerstaff," Absalom said. "She is married and lives in Arkansas. She is an aunt on the child's mother's side and as such under French law has the highest priority of placement preference for the purpose of adoption."

Sabine read the piece of paper.

"I don't care what that paper says," I said hotly. "I don't care who this Emily Bickerstaff person is. She's not getting Robbie. Courtney had no family. I'm his family."

Sabine turned to me, her face white.

"What?" I asked, reaching for the paper. "What is it?"

It was a laboratory DNA test result. It had Robbie's name printed on it along with Emily Bickerstaff of Little Rock, Arkansas.

I felt as my whole world was spinning around me, ready to

jump its axis and fly into the void. I was having trouble breathing. I actually pulled at the collar of my sweater.

"How did they get Robbie's DNA to do this test?" I asked, snatching up and flinging the sheet of paper at Joelle. "I'll sue you for illegal access! Did you break into my apartment? Or hire someone who did?"

"I do not have to break into anything," Joelle said, the first words she'd uttered since we'd stepped into the meeting room. "I merely found the pacifier the child dropped in the park one day."

My heart was racing as my gaze darted from Joelle to her lawyer. I literally felt the desperation welling up inside my chest.

"You followed us? You *stalked* us?" I asked, my voice rising shrilly. I turned to Sabine. "I want to make a formal complaint of stalking."

I know how that sounded, how weak and desperate. And I knew from the look on Sabine's face that it would do no good. In fact it would just make things worse.

"One final thing," Absalom said as she began to gather up her brief in the time-honored signal that the meeting was over.

"If rather than act in a way that is clearly in the best interests of the child your client instead attempts to bring this case before the US courts, I will be forced to file a statement of indictment alleging that she did not contact French child services in a timely manner."

She locked eyes with me. "Your attorney will explain it to you, Madame Baskerville, but in a nutshell it brings an allegation of child abduction against you. And in France that carries a prison sentence. So. Your choice."

I went completely still, with the lawyer's words ringing in my ears. She was telling me if I even tried to fight them on this I risked prison. For a moment I had difficulty focusing. When I finally turned to look at Joelle I saw she was smiling as me, her true purpose finally revealed.

As I stared at her, I felt for the first time since I'd met her something seismic that drew us together—a palpable bond that was greater than our connection to her husband and my father Claude, or the fact that we lived in the same beautiful apartment in the ninth arrondissement or even that we were inextricably fettered forever by French law.

No, the innate and undeniable connection I felt with Joelle was that I now knew what it was to hate someone so much I could barely breathe.

38

I think for the first time since I moved to Paris, I walked its streets and didn't see a single thing around me; not the pigeons, the sidewalk cafés, the entwined lovers, the skateboarders, the lacey silhouette of the black wrought artwork that formed Paris's historic architectural template. None of it. I walked home in a daze that clouded my vision and thankfully, at least to a certain extent, my emotions.

Every step I took from my meeting with Joelle and the lawyers felt like a fifty-pound weight was strapped to my legs.

Could they really charge me with child abduction? Who was this Emily Bickerstaff? Did she really want Robbie? How did Joelle find her?

I figured that my best bet was to track down Bickerstaff and talk to her myself. If I found out that Joelle had offered her money to take Robbie, maybe I could use that in my favor.

Unfortunately I'd had no time to debrief with Sabine over the disastrous meeting as she had another engagement she needed to hurry off to.

I got home at a little before six and Haley was ready and raring to be on her way. She had her skateboard with her and had already mentioned that she was going to meet a friend at a skateboarding park. If I'd had my wits about me I'd have made a bigger deal about the fact that she seemed to have made a friend.

But I was too stunned by my meeting with Joelle and her lawyer to respond normally. After saying goodbye to Haley, I dug out a nice bottle of Bordeaux, picked up Robbie, and walked downstairs with Izzy to Geneviève's apartment. I hadn't spoken to her in a few days and knew that there was every possibility she had plans tonight.

I knocked on her door and when she opened it I smelled the tantalizing fragrance of dinner cooking coming from her kitchen.

"Got time for a couple of lost Americans?" I said.

Izzy barked and jumped at Geneviève's knees before racing inside.

"Of course, *chérie*," Geneviève said, her face puckering into a worried frown. She held her arms out for Robbie but he was too rambunctious. I handed her the wine bottle instead and put Robbie on his feet and let him toddle into her apartment.

"Fix yourself a drink, *chérie*," Geneviève said. "I am making *choucroute garnie* tonight."

"That sounds great."

I went to the bar cart in her living room and made both of us a couple of gins with sweet vermouth and a dash of absinthe. I brought the drinks into the kitchen.

"What has happened?" she asked.

"Joelle found someone in the States who's a relative of Robbie's," I said.

Her eyes widened and she took a sip of her drink.

"Confirmed?" she asked.

She had a point. It certainly wasn't beyond Joelle's nasty proclivities to say she'd found someone when there was no one.

"I'll get on the Internet tonight and confirm it. But for now I'm acting under the assumption that this person exists."

"And she wants Robbie?"

"That is the million-dollar question," I said drinking half my glass down.

"*Chérie*, use my computer," Geneviève said. "Dinner won't be ready for another fifteen minutes."

I kissed her gratefully and brought my drink into the living room where she kept her laptop. It was password protected, but I knew the password. With one eye on Robbie, I spent the next fifteen minutes on my US people-finding site that I'd used when I was a skip tracer.

I'm not sure if what I found made me feel better or worse.

Emily Bickerstaff was a fifty-ish retired schoolteacher who didn't own her own house, which I thought was a red flag for someone who had made at least a middle-class income most of her life. She was active on Facebook—mostly with her students who'd graduated years before.

When I drilled down into those websites most people don't have access to, I also found out that she seemed to have dropped out of AA a few years back. I thought about that for a moment. Did that mean she was drinking again? My understanding of AA is that it was a lifelong commitment.

I glanced at Robbie who was sitting on the floor gnawing on one of Geneviève's fashion magazines and staring at *Jeopardy* with the volume turned off.

I turned back to the computer. I found a news article lauding Bickerstaff as T*eacher of the Year* for the last three years before she retired.

Oh, well, I thought with resignation. *The Lord giveth and the Lord taketh away*

She wasn't a lowlife. If she was recovered from her alcohol problem, she might even be a viable candidate as Robbie's guardian. I was dying to call her up and see if she really wanted

Robbie, but on the face of it she didn't appear to be someone who would be taking him for the money.

Joelle probably told her Robbie was living in France with a meth addict and she was his only hope.

"We are ready, *chérie*," Geneviève said.

I brought Robbie to his highchair which Geneviève had set up beside my place at the dining table. She'd placed a small portion of the sauerkraut and potato dish with the sausages cut up on the tray for him.

The meal was of course delicious. I tend to think any meal I don't cook myself is particularly delectable and not because I'm a bad cook or don't like to cook. But there is something so nurturing about having food set down before you that you didn't have to make yourself. Perhaps it's a feeling extending back from infancy when others did everything for us.

"Did you find out anything hopeful?" Geneviève asked, referring to my evening's Internet research.

"Not really. I'll call her either tonight or tomorrow and try to get a better feel for who she is."

"Are you sure she and Robbie are related?"

"The lawyer had a laboratory DNA test done."

"*Vraiment?*"

"Yeah, so unless the lab report was falsified—which would jeopardize the lawyer's career so I'm betting it wasn't—I'm going forward with the assumption that Emily Bickerstaff is legit."

"What can you do?"

"First I'll find out what my legal options are. It seems the French, like in the States, believe that children with no parents should be placed first with relatives if there are any."

I didn't have the heart or stomach to tell her I'd also been threatened with a charge of child abduction if I opted to fight Joelle and her lawyer.

"What about Catherine?" she asked.

"I think technically Catherine *would* qualify as a close relative," I said. "But as you know her husband would never agree to it."

"Even if it meant you would lose Robbie, otherwise?"

I'd been thinking of exactly this during my walk home this evening. If I called Catherine and told her what was going on, she'd move earth and heaven to save Robbie. But not only would she have to get Todd to agree—a very big if—but I'd have to face the fact that Robbie living with Todd was not the safest option for him. I don't know if Todd would physically abuse him but I'm pretty sure he'd make him feel seriously unloved and unwanted.

And if it never got that far? If Todd put his foot down and forbade Catherine outright from taking Robbie? Catherine would then have to make the decision that I knew she was nowhere near ready to make.

If she opted to stay with Todd and Cam, she'd end up hating herself thinking how she'd let me and Robbie down. She'd be eaten up with guilt.

I couldn't do that to my daughter. Even if it meant losing Robbie.

39

The rest of dinner with Geneviève was quiet and restful in a deeply restorative way, as is often the case when you mix home cooking with an old and loving friend. By the time I finished helping her clear the table and stack the dishes, Robbie was already nodding off.

I left him with Geneviève long enough to run Izzy downstairs to wet the pavers before I came back and brought them both back upstairs to my apartment—feeling stronger and more confident than when I'd knocked on her door.

Robbie did me the solid of sleepily enduring his bath without fully rousing and then going down after only one bedtime story—most of which he slept through. I put him down, kissed his sweet face, watching his thick lashes against his chubby cheek and saw as usual my late husband's face.

You're mine, dear boy. I won't let anyone else have you.

I had just settled back down on the couch with my laptop when my phone rang. I honestly thought it would be Sabine finally taking the time to reassure me. I was surprised to see it was Adele.

"Hey, Adele," I said.

"*Bon soir*, Claire. I have the files from Jean-Bernard's laptop if you want them?"

I sat up straight. Finally! A bit of good luck.

"Yes, absolutely!" I said.

"I can't talk now," she said breathlessly. "I am meeting Antoine for a drink. Tell me when they show up."

I opened my laptop and waited until I saw the email from Adele appear. Then I checked to make sure the attachments were there too.

"Got 'em," I said. "Have fun tonight, Adele. And thank you."

"*Pas du tout*," she said.

In all there were a total of ten files in the email that Adele sent me, most of them irrelevant. Jean-Bernard kept his household budget in an Excel sheet on his laptop and nothing seemed odd about either his income or how he spent it. He didn't own his Paris apartment, but few people did. (I knew very well how lucky I was.)

There were a couple of files that had to do with his university and his law school, several correspondence files that were unexciting and didn't lead me anywhere. It was in the case files where I felt that, if I hadn't actually hit pay dirt, then I'd certainly edged closer to where the treasure was buried.

A file entitled *Evelyn Couture* had six documents in it, each titled with a different month. Jean-Bernard's idea of a comprehensive filing system was to treat each meeting he had with Evelyn like it was an entry in a diary. While I probably wouldn't be able to ask Marie-France about that—since I'd effectively burned that bridge and then firebombed it for good measure—I could ask Julien if this was standard procedure. Whether or not I could believe what he told me was another question.

Six months ago when Jean-Bernard first started seeing Evelyn the entries started out very matter of fact and objective.

Evelyn shows signs of discontent and frustration. She's not eating well. Seems to have lost weight. Struggles with her cane. Possibly developing a bit of a crush on her caseworker. (Moi.)

By the end of his tenure with her, as evidenced in a document dated just two weeks before his death, Jean-Bernard seemed to be more prejudiced and subjective.

He wrote: *Evelyn is impossible to handle. Nothing I say makes her happy, nothing will satisfy her. I know she must be physically uncomfortable but when I offered to have the state physical therapist come out—which she qualifies for—she refused to speak to me. (Did I really once think she had a crush on me?)*

At this point I strongly believe another caseworker with fresh eyes (and new energy) is the answer. I've spoken to Julien Ricard to see if he'll swap with me. I've already told him I don't care who he swaps me for. I'll take two of his for one Evelyn. (Nobody can be a bigger PITA than Evelyn.)

I can't say I hadn't seen a little bit of the Evelyn Jean-Bernard was describing—along with the fraying of her relationship with her case worker—in the brief conversation I'd had with her.

I turned to the file titled *Zéro Petit*.

The first date that Jean-Bernard referenced with Zéro appeared to be right around the time he started at *Mieux Faire*. I realized I didn't know who'd handled Zéro—or Evelyn for that matter—before Jean-Bernard came to work there. That was another question I'd have to ask Julien.

The first document in Zéro's folder was dated a year ago and gave the basics of Zéro from an uninvolved, unbiased caseworker's perspective. But of course I knew that Jean-Bernard knew Zéro personally and so couldn't be unbiased. They'd been tight as ticks in college. Which was why it was so shocking to read Jean-Bernard write:

Zéro Petit shows all the hallmarks of a petty crook addicted to drugs. He shows little impulse control and appears perennially angry with the world for having caused his plight. He takes no responsibility for his situation and accepts help from me and Mieux Faire with resentment and acrimony.

I thought this particularly harsh on Jean-Bernard's part since it would be the rare individual who could take food stamps or even advice from the person who used to be a friend and equal. Of course Zéro was resentful! But for whatever reason, Jean-Bernard wasn't cutting him any slack.

I read through all the case study files—and there were nearly a dozen in addition to Evelyn's and Zéro's—but none that were still in Jean-Bernard's care or hadn't been moved to another caseworker over the last year.

Jean-Bernard's final entry on Zéro—written the week before Jean-Bernard was killed—read:

Zéro is more unpredictable and violent. He claims he's not using but he obviously is. I've tried everything to get through to him: shame, praise, threats, even bribery. Nothing works.

My final assessment is that Mieux Faire has done all it can for him and it is time to move on to another needy individual who is more deserving. I am aware that this means Zéro will lose his state entitlement status and all the benefits that that entails but after a year of working closely with him I believe there is no possibility of a successful rehabilitation for him.

I was stunned. Jean-Bernard was asking Marie-France to terminate Zéro which would also mean the termination of whatever meagre stipend he received from the State.

And they used to be good friends? What the hell had happened?

I shook that thought out of my mind. It didn't matter what had happened. It didn't matter what event had driven Zéro to take drugs or Jean-Bernard to want to give up on him. All that mattered at this point was that if Jean-Bernard went forward with his plan to cut Zéro from the program, Zéro would be in worse trouble than he already was.

If Zéro had known Jean-Bernard was planning it, it was also a motive for murder.

What was it that Jean-Bernard had written? *I've used every-thing on the man, shame, praise, threats, even bribery. Nothing works.*

I got a very vivid image in my head of Zéro's anger when he talked about Jean-Bernard.

I felt weary as I rubbed my eyes. It had been a long and basically frustrating day. Izzy snuggled closer to my hip and I dropped my hand to caress her. She shivered and I pulled the cashmere throw around her.

Before I closed out the last document in Zéro's file I saw a note at the bottom of the page which read: *Add to work diary: appt with Zéro on the 20th.*

I froze when I saw that. Jean-Bernard had never gotten the chance to add the note to his work diary which is why I'd not seen it there.

The 20th was the day Jean-Bernard died.

I shivered. *Had* the two men met that morning? I rubbed my eyes in weariness and Izzy lifted her head at the motion, ever ready to jump off the couch in the direction of the front door.

One thing my little furry friend was right about: it was time to call it a day. I wasn't sure what tomorrow had on tap for me but I knew I had to go back to Stalingrad to talk to Zéro. I don't know if he would talk to me but it was the only lead I had. I needed to at least try.

Just as I got up and slipped my driving moccasins back on, my phone rang. It was late, and except for a call from the States, I rarely got calls at this time of night. I picked up my phone and was surprised to see the call was Pierre Berger.

"*Bon nuit,* Monsieur Berger," I said formally. "Do you have news?"

I think it was his hesitation that told me that whatever he

was about to say wasn't good. In that split second, I stopped reaching for my coat on the hook in the foyer and held my breath, praying for what I didn't even know.

"It's Gigi," he said with a heaviness to his voice. "She tried to kill herself in her cell tonight."

40

After receiving the news of Gigi's suicide attempt, my evening got even longer. I had three separate phone calls with Berger in an attempt to see how I might be allowed in to see her in the clinic where they'd taken her. But there was too much red tape and in the end I had to be satisfied with Berger getting a message to her that I was thinking of her and to please be strong—and for Berger to keep me informed of Gigi's status.

Have you ever had one of those times in your life where you feel as if everything in your world is slowly but surely turning to *merde*? The only good thing I had going was that Gigi's attempt had not been successful. It's all too easy to see only the negative. I wasn't writing in the date of Gigi's funeral in my day planner and I needed to remind myself of that.

Boy, how is that for one seriously dark Pollyanna vibe?

After handing Robbie over to Haley in the morning, I set off to try and get something done today that would enable me to look back on this day as having moved the needle or at least provided some momentum. I needed a substantive clue or a lead. (A confession would work too.) I needed to find *something* to help get Gigi out of jail and back into some semblance of a life. As a mother myself, I was keenly aware that Gigi's parents had already lost one child.

I was determined down to the soles of my Ferragamos that they would not lose another.

I set up my surveillance at a café table near the produce and seafood stands in the outdoor market that I was sure the Zenns must use—unless they'd been and gone an hour ago and this was all for nothing.

I found myself mulling over the fact that Jean-Bernard had possibly met with Zéro the day he died. If that was true, not only had Zéro lied about not seeing Jean-Bernard recently but it meant he'd had an opportunity to poison Jean-Bernard—on top of already possessing motive and means.

Jean-Bernard would have had to leave Eloise's apartment early and gone straight to Zéro's or somewhere nearby—after which he could hurry off to the café to meet Gigi where I then met him.

It all fit.

Except. The drugs took effect within thirty minutes. Zéro would have had to meet Jean-Bernard *at the Tower itself* and even then...how would he have secretly drugged him?

Just as I was tempted to get up and knock on the Zenn's apartment door again, I saw them. The whole point of my thinking I might be able to recognize this couple after one brief interaction with them was because for someone with face blindness, the two of them share a singular feature that, for me, makes them stand out.

First, they were both incredibly short. It's not that the French aren't generally a short-statured people because they are, but it was highly unusual for both members of a *couple* to be so short. That and the fact of Madame Zenn's flaming red hair made picking them out of a crowd a no brainer. Even for me.

I threw down a few euros on my café table and hurried to catch up with them.

Just as Madame Zenn was dragging her *chariot* cart to the first produce kiosk to wait her turn, I sidled up to her and pretended we'd just bumped into each other.

I swear, you would be surprised how many people believe you just happened to come upon them.

"Madame Zenn!" I said with a big smile. "It's so good to see you again. And Monsieur Zenn."

Madame Zenn turned to look at me and for a moment I wondered if she might have face blindness too because it was clear she couldn't place me. While it's true I don't have stand-out identifiable features like flaming red hair, I would've expected my flamboyant American cheerfulness would make me memorable in most French setting.

"Claire Baskerville," I prompted. "The Canadian working with the police on the Eiffel Tower accident?"

Instantly her face clouded over which left no doubt that Madame Baldoche had been on the phone with her about me.

"I have nothing to say to you," Madame Zenn said.

"Okay. But I was just wondering if Madame Baldoche had mentioned to you that we'd spoken?" I asked innocently, glancing at Miguel who was beginning to edge away. That was fine with me. He'd already told me that he hadn't really seen anything that day.

"She told me!" Madame Zenn said whirling around on me, her face the picture of extreme annoyance. "How she could suggest that I was the only one who saw anything is beyond me! We all saw it! We all saw the man hit the young lady who then pushed him!"

I glanced around because her voice had caused several shoppers to turn and look at us. When Madame Zenn saw that we were becoming the center of attention, she pulled out of line and I followed her.

"But Madame Baldoche has recanted her statement," I said. "She now says she saw nothing. I need to ask you, Madame Zenn, if you're absolutely sure that you—"

"Yes! I saw what I saw! Marguerite Baldoche saw it too!"

"She says not."

I saw the anger and frustration building inside Madame Zenn and decided that probably wasn't a bad thing. Not that I like tormenting little old ladies. Technically, I'm a little old lady myself. But I needed her to shake loose of what she thought she saw and reconsider what she really did see.

Or didn't.

"Did she also tell you she lost the tickets to get in so that we were forced to buy them all over again?" Madame Zenn said, her face flushed pink with vexation.

"She didn't mention that," I said.

"I'll bet she didn't! Or that she accidentally threw her Métro ticket away and had to buy another one for the ride home?"

"Be that as it may," I said. "She said she didn't see anyone push anyone. And neither did Monsieur Baldoche."

"I saw what I saw!" Madame Zenn squeaked in shrill frustration, nearly beside herself now.

As I watched Monsieur Zenn hurry over, presumably to calm his wife, I also saw that a good portion of the gathered shoppers at the produce market were eyeing me with censure and open hostility. I decided that while this latest interview with her might not have made things worse, it certainly had not pushed the situation toward discrediting Madame Zenn as a witness.

Quickly making my apologies to both the Zenns, I slipped away into the crowd, hoping to lose myself before anyone grabbed a pitchfork.

41

M y second trip to Stalingrad was clearly going to be no more pleasant than my first.

At this time of day beggars sat on the street in front of shops, and the streets were sporadically populated by men and women in worn cloth coats not nearly thick enough to keep them warm. All of them watched me, their eyes dark, and unfriendly.

I stood with my back to a south facing brick wall along the street where I ascended from the Stalin Métro, and felt an unpleasant fluttering sensation in the pit of my stomach that was either nerves or a warning sign of fear.

I studied the street and watched the encroaching shadows deepen by the second.

The fact is, Paris has this amazing feature in summer that I'll probably never get used to, but that I absolutely love. In the summer months it stays light until nearly midnight, giving everyone long days of sunshine and extended hours to sit outside in cafés.

Unfortunately, the converse of this miracle was also true.

On a brittle January day like today, just after four o'clock in the afternoon, it was already getting dark.

I knew I probably should have held off on this excursion until tomorrow. I should at least have waited until it was daylight. But I was so determined not to end another day with no real movement forward that in my eagerness I put aside any sense of growing uneasiness—often known as *one's better judgment*—and so here I was.

I'd gotten Zéro's last known address from Jean-Bernard's case notes. He'd made a note of it a year ago and hadn't updated it, so I was hoping that meant that Zéro hadn't moved. Drug addicts moved often for a variety of different reasons, so it was actually somewhat ludicrous for me to think the address was still good. But if it wasn't, if Zéro was no longer there, perhaps there would be someone there who might tell me where I could find him.

I pulled out my phone and looked at the route I'd plotted to his address. Looking at the map, I had no way of knowing which street was more treacherous than the other. I thought of the illegal Taser in my dresser back at the apartment. I was in the process of kicking myself for not bringing it when I recognized a landmark from the last time I'd been here.

It was the corner that led to Evelyn's apartment and the last place I'd seen Zéro. The last thing I wanted to do was engage with Eveyln, so I stood on the corner of her street and looked down it to the small square in front of her building. Because the actual apartments were safely behind two sets of doors and a courtyard, there was no way to tell by looking if Evelyn was home.

But as it was nearly dark now *and* it had begun to snow again, I had to think it was a pretty safe bet that she was.

I noticed an alley on my map off the courtyard that seemed to connect with the street that led to Zéro's address. Because Evelyn's square was quiet—and because I was already associating it with her and therefore relative safety for some reason—I stepped away from the corner and walked to the courtyard and the alley.

Unfortunately it was completely dark now. I shivered inside my thin corduroy coat—again worn to look shabby so I would blend in and therefore it was not very warm—and shoved my hands deep into my pockets. A hush had descended in the little courtyard. It was the kind of quiet that I tend to associate with snow, which muffles noises, but still it was odd to register it in the middle of an urban scene. I felt a wave of budding trepidation.

I looked at the map on my phone again. The alley cut-through would definitely take me to the street that led to Zéro's apartment building. I looked around and was surprised at the sudden lack of people. There was only the cold, the falling snow, and the smell of diesel oil, urine and woodsmoke.

I hurried to the opening of the alley and away from the last glimmer of light from the street lamp in the courtyard. The alley was dark but I could see light at the end of it. I straightened my shoulders and thought of Gigi, alone, afraid, and so distraught that she tried to kill herself. I stiffened my resolve. As I walked down the dark alley, I told myself that unless someone had seen me enter, it was not likely that anyone was waiting for some clueless victim to come wandering by.

That's what I told myself.

You see, I believe that there is a point where it's smart to be careful and a point where it's foolish to let ungrounded fears determine your actions. I have to say I am always trying to tell the difference between the two. Frankly it did seem like this alley was in a gray area in that regard.

I made it halfway down the alley when I felt the phone in my hand begin to vibrate. I looked down to see I was getting a call from Haley. I slowed. I could hear car noises and even conversations coming from the end of the alley. A streetlamp illuminated the exit several yards ahead.

I answered the phone.

"Hi, sweetie," I said. "Is everything okay?"

"Are you coming home soon?" Haley asked.

I heard the anxiety in her voice and a splinter of panic pierced me. I stopped walking.

"Has something happened?" I asked, feeling my heart rate begin to speed up.

"Something's not right. Can you get here soon?"

Before I could answer her, the wedge of light dimmed. I jerked my head up to see a man had suddenly appeared in the alley.

My adrenaline spiked.

He was coming very quickly toward me.

42

I watched him come, knowing I couldn't turn around, knowing I couldn't outrun him or fight him. So I stood there, my phone in my hand, too shocked to even scream.

He reached me in seconds and reached out and slapped the phone from my hand. I dimly registered the sound of it hitting the ground.

He was of medium height with a crooked nose and a truncated jaw shaded by a day's growth of beard. I stumbled backward a step and he grabbed the front of my coat and slammed me into the brick wall. He brought his face close to mind. His breath was foul and smelled of fish and alcohol

"Why are you here?" he asked in a guttural, heavily accented French.

"See—seeing a friend," I stuttered, my heartbeat racing.

He held up a knife to my face and pressed the tip into my chin.

"Take my purse," I whispered.

I realized at some level that trying to dictate the speed of this encounter might possibly upset him. But I couldn't help it. I just wanted this to end it, for him to just get on with it.

"*Oui*, I will take everything," he said. "I will take you, too, eh?" He laughed in a belch of vomit-smelling breath.

I knew that one well-placed knee thrust up hard between his legs might end this—one way or the other. Because if I didn't do it with enough force or place it in the right spot, it would be the death of me.

But I also knew I couldn't let him decide how this played out. For one thing I was pretty sure we were working from different playbooks. Maybe my eyes gave away the fact that I was thinking of trying something because he suddenly stepped back, still holding the front of my coat at arms' length but the knife now at his side.

He could still bash my head against the side of the alley wall, stab me, or throw me down on the ground and rape me. But in this new position, I was now too far away to kick out.

I'd missed my moment.

Sometimes when something terrible is happening to you or even just something you're witnessing, the world seems to slow down and the audio dims. Maybe that's a result of watching too many movies but that's how I felt as this man stared into my face, threatening me. He was bigger than I was, plus he was a man and he had a weapon. He was using every unfair advantage he had to terrify me. A deadly irrational thought began to churn a slow vortex of fury through me.

He's getting nothing from me the easy way

A few people walked by the entrance of the alley, maybe they even paused to see what was going on but I was under no illusion that anyone would stop and help. I was the outlier here.

"Take your clothes off," he snarled.

"Go to hell," I said and spat at him.

I didn't have enough spit in my mouth and he was too far away for it to have reached him if I had, but that didn't matter. His eyes blazed in shocked fury. He knew what I'd tried to do.

His knife hand shot back to my face and I jerked my head

away, baring my throat to him, and swinging up my leg at the same time.

Hard between his legs.

It wasn't hard enough. But it gave me a few seconds. grace He groaned and dropped his hold on me. I flung my purse at his face and turned and ran.

I had no hope of escape. None. The courtyard I'd just come through was empty of people. Even if it had been full they wouldn't have helped me.

I made it two steps before I felt his hands on me. He flung me to the ground. The impact knocked the wind out of me. I pulled my knees into my chest and tucked my head, trying to make myself small. I squeezed my eyes shut.

The first kick exploded into my exposed hip like a runaway cement truck crashing into a wall. My body reverberated with the assault, the soundtrack of my world shutting off as I focused on the pain radiating through my hips and legs.

I gasped for breath, letting the helpless fear wash over me.

And then, nothing.

The volume of my world eased back up and when it did I heard the horrible gasping sounds as my lungs fought to take in a full breath without seizing. I opened my eyes.

Two sets of legs stood over me. Two men.

"Or what?" one of the men—my attacker—said in his thick patois.

"Or I kill you."

"I saw her first!"

I inched away from them, my back now against the wall. I stared up at the two men.

My attacker was massaging the area between his legs where I'd kicked him and glared at the other man. There was something about him that seemed to intimidate my attacker.

Suddenly, without warning the new man drove his fist hard

into my attacker's gut. The man bent over and fell to his knees, his knife clattering to the cobblestones.

Then the new man grabbed him by his hair and jerked his head up. He punched him square in the face, the blow landing like a solid thump of meat against meat. Blood spurted down the man's shirt. He fell over onto his back.

"Be glad I don't kill you right now," the new man said, his voice suddenly familiar to me.

My attacker scrambled to his feet and reached for his knife but the second man—whose voice I now recognized—shouted, "Leave it!"

My attacker hobbled out of the alley still cupping a hand to his groin.

I waited until Zéro turned around before I attempted to stand. He came to me with my purse in his hand.

"You have to be some special kind of stupid to come here at night," he said as he gingerly touched the cut on my jaw where the man had pressed the knife. "You're bleeding."

I felt like telling him that in my experience older women invariably got a pass even in what some would consider risky areas of town. But in the end I didn't have the energy to defend myself any more today.

"I needed to talk to you," I said.

He shook his head and held his hand out to help me to my feet.

"I do have a phone, you know," he said.

43

S tanding up was a little trickier than I'd expected, but with Zéro's help I managed to get to my feet. I knew I'd have a bruise on my hip the size and shape of Africa by this time tomorrow but nothing felt broken. Once Zéro got me on my feet he led me to a nearby café where he ordered *brik*, a fried pastry filled with cinnamon potato chunks and cumin green onions.

I could feel the eyes of everyone in the café burning into me. The idea that a lone white woman would be here after dark was as astonishing to them as it was starting to feel to me.

In my defense, I was just so driven by the thought of talking to Zéro—and if I'm honest, getting a confession out of him— that I didn't set out with the proper protective equipment for my quest today. For one thing, I should have known it would be dark by the time I'd finished interviewing the Zenns. And I should not have come into this neighborhood unarmed. Although frankly I'm not sure a Taser would have worked on the behemoth who accosted me in the alley.

"What was so important that you would risk your life to talk to me?" Zéro asked, watching me carefully over the rim of his demitasse cup.

I realized that presenting the facts to Zéro that Jean-Bernard was killed with a drug cocktail and not a plunge to his death might make him feel like I were accusing him of having access to such a cocktail. Which of course was what exactly what I'd been thinking when I set out this morning. But the more I sat here, my hip aching, the abrasions on the palms of my hands throbbing from where my attacker had flung me on the ground, the more I thought that I was probably not the best person to be asking Zéro these questions.

Except of course the police weren't interested in asking them.

"Look," I said. "I'm trying to get to the bottom of Jean-Bernard's murder because I'm hoping to help his girlfriend."

"That's assuming she didn't kill him."

"Have you ever met Gigi?"

He shrugged and focused on the *brik* before him.

"Because if you had," I said, "you'd have found it difficult to believe she could hurt anyone."

"I thought it was done in a moment of rage," he said, raising an eyebrow at me. His face was scarred but there was something in his eyes that told me he'd once been vulnerable. He'd had to shut off that valve of human emotion a long time ago.

"Even Mother Teresa could have a moment of homicidal fury," he continued.

"Maybe," I said. "And if it turns out that that's what happened, I'll accept it. But Gigi says she didn't do it."

We ate in silence for a moment. I could already feel my hip throbbing uncomfortably. The pain and the cold were more than one mug of hot coffee sprinkled with cinnamon could adequately address.

"It must have been galling to have Jean-Bernard be your caseworker, given your history with him," I said.

He cracked his knuckles and jerked his chin upward.

"So now you are accusing *me* of killing Jean-Bernard?"

"I'm trying really hard not to," I said. "I only want the truth."

"I didn't kill him."

"What happened to you?" I asked bluntly, feeling a combination of the cold and my injuries urging me on to a hot bath and an ice pack on my hip.

Zéro rubbed a hand across his face and looked away.

"You know Jean-Bernard and I were friends once?"

"I heard that."

"He went one way and I..." He let his hand drop into his lap.

How do you ask someone why they started taking drugs? Why they set out on their path of destruction? Was it a woman? A disappointment of some kind? Was it just falling in with the wrong people? Whatever it was it was more than I could ask him today. Not that I wouldn't comfortably cross every boundary that proprietary and common sense set down—I did just deign to walk through one of the worst sections of Paris alone and *at night* after all.

But just looking at Zéro's face told me that that subject was closed. Permanently.

"Jean-Bernard had a notation in his diary that he was meeting you on the 20th," I said.

"Wasn't that the date he died?"

I'd been hoping he wouldn't know or remember that. Drug addicts' memories are notoriously unreliable.

"It was."

"I didn't see him on the 20th."

I studied his face for a moment. He was either lying or telling the truth and right now I couldn't tell which.

The question I really needed answered was of course the trickiest. And since I was having trouble figuring out if he was lying to me or not, whatever answer he gave might not be the most helpful. But I still had to ask it.

"How long were you expecting to work with Jean-Bernard?" I asked.

"I don't understand."

"You are a service user of *Mieux Faire's*. Did you expect that to continue indefinitely?"

He frowned as if honestly perplexed by the question.

"Why wouldn't it?" he asked.

If he was telling the truth and was truly unaware of Jean-Bernard's intention to cut him loose—along with all the benefits he received from the state—then there went his motive.

If he was telling the truth.

"You act as if you hated him," I said.

"No. It was the other way around."

"Jean-Bernard hated you? Why?"

He narrowed his eyes at me.

"What do you know about him? His family?"

"Nothing."

He nodded. "Jean-Bernard could never forgive me for this." He made a vague wave to encompass the street.

"He felt as if you'd let him down?" I ventured.

Zero snorted which I took it as a *yes*.

I wondered if a little digging into Jean-Bernard's life would reveal to me a loved one with a drug addiction. Perhaps a beloved parent whose habit destroyed the family. It would make sense.

"Who was it?" I asked. "His mother?"

He looked at me with renewed respect.

"His father," he said. "It was only alcohol but he drove the family into poverty. Jean-Bernard's sister and his mother literally died of shame."

"That's terrible," I said.

"So how I live here? My lifestyle? For Jean-Bernard it was the ultimate betrayal."

"It's hard for people who don't suffer from addiction to understand."

Zero rolled his eyes. I could see our time had come to an end.

"Thank you for saving my life today," I said.

"I would suggest not coming back here."

He held his hand out and nodded at my phone which I'd picked up from the ground mostly intact. I handed it to him and he typed in his phone number.

"There," he said, handing it back to me. "Now you need never come back. If you have other questions, just call me. But I would still prefer never to hear from you."

"I understand," I said, taking my phone back. "Why did you save me?"

"I have some humanity left in me," he said, signaling to the waiter. "I'm not going to let a thug beat up a woman."

I watched him for a moment while I paid our bill, mildly grateful that he hadn't felt the need to say *old* woman. Maybe the word was hanging there in the air unspoken. Or maybe that was just me. I'd lived too long in the States where age meant more than it should. And none of it good.

It wasn't until after Zéro had walked me to the Métro station and seen me safely through the ticket stile in the direction of the ninth arrondissement that I remembered Haley's phone call.

I quickly found my seat on the train and with a churning stomach called her back. I could see that she'd called me a good half dozen times since my phone had been knocked out of my hand. My anxiety inched up as I waited for her to answer.

"Hey, what happened?" she asked when she answered.

"I'll tell you when I see you," I said. "I'm on my way now. What happened?"

"I guess it's no big deal because nothing's happened," Haley said. "Hey, Robster, wanna say hi to your mom?"

"Haley," I said impatiently, although a part of me was relieved and grateful that whatever had happened she was obviously taking it in stride. "What was it? Why did you call me?"

"Oh yeah, you got a note shoved under your door about two hours ago. It was pasted together like they do in old-fashioned movies, you know? Like for ransom notes? That's what Geneviève said anyway."

"What did the note say?" I asked.

"Yeah, that's the weird thing," Haley said. "Geneviève thought you should call the police."

The feeling of helplessness and fear came back as I waited for Haley to get the note.

"Okay here it is," she said finally.

I held my breath as I waited to hear.

"It's in French but Miz Rousseau translated it for me. It says *He deserved to die.*"

44

It was only a little after eight o'clock by the time I finally got home. Both Haley and Geneviève were in my apartment playing a card game when I arrived. Robbie was already bathed and asleep.

I shrugged out of my coat, wincing as I did, and Haley handed me the note. The letters were crudely cut out and pasted together from magazines and newspapers.

He deserved to die.

Did the author mean Jean-Bernard or Paolo? Clearly whoever sent this wasn't connecting the two murders. Was that odd? Why had I automatically jumped to the conclusion that the two deaths were linked?

And why was this note sent to me?

It had to be because of Jean-Bernard's death, I reasoned. His is the death I'm investigating.

"What happened to you, *chérie*?" Geneviève said as she walked over to me, a glass of wine in her hand. I was wearing slacks and the knee of one had ripped when I'd tumbled to the ground. A stain of dirt and blood streaked along the knee to the cuff.

"Whoa!" Haley said when she saw my pants.

"It's nothing," I said but by then their eagle eyes were roaming over me relentlessly.

"What happened to your hands?" Haley asked.

"And your chin?" Geneviève added.

"I fell," I said. "No biggie. My foot hit a cobblestone the wrong way. Have you called the police?" I wagged the note, already ruing the fact that so many of our fingerprints were all over it.

"We thought you'd want to see it first," Haley said, glancing at Geneviève as if to confirm this.

"Okay, good," I said, "I'll call them now. Are you staying the night, Haley?"

She shook her head. "Big algebra test tomorrow and I didn't bring my books."

I was a hair breath's from asking if she truly intended to go home and start studying at nine o'clock in the evening but I reminded myself that she wasn't my daughter.

"Okay," I said. "I'll call you an Uber. It's too late for the Métro."

"I don't mind," she said.

I punched in my Uber app and set up Haley's ride. Then I called the police and explained that I had received what I felt was a threatening note. When I hung up, Haley was hesitating in the doorway with her coat on.

"So you think it was a threat?" she asked, a note of unease in her voice.

"I only said that to get the police to take it seriously," I assured her. I made a point not to look at Geneviève who would be much less easy to fool.

"Oh. Okay," Haley said. "Well, see you tomorrow."

After Haley walked out the door, Geneviève turned to me.

"I'm going to wait with her downstairs until her ride comes," she said. "And *you* should get in the tub." She gave me a pointed look to underscore that she hadn't bought my story about falling.

After checking on Robbie, I did exactly what Geneviève suggested. After a long hot soak in the tub, I dressed in leggings and a velour hoodie on the slight chance that cops might be knocking on my door tonight. Then I curled up with my laptop, my faithful French bulldog who had spent my whole bath time watching me with worried eyes, and a glass of Syrah.

The first thing I did was research Zéro Petit. I'd done this before now but not comprehensively because I assumed Jean-Bernard's case notes would give me the real meat of Zéro's situation. But of course they hadn't. There had been no background at all in the notes.

I find people for a living. It's what I do. My skillset is tracking down cheating spouses or runaways along with a slew of other unsavory things a typical private detective might do—uncover credit debt, dig up job histories, detail criminal records. I also locate people trying to run away or skip town on their bills.

I used to liken what I do to a treasure hunter digging for gold, except the treasure hunter is really a kind of savior and the gold is often something gross and disgusting.

That might be a slight exaggeration, but it still accounts for why I dig with trepidation. I've found things I wasn't expecting to find and hope to never find or see again.

That turned out to be the case with Zéro Petit.

Born in Lyons, Zéro had gone to school with Jean-Bernard in Strasbourg—as I already knew. But what I didn't know was that it was Zéro and not Jean-Bernard who was the wunderkind. He was the one with the certificates, the science awards, the local paper touting him as their local boy wonder.

Which of course makes his story so much more tragic when it finally unraveled.

I found the truth in a series of newspaper articles from ten years ago—about the time Zéro should have graduated with honors but instead had spent a month in a mental facility after causing the death of a young woman. All the newspaper accounts exonerated Zéro and indeed no criminal charges were ever filed. He'd been driving down a country road at night when a teenage girl deliberately stepped into the path of his car. The girl—who had a history of mental disturbance and depression—died at the scene.

Riddled with guilt and self-recrimination, Zéro emerged from his stint at the mental health facility a changed young man with a brand new opioid addiction.

I felt a heaviness in my chest as sadness filled me. It had taken Zéro ten full years to morph from that broken young man to the hardened and embittered drug addict I'd had coffee with today.

We're all of us just one unlucky break away from total disaster.

I shook myself out of my gloom. The fact is, in my line of work, half the people I run into are seriously, chronically unhappy, dealing with problems that prompted my involvement in the first place. But I'm not a fixer. I'm a finder. Locating runaways does give me a certain amount of job satisfaction. But there was usually a good reason why the person ran—whether it was a teenager or unhappy wife or husband—and that I can do nothing about.

I got up from the couch with my empty wine glass and went to the kitchen to refill it. I also made myself a plate of toast with two soft-boiled eggs since I'd had no lunch or dinner today.

By the time I got back to the couch, feeding tidbits of buttered toast to Izzy, I felt a little better. Mentally, anyway. Physically, I could already tell that I was going to be virtually crippled tomorrow.

Those of us in our sixties can't bounce back from being tossed around a stone alleyway like we used to.

Next on my list of things to do was a long-distance phone

call to Emily Bickerstaff in Little Rock, Arkansas. I'd sketched out a brief bio for myself—fake, of course—and a few questions that I hoped Bickerstaff would answer before wising up and calling Joelle's legal team to complain about me—which could seriously complicate my legal case.

That threat of child abduction still buzzed worrisomely around my brain.

I glanced at Izzy. "Here goes nothing," I said as I pressed the number for Emily Bickerstaff that I'd found on my US people-finding site. It was eleven o'clock my time and since France was six hours ahead of the States, that made it six o'clock in the evening Emily's time. Like every good telemarketer knows, dinner time was the best time to catch people in.

"Hello?" she answered.

"Hello? Is this Emily Bickerstaff?" I said, hitting the southern accent that I legitimately own just a tad harder than usual.

"Who is this?"

"My name is Amanda Dawson," I said. "I used to work with Courtney Purdue in Atlanta. Do you have a minute?"

"Oh!" Emily said. "Oh, yes, of course."

"I'm sorry to bother you," I said, "but I was contacted a few weeks ago by a French lawyer who was looking for relatives of Courtney and she sent me your name."

That of course was a complete lie. There was no way a lawyer would pass on Emily's personal contact information to anyone. I don't know if Emily knew this but I was hoping she didn't.

"Oh, yes, about Courtney's little baby," Emily said. "they've contacted me, too."

"Oh, my goodness!" I said. "Robbie must be so big by now. I haven't seen him in a year since Courtney went to France."

"Well, you're one up on me, then," Emily said with an infectious laugh. "I haven't even seen pictures."

"I might have one or two on my phone. If you want I can send them," I offered. "Of course they're old now."

"That's okay," Emily said. "I guess I'll see him for myself soon enough."

"So is it true you're going to take him and raise him?" I asked.

"Well, that has yet to be decided," Emily said. "I mean, obviously I want to do everything I can for little Robbie but I'm hoping they'll find someone else. Honestly, I've never had kids myself and I'm fifty-six. It would be a serious lifestyle adjustment, let me tell you!"

She sounded genuine and warm. She sounded like someone's fun and quirky aunt.

I laughed. "I can only imagine. Do you think they will find someone else?"

"Well, they need someone who's blood related and so I'll bet I'm it," Emily said. "My sister—Courtney's mom—and I had no other siblings and I never had kids so I'm sure I'm all there is."

"That must have come as quite a shock to you," I said, looking at the next question on my list which would be little harder to pull off without Emily getting suspicious.

"You can say that again!"

"So do they just expect you to take him in and clothe and feed him? I mean, do you even get custody payments?"

I could only hope that Emily imagined that Courtney's girlfriend was as insensitive and basically clueless as Courtney herself was to ask such a question. Otherwise, she was going to hang up on me.

In truth, her voice did sound much less friendly.

"They certainly didn't suggest paying me to take care of my own nephew," she said stiffly.

"Oh, no," I said. "I didn't mean it like that. It's just that I've got three nephews myself and I can't imagine dealing with them for a whole evening let alone full-time."

I could hear Emily's tone soften then.

"Well, you're right, it's a daunting prospect. But the thing that comforts me is the fact of where I'm living here in Arkansas."

"What do you mean?"

"Our foster care system is considered one of the best in the country."

I felt a sudden coldness hit me in my core.

"You mean...so you're saying—"

"If it doesn't work out," she said, "I'm confident little Ronnie will do just fine in our state care system."

45

The next morning I woke up to the sounds of Robbie calling for me. I sat up in bed and instantly my side seized up and my hip began to throb. I don't know why I didn't ask Haley to come into work today. I groaned as I swung my legs out of bed and groped for my robe and slippers.

I limped over to the guest room and found Robbie standing up in his crib, his diaper off and on the floor. He was grinning at me and Izzy both.

"Good morning, handsome," I said, smiling back at him in spite of my need to run to the bathroom and consume a half jug of hot coffee before my day started.

Which was not going to be possible.

I picked him up and set him on the floor since I didn't trust myself to carry and walk with him due to my newly acquired aches and pains. He immediately ran into the living room where I caught him and deposited him in his playpen. He was not happy about that but there was no help for it.

I wasn't the only one who needed a little relief this morning as Izzy pointed out to me by running to the door and barking. I glanced at the living room window which twinkled in the sun from last night's frost. I'd need to take Izzy downstairs in my slippers and hope there was a dry spot to walk on that wouldn't ruin them.

Before I snapped her leash on I turned on my automatic drip coffeemaker, grateful I'd decided to load it up before I fell into bed last night.

I'd had trouble sleeping after my phone call with Emily Bickerstaff. All I could think of—when I wasn't thinking of how the coldhearted bitch intended to throw Robbie into foster care —was that if Joelle *hadn't* offered Bickerstaff money then I had no leverage at all.

Or maybe Joelle did offer her money and Bickerstaff was keeping that part of the arrangement to herself?

I hurried down the stairs with Izzy in my robe and slippers, the indignant howls of Robbie curdling the air behind me.

I'd be able to find out for sure about the money as soon as Joelle wired the money to Bickerstaff. But since—if that happened—it would likely happen *after* Robbie was removed from my custody and flown to Arkansas, it wouldn't really help.

After Izzy had done her business I went back upstairs and slowly, painfully pulled on a pair of jeans and an oversized cashmere Fisherman's sweater. I put on Saturday morning cartoons to keep Robbie happy—and wondered how many times in the future I'd be doing this in order to get a little peace. Then I gave a short prayer of hope that I would in fact be doing this with him many more times in the future.

I drank my coffee in the living room and tried to no avail to drown out the idiotic drama of the big dinosaur Barney's search for the cookies that a giant blue rodent named Mister Rat had purported to have stolen.

Nothing like leading the witness when it comes to establishing stereotypes, I thought.

I opened my laptop to finish the research I'd started on Julien Ricard last night until I had become too tired and achy to finish. Julien had no Facebook, Instagram or Twitter presence which was not all that unusual although it was extremely unhelpful for my purposes.

I read for twenty minutes straight, only stopping to pick up the occasional soft toy that Robbie had flung out of his play pen.

After several minutes of researching the law firm CDB I realized what an incredible first job it had been for Julien. Not only did the firm support diversity with a mission statement of all-inclusion, but they paid new hires nearly twice as much as the other big firms.

The question wasn't how had someone like Julien gotten employed there—since Marie-France and Jean-Bernard both said Julien was a superstar in his own right. The question—no, the mystery—was *why did he leave?*

My phone rang and I saw it was the police, probably responding to my call the night before. I picked up.

"Yes?"

"Is this Claire Baskerville of rue de Laborde?" The woman's voice was young.

"It is."

"You made a call yesterday about a threatening note you received?"

"Correct."

"We need you to bring the note into the nearest police station."

As bad as my relationship with the police was I did at least think they would come to my apartment to take my statement and, if not dust the hallway for prints, then bag the note themselves. I wondered for a moment if Muller had anything to do with this egregious dismissal of my appeal for help.

"Fine," I said. "Should I just pop it in a baggie?'

"*Pardon?*"

"Never mind."

I hung up and looked at Izzy who was watching me questioningly with her head cocked.

"You and me both," I said to her.

Suddenly the door erupted in a staccato of knocking which ignited Robbie and Izzy into a squealing bark-fest and nearly gave me a heart attack.

"I'm coming!" I shouted with more annoyance than an unexpected Saturday morning visit should have warranted.

I looked through my peephole and then swung open the door for Haley, who marched across the threshold with her skateboard under one arm.

"Hey," I said. "I didn't expect to see you today."

"I know," she said as she went to the playpen, dropped her skateboard and picked up Robbie, who flung his sticky hands around her neck. "I thought Robbie probably needed some park time!"

Even with the snow mostly melted and great tufts of yellowing dead grass making a valient effort of poking up through the slush, Parc Monceau was its usual beautiful tableau. The park was a four-block walk from my apartment and in my condition I'd been tempted to let Haley take Robbie on her own. But in the end, achy and tired or not, I decided I could use the fresh air.

Besides, Haley was doing all the heavy lifting with Robbie —literally—so all I had to do was hang on to Izzy's leash.

So many moments during our walk around the park—it was too cold to sit anywhere—I couldn't help but marvel at how good Haley was with Robbie.

And I couldn't help but think what would happen if I lost him to that Arkansas woman who saw putting him in foster care as an acceptable alternative to her lack of love and caring.

I couldn't let that happen.

I suggested to Haley that we hit a *brasserie* on the way back to the apartment. I happened to know she was a big fan of *raclette*—the cheese and roasted potato dish that most French people are rightly obsessed with.

"I'm so glad you decided to come over today," I said. "I fear Robbie would be binge-watching Barney all day if you hadn't."

"Yeah," she said, adjusting Robbie's hat which made him squeal and try to snatch it off again. "I thought maybe I'd spend the night too if that's okay."

I'd seen her overnight bag in the hallway when we left for the park so this wasn't a big surprise.

"That sounds great," I said. "Everything okay at home?"

"Oh, yeah. My folks went to Basel for the weekend only I didn't want to go."

At thirteen Haley was arguably old enough to spend the weekend by herself. So why was I really starting to hate her parents?

"Well, Robbie and Izzy and I are delighted you're with us," I said as we turned to head toward the park exit.

"What do you think the note was about?" she asked.

"I'm sure it's nothing."

"A weird kind of nothing. Geneviève was totally freaked out."

"The police will get to the bottom of it. It might be some malcontent in the building."

She turned to look at me with a frown.

"That's someone who's unhappy with their life," I explained, "so they want everyone else to be unhappy too."

An image of Joelle came to mind. The constant gurgling of a small waterfall nearly camouflaged the sounds of traffic on the perimeter of the park. A few ducks splashed noisily along the edge of the pond.

"I think my dad's screwing someone," Haley said as she tugged Robbie's hat back down on his head.

It's official. I hate both her parents.

I hate her mother for being clueless and disconnected with Haley. And I hate her father for being a prize dick.

"Are you sure?" I asked.

"Maybe I should hire you to find out," she said with a half laugh.

I wasn't sure she was joking.

"How does that make you feel?" I asked. As soon as the words were out of my mouth I knew they were a mistake.

"You sound like a shrink. It makes me feel like crap. Duh."

We walked without speaking for a few moments, just the sounds of Robbie talking to himself and Izzy's panting as she trotted to keep up.

"You can stay with us any time you want," I said.

"I know," Haley said, which surprised me. But it pleased me too.

I wondered if I should call her father but decided that Haley would probably see that as a breach of confidentiality.

"You could talk to him," I said. "Tell him you know."

She looked at me. "You think I should?"

But I didn't know her father and I had no idea what she should do in this situation.

"Catherine's father cheated on me. But of course she didn't know about it at the time."

And she was a grown woman by the time she did.

"Lucky her," Haley said.

As we reached the exit, we stopped under the majestic wrought-iron and gilt gate and I saw I was getting a call from Sabine.

For a moment I felt a twinge of guilt that Sabine was calling because she had somehow found out I'd called Emily Bickerstaff yesterday. But I was almost positive there was no way that call could be traced back to me.

"Let's do Café Le BonBon for lunch," I said to Haley. "You go on. I need to take this."

She nodded, leaned over and scooped up Izzy and settled her in the stroller with Robbie who instantly began to pat the dog clumsily on the head.

"Hey, Sabine," I said, answering the call.

"Bonjour, Claire. I am calling to make sure you are not too disconsolate about the meeting on Friday."

"So you're not discouraged?"

"I knew they had a case, Claire."

"But you didn't know they'd dug up a blood relative?"

"I feared it, yes."

"You didn't mention it to me."

"I did not see how it would benefit our case to upset you."

"*You* seemed freaked out."

"I'm not at all."

"Are you confident we'll win?"

"I'm not that either. I am just calling to tell you not to lose heart. We still have a few tools in our bag of tricks."

Why did that sound like exactly what a lawyer *would* say when they knew their client was probably going to lose?

"So you think our case is still viable?" I pressed.

"Let's just see how we go, shall we?" she said.

Boy, it's a good thing Sabine hadn't decided to go into medicine. With a bedside manner like hers, all her patients would strangle themselves with their own IVs.

A moment later Sabine dropped the bombshell and her real reason for calling. And that is the only excuse I have for why I didn't ask her about the threat Absalom had made to have me charged with child abduction.

. . .

"Now do not get upset," Sabine said, her words sending a shiver of terror through me. "But Absalom has petitioned the court to have the case presented to them."

I felt as if I'd been gut-punched. I stopped walking.

"But Robbie and I are both Americans," I said, feeling desperate for anything to hold onto in the way of hope. "The French courts have no jurisdiction on his adoption, right?"

Once things went from a simple matter of filling out the right paperwork to actually having to fight in a legal court setting to keep Robbie, I found I had little hope that a *French* court was going to decide in my favor.

"That is unclear," Sabine said. "But whether the case is heard in a French court or a US one I fear it will now involve months of exchanges and documentation from both our countries' family law bureaucracies. You should prepare yourself, Claire. For an international case like this it will take months to get a viable adoption case constructed and scheduled before a family judge."

"And where is Robbie all this time?" I asked helplessly.

"In foster care," Sabine said. "Perhaps in France, perhaps not."

46

It is my belief that no matter what kind of otherwise crap day you are having, you can always count on seasoned fried potatoes and onions draped in fragrant *raclette* cheese to firmly and completely give you the will to go on.

After lunch, Haley and I walked back to the apartment, with Robbie and Izzy both napping cozily in the stroller. I helped Haley get the stroller upstairs, then decided that, fortified by my good lunch and two glasses of Malbec, I had the strength to enact a plan that had started to come together in my brain ever since I'd hung up with Sabine.

The more I thought about Sabine's reluctance to give me hope and the more I thought about what Emily Bickerstaff had in mind to do with Robbie, the more I began to believe that I was going to have to take things into my own hands.

I didn't know Sabine's legal strategy but if I had to guess, it was going to be more of a reaction than an actual direction. That was particularly disheartening because Joelle's lawyer looked like she had all kinds of potential legal tricks up her sleeve.

As I hurried downstairs, engaging the Uber app to call for a ride, I couldn't help but think that for me to do nothing would mean that whatever plan Joelle and her attorney had created would be the one that would carry the day. I wasn't sure if I could stop whatever they had in mind.

But I knew I had to try.

~

An hour later I walked into the main Préfecture de Police on the Île de la Cité and marched up to the waiting room receptionist. She looked up but didn't ask if she could help me. I pulled out the plastic baggie with the pasted-together note inside.

"I was told to hand this in here," I said. "It's a threatening note that was delivered to my apartment."

The woman took the bag, read the note through the bag and glanced at me, her expression clearly indicating that—in her opinion—the note did not at all read like a threat. I didn't feel the need to justify it to her. I filled out the form and was quickly on my way, already pushing the button on my phone for my next Uber.

Traffic was light for a Saturday and I arrived at my destination in front of Joelle's apartment building within twenty minutes.

Joelle's apartment building was on the corner of rue Blanches and rue Moncey. Like my own building, it was a classic Haussmann. There was a café on the corner and a line of shops, boutiques, hair salons, wine stores and pizza kiosks on the facing street.

I scouted out the street from the first café I came to and decided it would work. I sat down at a table on the very cold terrace and ordered a large café Americano with a shot of whiskey.

And then I waited.

When I think of all the surveillance I did back home, usually from my car, I am amazed I was able to get any work done at all. Or maybe being a private investigator in America is a young person's job—living in your car, crawling under bushes, hiding behind garbage cans—whereas in France, I thought as I sipped my hot drink, the job is so much more civilized.

I kept my eyes glued to the front door of Joelle's apartment building and signaled to the waiter to bring me another coffee.

I had two things going for me on this particular stakeout. One was that I was confident I would recognize Joelle on sight. I'd seen her enough times by now plus she had a distinctive look: auburn hair, mean expression and tight, form-fitting clothes.

The second advantage I had was the fact that over the past several months I had made a fairly detailed outline of Joelle's basic weekly schedule. I knew where she got her hair done and when. Same for her nails. I knew the different times of her yoga and Pilates classes and the times she most preferred to go.

Unlike when I was waiting for the Zenns just hoping to catch them, I knew that in roughly two minutes Joelle Lapin would leave her apartment building, her yoga mat under her arm, and stride past me and this table. I eased back into my seat and got ready. I signaled to the waiter for my bill and dug out the exact change. Once he arrived, I paid him, stood up, buttoned my coat and collected my handbag.

Then I stepped out onto the street at precisely the same moment that Joelle was passing.

"Well, what a surprise," I said to her.

She kept walking but looked at me as if at first she didn't recognize me. When she finally did, her pace slowed and then stopped.

"What are you doing here?" she spat.

"Going to yoga class?" I nodded at the mat she clutched in her arms.

"This is harassment. I'll file a complaint against you."

"I talked to Emily Bickerstaff."

Joelle's face looked pinched but showed no more than annoyance.

"She said you offered her money to take Robbie," I said. "That's child trafficking."

She reached into her purse and pulled out her telephone which she held up to me. I watched her activate the recording function on it.

"Repeat that, please," she said, "for the benefit of my lawyer."

I had to give it to her. She had ice water in her veins.

"If you pay Bickerstaff any money," I said slowly for the benefit of the recorder, "I'll be watching. I'll have you arrested as soon as the money shows up in her account."

"You are a sick and desperate individual," she said, holding the recorder close to my face. She was smiling. She knew she was winning.

I guess I'd hoped my little gambit would cause her to collapse into a mound of terrified tears and self-recrimination. When this didn't happen, I had only one last card to play. It was true I'd planned this scheme ahead of time in case she left me no other recourse, but it didn't mean I was proud of what I was about to do.

All I can say is desperate times call for desperate measures.

"Why are you doing this to me?" I said, raising my voice. "What do you care if I have this boy?"

"I am astonished at the ego for you to assume that you are the only one who can care for him."

She was clearly speaking for the benefit of the recording she was making.

"I can do a better job than institutionalizing him," I said.

"I guess we'll never know."

"Do *you* want money? How much? Tell me and I'll pay you."

She smiled and inched the recorder closer to me. My suggesting that I would pay her was gold for her case and we both knew it.

"I don't want your money," she said. "I only want what's best for the child."

I laughed.

"Your problem, Joelle, is you can't bear the thought that Robbie might get what you never got. Someone who loves him."

"You don't know anything about me," she said, her body stiff with tension and barely repressed rage.

"I know you're a dried up old gorgon who only lives to make others miserable," I said. "I know Claude didn't want to procreate with you."

"Shut your mouth! I'm recording all your insults! You're just proving my case of what an unsuitable caretaker you are."

"How about recording the little matter of your illegitimate child?" I said, watching her face whiten as I hit the exposed nerve. "I was thinking it might be kind of heartwarming if I were to reach out to her. If you're too shy I'll be happy to."

"That's black mail! *Also* recorded!" she shrieked, unmindful of how we were attracting attention of passersby.

"Let's just picture the heartwarming Christmases going forward, shall we? Your illegitimate daughter finally gets to meet the woman who abandoned her. Maybe she'll get an explanation for all the innate evil that resounds in her own heart. She'll finally be able to understand why nothing in life can make her happy or—"

I saw the slap coming from a mile off but instead of dodging it I tilted my face to more firmly connect with her hand. The slap itself wasn't that forceful but I rocked back a step at its impact. Then I touched my cheek with my hand, partially to hide the smile that was forming on my face.

"That's assault," I said quietly.

She stared at me, her face flushed, her eyes darting from my cheek to my eyes. The look on her face was akin to how Mr. Rat looked when he was confronted by Barney and all the children who'd had their cookies stolen.

Caught in a trap for the whole world to see.

"Prove it," she said, her eyes on the red blotch in the shape of her hand as it blossomed across my cheek.

I pointed over her shoulder to the CCTV camera on the street. Joelle turned to look and her body stiffened when she saw it. She turned back to me.

"You bitch," she said. "You did that deliberately."

"See you in court, Joelle," I said as I rubbed my cheek again for the benefit of the camera before turning away to walk down the street.

47

I know what you're thinking. You're thinking that was a low blow, a calculated and diabolical plot and totally beneath me. My response to that?

I would've done much worse to keep Robbie.

I think Joelle's biggest deficiency among her many was that since she was never a mother herself, she had no idea the lengths a mother will go to protect her child.

I shivered and ducked my head into the cold wind that threatened to push me off the sidewalk. Since Haley was staying overnight tonight, I thought I'd go to a bit of an effort for dinner. I'd already started stocking up on snacks—chips and chocolate—the very things I normally try to stay away from, since all the walking that Paris has to offer in the end does not counteract a daily *profiterole* habit.

I spotted the Monoprix up ahead and decided to get my dinner shopping done now before I got on the Métro heading for home.

As usual in the late afternoon, the grocery store would be crowded with shoppers on their way home from work. But it would be worse in an hour if I waited.

I entered the store, stamped off the slush onto the store entrance mat, and grabbed a wire basket. I saw a few rotisserie chickens slowly rotating, their luscious sizzling juices falling onto the fried potatoes laid out below. I've had this meal hundreds of times since I moved to Paris, usually with a nice green salad, and there are few things to compete with it for sheer comfort food.

I now knew Haley liked pizza, lasagna and Indian food. But roast chicken and potatoes was a no-brainer—especially if I picked up a nice chocolate *gateau* in the bakery department. I pointed out the chicken I wanted to the server behind the counter. She wrapped it up with a healthy scoop of the fragrant potatoes.

Then I went to the produce section to get enough greens to offset the meal. I was just heading to the *patisserie* department when I saw her.

Marguerite Baldoche. In the yoghurt aisle with a shopping basket. All alone.

As soon as I saw her, I realized I'd been looking at my interviews with her and Madame Zenn all wrong. It wasn't the questions I asked Madame Zenn that mattered. It was what she and Madame Baldoche *said to each other afterward* that was the key.

I had only upset Madame Zenn yesterday morning. That meant she'd had plenty of time to call Madame Baldoche to rant.

One thing I knew, if I knew anything, was that when you mixed emotion with playback, things got amplified.

I approached Madame Baldoche and put on my obnoxiously cheerful American face in preparation for greeting her.

"Bonjour Madame Baldoche!" I sang out, stepping close to block any route of retreat.

She was startled to hear her name trilled out in a public place when she was clearly having a quiet shopping moment and at first just stared at me uncomprehendingly.

That lasted all of five seconds.

"I have nothing to say to you," she said, twisting around in an attempt to walk around me.

I blocked her exit with my body.

"Your friend Madame Zenn told me that you absolutely *did* see Gigi push her boyfriend, no matter what you said to the contrary."

"How dare she!" Madame Baldoche burst out, her cheeks mottled with rage. "Does she believe I cannot think for myself?"

"Clearly she doesn't," I said, shaking my head as if in mutual commiseration. "She also told me how forgetful you are. She mentioned the entrance tickets." I winced dramatically. "*And* the Métro ticket."

I have never seen a sweet little old lady transform so fast into a whirling tornado of fury. Her eyes glittered as she took a step toward me.

"Did she also tell you that *she* left her glasses on the Métro and her husband left his wallet at home? Unless *that* was not an accident? Because my husband says he's done it before! The cheapskate!"

With that she pushed past me, banging my sore hip with her wire grocery basket. But I didn't care. In fact, I was downright giddy with what had just happened.

Call me persnickety, but it does seem to me that someone who wasn't wearing her glasses wasn't going to be a very good eyewitness for the prosecution.

As I carried my dinner goodies home, being mindful of where I stepped on the slushy sidewalk, I decided to tempt fate by texting and walking at the same time. I was so excited with the news I'd discovered that I needed to tell Pierre Berger as soon as possible.

<call Bernice Zenn and pressure her about what she saw that day> I texted him. I continued walking and glanced at my phone every few seconds until I saw his answering text.

<She saw what she saw>

I stopped in order to text a longer message, knowing he wouldn't pick up if I tried to call him.

<Ask her how well she can see without her glasses b/c she wasn't wearing them that day!>

I didn't bother waiting for a reply. I was tempted to go back to Madame Zenn to confront her with what I'd found out but I'd probably pushed the old girl as far as I could. It would really be better coming from Gigi's lawyer at this point.

Just as I turned down my street I saw I was getting an incoming call from Sabine.

I felt a chill on my skin that had nothing to do with the weather.

"Hello?" I said into the phone.

"Have you lost your mind?" Sabine said in lieu of a greeting.

"Hi, Sabine," I said. "What's up?"

"I just got off the phone with Mireille Absalom," she said. "She wanted to tell me that if I dared to bring a complaint of assault against her client, she'll counter with a charge of stalking. What the hell did you do? I didn't think I had to tell you to stay away from Joelle Lapin!"

Honestly on one hand I wasn't surprised. Joelle was a worthy adversary and of course I should have known that it wasn't likely she would let a little thing like an assault charge stop her in her quest to destroy me. I suddenly felt very tired.

It was too bad though. I'd had a whole blessed hour where I thought, I hoped, that I might have gotten the Joelle problem in my rear view mirror. I thought of Robbie at home with Haley and I felt a hollowness develop in my chest.

"I made a mistake," I said. "But the blood relation they found intends to put Robbie in foster care."

"*Mon Dieu!* Do not tell me you contacted her!"

"I gave a false name," I said meekly.

I heard the breath that Sabine sucked in as if attempting to calm herself before continuing our conversation. I didn't blame her. I'd made a mess of things.

"Claire, this case is not completely hopeless. But you must leave it to me. Do you understand?"

I assured her I did and we left it at that. I knew she was focused on trying to win this case for me—no matter how long it took. What she didn't seem to appreciate was that sticking Robbie in foster care for six months—whether here in Paris or back home in the States—until the matter was resolved meant I'd already lost.

Sabine wasn't addressing that piece. She didn't see *that* as something that needed fixing.

It was pretty much all I could see.

A few minutes later I stopped at a *boulangerie* not far from my apartment for *pain au chocolat* and *viennoiserie*—two favorites of mine. I had been so distracted after my conversation with Madame Baldoche that I cashed out of Monoprix without looking at their pastries.

In the evening at any bakery, there isn't usually anything good left on the racks. But I could see in the display case that there were still a couple of *viennoiserie*.

While I waited in line trying not to feel completely rotten about my chances of keeping Robbie—and how I'd definitely succeeded in making those chances even worse—I was surprised to see I was getting a call from Julien. I have to say that since I spoke with him in the park yesterday, I'd had to fight an inexplicable and growing feeling of antipathy toward him.

This was purely my gut speaking since I had no real

evidence to line up against him. But I've trusted my gut in the past and almost always been glad I did.

"Marie-France still isn't calmed down after your visit," he said when I picked up.

"Murder has a way of doing that to people," I said. "I'm sure Jean-Bernard and Paolo's parents aren't very calm right now either."

"I feel bad about the way our meeting ended yesterday," he said.

"Is there a point to this call, Julien? Because it's been a long day."

"Paolo broke up with me the night he died."

He's telling me this because I told him I talked to Paolo that night and he's finally realized there was no way Paolo didn't tell me.

"Oh, really?" I said with as much disdain and boredom as I could force into my voice. "Are you sure about that, Julien?"

He hesitated.

"No," he said finally. "It was me. I broke up with him."

My personal belief is that if the truth has to be pried out of you with a crowbar it doesn't really count as honesty on your part. Maybe my silence said as much to Julien, because right then he did the strangest most un-Julien like thing I can imagine.

He started to cry.

"I can't believe I told you Paolo confessed," he said. "He didn't. I don't know why I said that."

It distressed me to hear him cry but I couldn't fill the pause in the conversation. I literally had to dig my nails into the palms of my hands to prevent myself from doing it.

"He was becoming clingy and needy—"

"His sister had just been arrested for murder," I couldn't help but interject.

"I know! I can't believe how insensitive I was. It's just that I was ready to move on before all this happened and then when it happened, well, it wasn't Paolo's best look and I just...I just hate myself."

He wept audibly for a few seconds more.

I don't want you to think I'm totally hard-hearted but I just couldn't believe these tears were real. Not that they sounded fake. They didn't. They sounded genuine but a fake crier would make sure they did, wouldn't he?

"Please, let me help you, Claire," he said, sniffling. "Please let me try to make it up to Paolo by helping to find out who did this to him."

It was my turn next in line at the bakery so I quickly assured Julien that I would use his help in whatever way I could and I thanked him for his offer. And then I disconnected.

Not only did I need to give my full attention to the baker's assistant behind the counter—remember the French take these kinds of transactions very seriously—but, given how I felt, I didn't want to talk too much longer with Julien.

I knew that the longer we talked, the more likely he was to realize that not only did I not believe what he was telling me, I didn't trust him and his sudden desire to help me as far as I could fling a *bouquiniste's* metal shed.

48

D inner was simple, homey and comforting. Roast chicken and fried potatoes, served with warm bread and a peppery green salad.

I'd stopped by Geneviève's apartment to see if she wanted to join Haley and me for dinner. It was a rare Saturday night that Geneviève didn't have plans, and tonight was no exception. She had a fairly large social circle, comprised of mostly older women like herself, and liked to keep busy.

So it was just me and Haley. While I was assembling the meal and tossing the salad, Haley gave Robbie his bath and then took Izzy downstairs and walked her for a few minutes.

Honestly, the girl was becoming harder and harder to live without.

When Haley was here I felt like the Queen of England, strolling in to tousle my young charge's hair, kiss his cheek, and then go back to my life, while the hired help wiped the stewed prunes off his cheek, read him the interminable bedtime stories and got half-drowned trying to give him his bath.

Hey, when I was thirty I did my time with Catherine. But at sixty-three, I'm not going to beat myself up because I don't have the energy to be Mary Poppins after a long day.

When I put our dishes down on the table, Haley brought Robbie in to play in his playpen while we ate. Even though she'd spent the whole day with him, she still managed to watch him with real interest throughout dinner. It was almost like it wasn't a job for her. Like she wanted to be with him. I know she didn't have any siblings herself. I wondered if she was thinking of Robbie as a little brother.

I'd been giving it some thought and had decided that if she was up for it when summer came, we might try a live-in situation—at least until school started back again in the fall.

After dinner, I did the dishes while Haley played with Robbie and then read to him. Once he went down for the night, I asked if she wanted to watch television with me but she made a face.

"None of the shows are in English," she said. "And I hate subtitles."

"It's a good way to learn the language," I said.

"I'm hoping I can get through my time here without having to."

"You don't want to learn French?"

I was genuinely surprised. Maybe because learning new languages was so much easier at her age, it shocked me that she wouldn't want to take advantage of that feature of her youth. And also that she didn't want to unlock the secrets of the language spoken around her. It must be difficult to live here and not know what was being said.

I knew Haley would enjoy living in France so much more if she would try to learn the language. I suppose her parents had tried to encourage her.

"You know, studies have shown that learning a foreign language is good for your brain," I said.

"My brain's fine."

That was frustrating. Why be satisfied with *fine* when with a little effort you could be great? Bob and I never had a problem with Catherine not wanting to do her best. She always met or exceeded expectations.

I wasn't quite sure what to make of someone who was happy to rock along in the middle lane.

In any case, Haley retired with a book and I decided to craft a letter to Gigi with the hopes that Berger could get it to her.

I'd thought about Gigi on and off all day, wondering how hopeless she must have felt to have tried what she did. I prayed that her parents didn't know about it but of course they would have been told.

I took a couple of ibuprofen to counteract the steady throbbing ache in my hip and curled up on the couch with Izzy and my stationery pad. But I found it hard to concentrate and my mind kept coming back to all the things that felt like they'd been pressing in on me all week.

I'd have to put in the plus column how I'd managed to dismantle all five eyewitnesses to the so-called push off the Eiffel Tower.

In the minus column I'd have to list how I handled Detective Muller and honestly Joelle too. Come to think of it, I'd also done a scorched-earth treatment on Marie-France which made her no longer a usable resource for me.

Then totally separate from everything else was the fact that I hadn't heard from Catherine this week and she'd only tersely responded to the few texts I'd sent her. It was possible she was just busy. It was possible she was having a difficult week with Todd and connecting with me only made that difficulty more complicated for her.

And of course there was Jean-Marc.

Regardless of the fact that he'd turned me down when I reached out to him, I couldn't stop thinking of him. He'd been such a big part of my entry into Paris and also my struggles in regaining trust in the male of the species. Jean-Marc had been a wounded creature when I met him. Unfortunately, the last wound he'd been dealt had been hand-delivered by me.

Even more bizarrely? I've been thinking a lot about Bob this week too. I don't think the thoughts I have of him are about me missing him but rather about how he was such a big part of my life for so many years. Every Christmas, birthday and major holiday in the last thirty years included him in a very exclusive party of three. Sharing the joy of our dear Catherine was inextricably coupled with him.

You can't just wipe out a past life, no matter how intriguing and exciting your new one is—or how painfully the past life ended. I'm happy in Paris and I'm also happy not to be living with someone who couldn't be true to me.

But that doesn't mean I don't think of that old life with regret and even longing more times than is good for me.

And if all those things crowded into my brain weren't enough, then there's the issue of my father, a man who never reached out to me in my whole sixty years on this planet. I'd met him only once, and that was when he tried to manipulate and control me.

He was a man I was sure was unapologetically responsible for my husband's murder; a man who ordered the kidnapping of Robbie and was the source of the worst four hours of my life; a man who would justify anything he cared to do to me by his biological relationship with me.

Finally, he was a man I feared, and whose recent silence I feared even more than the turmoil and violence he'd wreaked last summer.

So yes. Lots to think about.

It was close to ten o'clock by the time I came back upstairs after taking Izzy out for her last call of the day. I rinsed out my wine glass and wondered when I'd started to default to that instead of the peppermint tisane I used to end my day with. I made a mental note to switch back and also to make an effort to make it to yoga class more often.

I was just about to begin my nighttime regime of floss, moisturize, brush and downward dog when my phone vibrated. I saw it was Berger.

"Hello?" I said.

"You were right," he said. "Madame Zenn recanted her statement. Upon reflection she didn't see anything."

I felt a wave of relief and satisfaction.

"It was the eyeglasses, wasn't it? You asked her how she could see anything with no glasses? So how does the case look against Gigi now?"

I settled down on the corner of the couch hoping to finally get a proper debrief from him.

"I can't get into it," he said. "But if you can come right now you can visit her in the infirmary."

I sat up straight, my toothbrush still in my hand.

"Right now?"

"Sorry for the late hour but it's now or never. Can you come? She's asking for you."

I looked in the direction of Haley and Robbie's room.

"Let me call you back," I said and disconnected.

I went to Haley's room and knocked lightly on the door so as not to wake Robbie.

"Come in."

She was lying on the bed reading *The Hidden Life of Trees* when I came in.

"Gigi's lawyer just called," I said. "He wants to know if I can go down to the police infirmary to see Gigi. Right now."

Haley shrugged. "It's fine with me."

"You sure you don't mind?"

I was well aware of how unsettled she might feel after receiving the threatening note under the door.

"Go if you want to. Me and Robbie are good."

I glanced at Robbie sleeping soundly in his crib. I knew they were safe. I knew that Haley could handle any emergency as well as I could especially if it only involved dialing the police.

"I won't be long," I said.

49

By the time my Uber pulled up in front of the police infirmary on rue de Angleterre, it was after ten o'clock. It was way past visiting hours, which I suppose is the reason Berger was able to get me in. He was waiting for me in the waiting room. He was on his cellphone and, holding a digital tablet in his other hand, still managed to hold up a finger to me to indicate he would be a moment longer.

The waiting room was empty. Even the receptionist had gone home, although I could see a police officer standing in the nearby hallway.

Finally Berger hung up and turned to me.

"She's physically fine but they have her on some sort of calming drug. I've already seen her, but there isn't much more I can do here."

Before I could reply, the policeman in the hallway stepped into the room and snapped his fingers at me.

"Just win her case," I said to Berger before walking over to the unsmiling policeman.

He led me down the hallway that smelled strongly of astringent chemicals and past medical personnel at nursing stations on their computers. I could hear the bleeps and pings of diagnostic equipment.

The policeman led me into Gigi's room, told me I had twenty minutes, and left.

A lamp was on by the far wall that allowed me to see the room clearly. There was a sink, a bedside table and a bed. I could just make out the form on the bed.

"Claire?" Gigi called faintly as I approached. She swung her legs out of bed and started to stand, but I hurried to her and put a hand on her shoulder.

"Hey, Gigi." I put my arms around her and just held her for a moment. I didn't know whether her parents had come to Paris to see her, but I knew there was a good chance mine was the only friendly face she'd seen in days.

"I am so glad you came," she said.

I had never seen Gigi looking so frail. Her hair hung around her shoulders as if she hadn't combed it in days. I thought I could feel her shoulder bones through the hospital smock.

She pulled away first and her eyes searched my face.

"I just can't believe it," she said. "Paolo."

"I know. I am so sorry, sweetheart."

She shook her head and wiped the tears from her cheeks.

"You got to meet him, didn't you?" she asked.

"I did."

"He was older than me so I didn't see him a lot growing up but I always knew he cared."

After a moment, I handed her a tissue and helped her get back in the bed.

Berger had told me that she'd taken pills to kill herself, but the doctors believed it to be more gesture than a truly committed attempt. The pills were ibuprofen that she'd hoarded for several days.

"Have you seen your parents?" I asked.

She shook her head. "Papa had another attack. Not a bad one but they couldn't come. I talked to them on the phone."

That was at least something.

"Gigi, you know I'm working with your lawyer Pierre Berger to try to get to the bottom of what really happened that day at the Eiffel Tower."

She looked at me in desperation.

"If they know it was a bad panel, why can't they just let me go?"

"Because it wasn't just a bad panel," I said gently. "Jean-Bernard had taken an overdose of an illegal street drug beforehand."

She stared at me. "Jean-Bernard didn't do drugs."

"There is a possibility that he didn't take the drug deliberately," I said.

She blinked at me.

"So they think I poisoned him? Before pushing him off the Eiffel Tower?"

I could see she was edging toward hysteria. My intention here was not to fill her in on what was happening but to give her succor and to possibly get information from her that might help her.

"Gigi, listen to me. Nobody is accusing you of poisoning Jean-Bernard."

"Just pushing him to his death!"

"The last time we spoke, you told me that Paolo and Jean-Bernard hated each other."

She nodded. "Mostly because of me."

"Mostly but not all?" I prompted.

"Well, there was the Julien thing."

I was suddenly very alert.

"What about Julien?"

"Well, you know, because of how Julien left his last job. Paolo never really forgave Jean-Bernard for that."

I felt a stillness settle in my chest at her words.

"What do you mean? How did Julien leave CDB?"

She made a face.

"I'm sure Jean-Bernard didn't mean to do it. He was probably drinking and not paying attention to what he was saying, you know?"

I waited.

"One night Julien and Jean-Bernard were out clubbing and —this was before Julien and Paolo got together—Jean-Bernard snapped a picture of Julien kissing some guy."

"Why did he do that?" I asked.

"Just fooling around. I told you, he'd been drinking. But then somehow it got posted to Jean-Bernard's social media feed."

Somehow?

"And the next day CDB fired Julien," she said with a weak shrug.

50

I stared at Gigi, my mouth open in surprise.

Jean-Bernard got Julien fired from his dream job? *That's* the reason he wasn't at CDB anymore?

Gigi could see she'd shocked me with her statement.

"I mean the law firm—the one that's supposed to be so progressive, right?" she said. "They made up some other reason for why they did it," Gigi said. "But Paolo said that Julien heard from one of his friends who worked there that it was because of the photo. They thought Julien wasn't discreet and would make them look bad."

I still hadn't said anything and Gigi finally noticed.

"You're thinking this makes Paolo look guilty, aren't you?" she said. "You're thinking this means Paolo had a motive on top of Jean-Bernard's treatment of me."

But that's not what I was thinking.

I was thinking I had just found the best solid gold motive of the entire bunch.

And it pointed directly at Julien.

Julien, with no alibi and the best motive of all for murder.

A few moments later the policeman came in to tell me my

time was up. I gave Gigi a hug and told her I had every reason to believe she would be out of here and home soon.

I did, too. Now that I had the motive-to-end-all motives, I just needed some evidence to pull Detective Muller's focus away from Gigi and onto the person who really killed Jean-Bernard—Julien Ricard.

As I was walking away from the clinic it occurred to me that Julien probably also killed Paolo because Paolo either knew too much or had threatened to go to the police. After all, his sister was being held for a crime that his boyfriend had committed! If Julien had refused to turn himself in, I could easily see the ensuing altercation turning violent and then deadly.

The Eiffel Tower was glittering and twinkling in the distance, symbol of this magical city I now called home. For a moment I was stunned by its iconic magnetism.

Speaking of which, I didn't feel like going home just yet. The air was cold but it was a good cold that felt restorative and energizing as I brought each breath into my lungs.

I decided to walk for a bit. This was a decent section of town and it was only a little after eleven. All the cafés and restaurants were still open, and people still filled the street.

I walked until I came to a busy café and settled in at a free table. I ordered a nightcap and watched the scene before me while I pondered what I now knew.

With all the eyewitnesses basically discredited, it was clear that the reason nobody saw Gigi push Jean-Bernard was because she hadn't. Or at least it was not a shove that could be considered lethal force. Jean-Bernard had been drugged such that the slightest breeze would have carried him over the top.

I hoped mightily that Berger was setting up his defense based on this. Proving Julien's involvement was Gigi's best and maybe only chance to prove her innocence.

I tried to think how I could either get Julien to confess or otherwise prove what he'd done. It wasn't that late and I was tempted to call him and ask him again if he really considered Jean-Bernard a friend, because clearly that was a lie.

A man maliciously gets you fired from the job of your dreams? Who forgives that?

No, Julien had been biding his time, waiting for his moment. And then when he acted, the fact that Gigi had gotten caught in the crossfire was just a regrettable necessity.

My phone dinged indicating an incoming text and I saw it was from Adele.

<*Friend of mine said your note showed three sets of prints*>

I felt my shoulders sag with disappointment. Three sets meant mine, Haley's and Geneviève's. Whoever left the note had wiped it clean before delivering it. I thought back to the message in the note. *He deserved to die.*

That sounded like Julien's handiwork. But unfortunately there was no way to prove it unless I got him to admit he sent it.

I finished my drink. There was nothing more I could do tonight. Any more planning or scheming would best be done after a good night's sleep. I paid my bill and stood up just as my phone dinged again, indicating another text message.

<*Come quick. I am in trouble*>

It was from Zéro.

Quickly, I called his number but the call went to voicemail.

What kind of trouble could it be that Zéro would reach out to me? Did it have to do with the case? I hesitated for a moment as I tried to think what would happen if I called the cops. Would that just end up endangering him?

Another text came through.

< *rue de Tanger. NO flic!*>

I flung down five euros for my drink and left the café, already clicking the Uber app icon.

51

I sat in the back of the Uber and stared out at the passing street scenes.

The streetlights outside became fewer the more we drove until it felt as if we were driving into darkness itself. Zéro had saved my life yesterday. He wouldn't be begging for me to come back to his neighborhood if he wasn't in serious trouble.

I thought of Jean-Marc. If he were still in town and if we were still friends, I could call him for backup.

If, if, if.

I was on my own.

And I'd better get used to it.

I continued to text and to call Zéro's number but he didn't answer. I read his two texts over and over again but could get nothing more out of them.

What could possibly be happening? How did Zéro think a sixty-three-year-old woman could help him?

Everything about this errand was mad!

I had just come to the point where I realized what I was doing was insane and was about to tell my Uber driver to turn around when he stopped the car and told me to get out. We were at least two blocks from rue de Tanger—if I was still going there, which I'd now decided that I wasn't.

"I've changed my mind. I need you to take me home," I said.

"No, Madame," my driver said tersely. "You must get out."

I could see his eyes in the rearview mirror and saw what I should've seen before now. He was a nervous wreck and very uncomfortable with being in this part of the city.

"Just turn around," I said, trying to keep my voice calm.

"Get out!" he shrieked. "Get out of my car!"

Realizing that I wasn't going to be able to reason with him, I gathered up my bag and got out of the car.

I stood there on the street in a panic. How was I going to get home? The Métro stopped working at one o'clock. It was already five past the hour.

I punched in the icon for another Uber and saw there were no Ubers available.

I felt suddenly thirsty with a tightening sensation in my gut. There was minimal traffic on the street and no pedestrians. I walked quickly to the shadows, hearing my footsteps echoing loudly in the street, and stood under a tattered awning of what looked to be a small boarded-up shoe store. My heart was pounding.

Suddenly my phone dinged and I jumped at the sound. I pulled my phone out of my coat pocket and saw another text message from Zéro.

<Hurry>

I called 17, the statewide emergency police number.

"There is an emergency at rue de Tanger," I said in a low voice.

"Speak up, Madame," the dispatcher barked. "What is the address and what is your emergency?"

Frustrated, I hung up and texted Adele, my hands shaking as I did.

<*Need you to send the police to rue de Tanger*> I texted her.
<*Tell them a woman is being assaulted*>

<*They won't care*> Adele texted back. <*What woman? YOU?*>

<*Tell them whatever you have to*> I texted furiously back <*just get them to come!*>

I heard the sound nearby of something scraping on the paver-covered sidewalk and felt my stomach lurch. I pressed back further into the wall hoping the shadows would cover me.

I scanned the street and saw a shadowy figure move down the street. I didn't think he'd seen me but I held my breath until he disappeared.

The scraping sound happened again. I knew fear made one hypervigilant to sound. Was I really hearing it? My heartbeat was pounding in my ears.

My phone vibrated in my hand and I looked down to see I was getting a call from Haley.

"Yes?" I whispered into the phone. "Haley?"

"Where are you?" she asked, a thread of fear in her voice.

"What's the matter?" I said, forgetting to keep my voice low.

"Someone's in the outside hallway," Haley said, her voice rising shrilly. "They're trying to get in."

52

"Call the police," I said, my heart pounding.

"Don't hang up!" Haley said, her voice wobbling and reminding me that she was still just a child herself.

"It's okay, Haley," I said firmly, allowing my voice to be confident—but unfortunately loud. I heard it echo off the dark wet streets around me. "Call the police *now*."

"Okay." She disconnected and I stood there quaking and staring at my phone. Is this why I was lured here? So that someone could go to my apartment?

Suddenly the scraping sound was right next to me and I whirled around to see the shadowy figure I'd seen before was no more than five feet from where I stood. I had only one way to run—and that way would be blocked by him in two steps.

"Don't be afraid," he said, stepping out of the shadows. "It's only me."

Julien stood before me, missing his coat and his scarf, his cheeks chapped red from the cold.

"Julien," I said in astonishment. "What are you doing here?"

"I told you I wanted to help," he said stiffly. "Are you looking for answers here?"

Now was not the time to tell him I knew he'd killed two people.

"I...I had an argument with my Uber driver," I said. "He abandoned me here."

"That's difficult to believe." He took a step closer to me.

"Look, Julien," I said, making my voice sound stronger than it felt. "I'm an American citizen. If you hurt me my embassy will prosecute you to the fullest extent of the law."

Julien rubbed his forehead and looked around as if bewildered.

"I have two detectives," I said firmly, "a crime scene tech, an attorney and at least three other people who know the details of what I've discovered about Jean-Bernard's killer. If I end up dead, all of them will be looking for you."

"Me? I had nothing to do with Jean-Bernard's death! I told you. I only want to help!"

Was he playing games? Was he hoping I'd let my guard down?

"Stop it, Julien," I said. "I know the truth. I know you hated Jean-Bernard and that you lied about it. I know he lost you your dream job at CDB. Okay?"

He watched me silently, his eyes glittering.

"I suppose it was only a matter of time before you heard that," he said.

"I get it," I said. "How could anyone forgive something like that? I truly understand."

"You're wrong. I didn't kill Jean-Bernard."

I'm not sure what he gained by saying this unless there was a ghost of a chance he didn't intend to kill me?

"I mean, yes, I was wrong to tell you we were friends when we weren't anymore, but I swear I didn't hate him."

"Then why are you following me?"

"I told you! To help you!"

"That's great," I said, my eyes glancing to the right. There was a broken wooden fence there. I might be able to slip through where the slats were missing. But Julien was young and in good shape. He'd catch me easily.

"You have no idea the guilt I feel over what happened to Paolo," he said.

I'll bet. Murdering someone does bring with it a certain amount of guilt.

"If there is anything I can do to help find his killer—or even Jean-Bernard's—then I want to do that."

"Did you follow me to the infirmary tonight?"

Keep him talking. Make him believe he's winning me over.

"I did. I waited outside and then followed you to the café. When I saw you get in the Uber I grabbed a taxi and followed you here. My taxi let me out about twenty meters from where your Uber stopped. I thought for sure you saw me."

I was so busy going toe to toe with my Uber driver I hadn't noticed.

"Okay, great," I said. "You'll be a much appreciated addition to the team." I smiled at him and then let my eyes go over his shoulder as if I were seeing something behind him.

It's an oldie but it always works.

Sure enough, he turned to look.

I pushed off the brick wall and sprinted down the sidewalk, knowing my only chance was to find a hiding place before he saw me. I turned and darted into what I thought was an alley but was only an alcove. But it was too late to turn back. I saw a line of garbage bins at the back of the alcove. They were a natural hiding place.

But also an obvious one.

I heard his footsteps coming, not hurrying. Just before I knew he would appear at the mouth of the alcove I flung my purse at the bins. They hit with a crash as I slid into the shadows by the opening. I forced my labored panting down into my throat and held my breath cutting off the sounds altogether.

Julien raced past me to the garbage bins where he began to search for me behind the cans, overturning them and throwing the lids behind him.

I hadn't expected him not to care about making noise.

But I should have. He was behaving exactly true to form—like a person with nothing to lose.

I felt a strong urge to run away while he was busy rampaging through the bins but I found I couldn't move. I saw the precious moments I'd created with the diversion slip away in my frozen panic.

The sounds of his noisy search of the bins went on and on and still I couldn't move. As soon as he turned around to leave he'd see me.

I carefully unbuttoned my coat and eased my shoes off. They made too much noise and increased the chances that I would trip on the cobblestones.

I took in a huge and unfortunately audible breath which galvanized me. I turned and ran toward the street, accidentally kicking a garbage can lid in an earsplitting clatter. I heard him curse behind me.

I hadn't reached the street when I felt his hands on me. I slipped out of my unbuttoned coat—shoeless and now coatless.

I made it another two steps before an iron-like arm caught me hard around the middle and dragged me back into the alcove.

He pushed me face first into the wall, his arm still around my waist. My heart pounded in terror, both of us panting and unable to speak.

Finally he turned me around to face him, his eyes probing mine. For one second as I looked into his eyes, I saw something that made me think that maybe I was wrong.

I opened my mouth to say something. I'm not even sure what, when a loud bang exploded in the close space around us, the sound of it tearing into the air and reverberating all around us. Julien gripped me hard and it was then that I realized that he'd flinched violently at the sound.

Or its impact.

He released me and crumpled to his knees before falling forward. Confused, I watched the blood pool around him where he lay. And when I looked up I saw a well-dressed older woman standing in front of me with a gun in her hands.

I had no idea who she was until she spoke.

"Is he dead?" Evelyn Couture said.

"Thank God," I said, beginning to tremble in the aftermath of what had just happened. I bent down, using the wall for support to pull my coat off the ground. It was getting soaked with Julien's blood.

With frozen fingers, I pulled it around me and eased down to my knees beside Julien. I felt for his pulse. It was faint but there. From the position in which he lay I could easily see the bullet's point of entry in his back.

I pulled up his jacket and pressed hard on the wound to try to staunch the blood. With my free hand I fumbled for my phone in my coat pocket but before I could reach it I realized two things.

One. Evelyn was still just standing there staring at me.

Two. She was dressed differently from the last time I saw her.

I glanced up at her.

Make that three things.

She wasn't using her cane.

Evelyn stepped over to me and held out her hand. For a moment I thought she meant to help me to my feet.

"Your phone," she said.

"He needs an ambulance."

"Give me your phone and step away from him."

"He'll bleed to death!"

She aimed the gun at me.

I swallowed hard and backed away, my hands covered in Julien's blood. My phone still in my hand.

"I don't understand," I said.

"You don't understand why I would pretend to be crippled, elderly and needy?" she asked. "I would have thought it was obvious."

"It was so you would qualify as a client of Jean-Bernard's," I said.

"I was more than that to him," she said. "But we had to play the game. But I had a plan. A marvelous plan of transformation and rebirth. We were going to be so happy."

All of a sudden I remembered the photo in Evelyn's living room. Something about the photo had tickled my brain when I laid eyes on it. It was almost like I'd seen the young man in the photo before—which I now realized I had.

It was Jean-Bernard. Years ago. Had Evelyn and Jean-Bernard known each other before?

"So let me guess," I said. "You tossed aside your cane and your gray wig and revealed your true, non-decrepit self to Jean-Bernard. I take it, he was less than thrilled?"

"He said I'd lied to him! He said he couldn't date a client! He looked at me like I was a monster! Or insane."

"So you killed him."

"Shut up," Evelyn said, never dropping the aim of her gun from my chest. "You don't know anything about me. If you'd gone where I told you to in the text I wouldn't have had to come looking for you. As it is, we can't stay here."

A sick feeling curdled in my gut.

The text message hadn't been from Zéro.

"If you're thinking Zéro will repeat his big savior act, you can forget it," Evelyn said as if reading my mind. "I killed him an hour ago."

A stab of cold fear pierced me. What she said had the ring of truth to it. How else would she have access to Zéro's phone?

I tried to rally, to think. Adele had phoned the police ten minutes ago. Unless they ignored her, they might be on their way. Except I'd given Adele the wrong address. I'd sent her to rue de Tanger, the address I'd been sent in the text message.

That wasn't where I was now.

Nobody was coming.

"So it was you who sent me the text," I said trying at least to stall for time.

"That's right, using Zéro's phone after I killed him."

"Why?"

"I would have thought that was obvious. Because I don't

want to go to prison for killing Jean-Bernard and the other guy."

The revelation was immediate and appalling. And I should have realized it sooner.

"You killed Paolo," I said.

"I'll bet you'll never guess why."

She moved closer to me, her gun arm never wavering. As I stared at her I knew there

was no doubt that it was Evelyn on the CCTV camera outside Paolo's apartment building the night he was killed.

"He came by here last week," she said. "He must have followed Jean-Bernard—one of the few times I get him all to myself and this pervert comes and hogs all his time! The two of them spoke forever outside my apartment and when I got tired of waiting I came downstairs and saw them embracing! I could see he was trying to take Jean-Bernard away from me."

"You thought Paolo was trying to turn Jean-Bernard gay? That's why you killed him?"

She was insane.

"I didn't want to," she said heatedly, brandishing the gun. "That's on Jean-Bernard. He made me do it."

"How did you do it?"

"I gave him some pills and told him it was for his headaches. He used to get migraines."

"But it wasn't headache medicine."

"No. It was *krokodil*. Pretty easy to get around here. I told him to take three. I had no idea when he'd take them."

I groaned. That explained why the drug was taken during Gigi's window of time. No one had dropped the drug into Jean-Bernard's food or drink. He'd unwittingly poisoned *himself*.

In fact, if prompted, I would bet that Gigi might even remember a moment before they got in the elevator of the

Eiffel Tower where she might have seen Jean-Bernard take a few pills for a headache he felt coming on.

"And then you used the same drug on Paolo?" I asked.

"I couldn't let him get away with ruining my life, could I?"

Julien groaned. I wondered if the police would get here before he bled out. I wondered if they would get here before she shot me.

"Why did you lure me here?" I asked.

"Why do you think?"

"I have no idea. What did I ever do to you?"

"You are so oblivious!" Evelyn said angrily. "Like all Americans! You really do think you are the guardians of the world, don't you? You barge into people's lives, rearrange everything, ruin everything! And then leave! But not this time. Drop your phone."

It had given me some courage to feel it in my hand but I tossed it to the ground, hoping it wouldn't break in case I got the chance to use it later. Evelyn pulled out her own phone.

"Now. About the little drama playing out in your apartment. You do know your babysitter has a visitor, yes? Want to take a listen?"

I took two steps toward her. She cocked the pistol and I stopped.

"Why would you want to hurt an innocent girl and child?" I asked, my terror ramping up into my chest.

Evelyn twisted her mouth into an ugly semblance of mockery and repeated my words back to me.

"*Why would I want to hurt an innocent girl and child?* I'm doing it because you came into my home and acted like I was nothing but a loser charity case to Jean-Bernard. I'm doing it for the pleasure of seeing the look on your face. Just before I kill you."

She held up her phone.

"This is a video taken a few minutes ago. Everything has

already happened. My man was paid upfront to kill both of them. And you can't do a damn thing about it."

She stood before me holding both arms straight out toward me, one holding the phone in a horizontal position and the other holding the gun.

But my eyes were glued to the video. I couldn't help it. I knew I should be thinking of rushing her or distracting her but as soon as I saw the hammer hit the lock on my apartment door and then swing open, I could only watch in mesmerized terror as the unthinkable drama unfolded. I heard Haley screaming in the background and Izzy's barking until they were suddenly cut off with a painful yelp. And then silence.

"*And your little dog too*," Evelyn said gleefully. "One down. Two to go."

The fury inside me quickly began to overwhelm the horror. That this monster could snuff out the lives of these two precious children like they were nothing was...incomprehensible.

It's true what they say. I saw red and everything else fell away.

Everything except my fury.

Which didn't mean that habits long ingrained in me didn't kick in even without my realizing it.

"Look!" I said, pointing at the video screen. "Your guy went to the wrong apartment!"

"Eh?" Evelyn frowned and turned the phone around to see the screen.

That's when I charged her.

54

H aley crouched in the bathroom, her hand holding Izzy's mouth shut to prevent her from barking and giving away their location. Robbie sat in the bathtub, blinking and looking around with curiosity.

Haley felt herself trembling. The urge to crouch down and make herself small was intense, nearly irresistible. She licked her lips and realized she was holding her breath. Suddenly, she heard the muffled sound of a gunshot.

At first she thought it came from outside the building, maybe a car backfiring?

But no. It sounded more like a gunshot from a television program, muted and distant. And then she heard his voice, deep and cold and robotlike. As soon as she heard him, Haley realized even without understanding his words that he was talking the way one does when narrating a video.

The guy was inside the apartment walking through his actions.

He's videotaping it.

Izzy whimpered and Haley removed her hand and put the dog in the tub with Robbie. She held her finger up to Robbie and he went instantly still. They'd played this game many times. Robbie was good at it. Tonight he'd need to be perfect.

Stay quiet and the monsters can't find you.

She crept back to the bathroom door and tested the lock. It was the kind you could open with a hairpin.

Or a good kick.

She put her ear to the door. He was still speaking.

What is he saying?

Where had the gunshot come from?

His voice became louder as he moved from the foyer through the living room. He'd go to Claire's bedroom next. And then the guest room. After that the only place left would be the ensuite bath where she was. She glanced at Izzy and Robbie in the bath. They were both watching her.

"*Je sais que tu es ici, ma petite,*" the man said, louder now.

She felt her insides turn to ice.

He's talking to me.

"*Allez maintenant et ça ne te fera pas de mal.* "

She had no idea what he was saying but his tone was cold and taunting. Whatever he was saying, it was bad.

She listened as his footsteps moved down the hall pausing at the guestroom, her emotions vacillating between terror and panic.

She stood up slowly and stood between the bathtub and the door. Behind her, Izzy growled deep in her throat but Haley knew it didn't matter about the noise anymore.

In seconds he was outside the bathroom door. The man knew they were inside.

"*Ouvre la porte,*" he said, his voice deep and menacing.

Not understanding him made it worse, made it a million times worse. It made him sound mysterious and evil with possible content to ease or soften his meaning.

His intention.

Haley wiped her damp palms on her jeans and backed up

until her legs touched the back of the bathtub. She felt Robbie reach over and gently tug at her pant legs.

I'm cool and calm, she told herself, trying to override her panic. She focused on the doorknob and watched it as it slowly started to turn.

She glanced around the little bathroom one last time. She saw the tiny ceramic sink, the oval sweetheart mirror with the etched flowers on its border, the old-fashioned ceramic light switch. She saw Robbie in the tub, watching her, his trusting and solemn eyes on her.

The man continued to talk to her, his voice low and abrasive, his words incomprehensible.

The doorknob rattled and then made a loud click as the lock broke. Haley felt a rush as if all her nerve endings screamed at the same time as the lock breaking.

She set her jaw as she watched the door inch slowly open. And she felt a rush of adrenalin course through her. Because that was when she knew she was ready for whatever happened next.

In fact she had never been more ready in her entire life.

———————

55

The gun went off in my ear, deafening me immediately. But I was too far gone to care. My hands connected with Evelyn's throat and I dug my nails into her neck and squeezed with every ounce of weight and strength that seven years of regular Pilates classes had given me.

I brought my face close to hers and saw her eyes bulge frantically as she fought to peel my hands from her neck.

For me, everything that happened after that happened in a penumbra of eerie silence. I didn't hear the gun fall to the stones at our feet, I didn't hear Evelyn's desperate gasps in her attempt to breathe while I choked off her air, I didn't hear her agonized gurgling sounds.

I only took my hands from her neck when I felt her shoulders sag against the brick wall and I wasn't strong enough to hold her up. I took a step back and watched her slump to the ground and saw she wasn't holding the gun anymore. I saw it next to her knee and picked it up.

With the solid feel of it in my hand I walked back to her and kicked her shoe to get her attention. She was holding her throat with her hand. Her eyes had been shut but quickly fluttered open. She looked up at me, standing over her. She looked at the gun in my hand.

My world was still totally silent. I saw her lips move but the words didn't reach me. She still held her phone in her other hand.

I used the gun to point to it.

"Tell the man to leave them alone. Tell him *now* or I'll shoot."

I couldn't hear my own voice. Evelyn looked at me with a strange expression on her face. I have no idea what my French must have sounded like to her. I pointed again to the phone in her hand.

"Call him!" I shouted.

Evelyn's face slowly twisted into a demonic smile and her lips moved.

In frustration I pointed to my ear.

"I can't hear you!"

That actually made her laugh and then wince as the laugh triggered pain in her throat. She held up her phone and then soundlessly mouthed the word *Non* as she shook her head, over and over again.

Non she would not call. *Non* she would not stop him.

I stared at her and for one terrible moment I didn't know what to do.

It was either already too late or it was happening right now and I was powerless to stop it. I felt nearly insane with my helplessness.

Watching Evelyn deny me, watching her cold-bloodedly refuse to stop the horror that was happening in my apartment, I thought I would go mad.

Instead, I took careful aim and pulled the trigger.

56

Evelyn was writhing on the ground, her mouth open wide in a howl of agony that I could just barely hear. Her screams were faint—as if they were coming from a long way off.

I had shot her in the knee.

I picked up her dropped phone and found the number the video had been sent from. The blood pounded in my ears as I tried to think. I couldn't call the man and tell him to stop or I'd kill his client. My French was passable but not if I couldn't hear myself speak.

I turned to Evelyn and tossed the phone to her. She was holding her bloodied knee and rocking from side to side. I knelt beside her and jammed the gun barrel into her other knee.

"Call him!" I screamed.

But it was no use. She was too far gone.

A crowd had formed at the mouth of the alcove. The gunshots had done what all the bashing of garbage cans and shouting hadn't managed to. People were gathered and creeping slowly around us. I was not afraid. I had a gun and I obviously wasn't afraid to use it.

"Call an ambulance!" I shouted, not at all sure what my words sounded like, only hoping they were intelligible.

I turned back to Julien, who was lying very still on the ground. Kneeling beside him, I could tell he was still breathing but I had no idea how much longer he could hold on.

The crowd had now grown to at least twenty people. Two were attempting to give first aid to Evelyn.

And then I heard the sound that must truly be the most wonderful sound in all the world when you really need to hear it. It was a police siren.

I sat back on my heels, my hand on Julien to feel the faint rise and fall of his chest, and I saw someone separate himself from the crowd. There was something about the way the man walked toward me that made me believe he knew me.

"Zéro?" I called. "Is that you?"

"*Oui, c'est moi.*" He came over and knelt by Julien.

Tears of relief welled up in my eyes.

"Evelyn said she stole your phone," I said. "She said she killed you."

He glanced at Evelyn who had stopped screaming. He frowned. "Really? I thought I'd lost it."

"I need your help," I said. "Please."

He looked at me warily.

"I need you to get me my phone from over there against the wall."

He got up and skirted the crowd, and fetched the phone and handed it to me. The screen was cracked but it still functioned.

"And I need you to take this." I said, handing the gun to him.

He acted as if he'd known all along I would give it to him.

Or perhaps he was already planning on taking it from me. He stood up. My hearing was nearly fully back. The police would be here any minute.

"This time I really must ask you not to come back," he said, wagging a finger at me.

"No worries," I said to him. "I'm glad you're alive by the way."

He shrugged and then disappeared into the crowd.

I took in a long breath to fortify myself and then looked at my phone and prayed as I have never prayed in my life. I was terrified to call. I didn't dare ask Geneviève to come upstairs either. Should I call Adele?

Suddenly my phone rang. It was Haley's phone calling.

My blood ran cold at the sight.

Was it the killer calling to gloat?

With trembling fingers I pressed *Accept*.

"Haley?" I said, tremulously.

"Everything's under control here, Missus B," Haley said. "Cops are on their way and the threat has been neutralized. Or maybe dead. It's one or the other. I'm gonna let the EMTs sort that out."

"Wh-what?" I stuttered in relief and disbelief.

"Remember that heavy metal towel rod you had propped up behind the bathroom door? Well, I did a Hank Aaron on the guy and he never knew what hit him. The floors are a bit messy but I figure it's the bathroom so at least no carpets were damaged."

A part of me was able to register that this was the most I'd ever heard Haley talk.

"Are...are you okay?" I managed to get out.

In the background I heard Robbie babbling, "Chief! Chief!"

"Hey!" Haley crowed. "It looks like the little man finally came up with my nickname!"

And I began to laugh where I sat on the ground next to Julien just as the police and two ambulances pulled up.

I laughed and laughed until my laughter turned into shoulder-wracking glorious sobs of relief.

57

I didn't have much hope I'd get home before dawn, and I was right.

As soon as the ambulance loaded up both Evelyn and Julien to take them to the Hôtel-Dieu behind Notre Dame Cathedral, I was taken in a police van downtown to tell my story.

At one point, the thought did cross my mind that one way to get a ride out of a dodgy area of town was to be involved in two near-homicides. In any case, I called Geneviève to have her go upstairs to wait with Haley although the girl did not sound as if she needed hand-holding.

The police arrived at my apartment and I was able to speak to the detective in charge who had called Haley's parents who were now speeding home from Switzerland.

I spoke to Haley a few more times during all this and she assured me that Robbie had finally gone back to sleep. But Izzy was powering through, barking at the paramedics, the detective and other police personnel.

While I was sitting in the hallway at the *préfecture* waiting to give my statement for the second time to someone totally different, I was able to talk longer with Geneviève who assured me that Haley was fine and that the man whose head Haley had cracked open with my towel rod appeared to have survived the encounter.

I was relieved about that. Not that I cared if that scumbag stuttered or soiled himself for the rest of his life, but I didn't want Haley tortured with thoughts that she'd killed someone. It might not bother her now but it might later.

"Madame Baskerville?"

I looked up to see none other than Detective Monet, who'd taken my statement when Paolo was killed. When I stood up, I looked behind her to see if Muller was there. But he wasn't.

As I followed her to the interview room, I began to feel the full effect of my long and horrifying night. Before I entered the interview room, a police assistant stopped me and asked if I'd like a coffee and something to eat, and I gratefully accepted.

When I sat down opposite Monet I felt my knees give way which made her look up and for a moment she saw I was exhausted.

"I've given my statement already," I said. "And you must be aware that there was a break-in at my apartment tonight. A killer was sent by Evelyn Couture. My sitter is still there on her own."

Actually Haley was there with a detective, two police-women, and Geneviève but I still needed to be there too.

"I know, Madame Baskerville. I will try to make this quick."

"Can you tell me the status of Julien Ricard?" I asked, holding my breath in fear of the answer.

"Monsieur Ricard is in surgery," she said.

That was all I was going to get out of her and chances are it was all she knew. The fact that he was in surgery I decided to take as a good sign. I'd been wrong about Julien. I felt bad about that.

My phone rang and I saw it was Pierre Berger. I'd called him twice since midnight and was surprised to hear from him now at four in the morning.

"I need to take this," I told Monet. "It's my lawyer."

"You are not being charged," she said.

"I still need to take it," I said, clicking *Accept* on my phone. "Can you get Gigi released?" I said into the phone. "Someone has confessed to killing Jean-Bernard." I looked at Monet to see if she would confirm this but she was focused on the documents on the table before her.

"I heard," Berger said. "Gigi's still in the infirmary but her release is in process."

Suddenly I didn't feel quite as exhausted as I had just a moment before.

"Great. Thank you, Pierre."

"*Pas du tout,*" he said and disconnected.

I looked across the table at Detective Monet.

"You already know what I'm going to say," I said. "You probably have it written down right there in front of you."

"I need to hear it from you again," she said. "And then one of my men will drive you home."

Just then the door opened and the assistant entered with two steaming cups of coffee and a plate of *profiteroles*. My stomach growled. Once I'd eaten half a *profiterole* and taken a restorative sip of coffee I turned back to the detective.

"Where's Inspector Muller?" I asked.

"You do know that I ask the questions, yes? I'm sure they don't do things that differently in the States."

"It's just that the Jean-Bernard homicide was his case," I said. "Shouldn't he be here?"

"Inspector Muller has taken an unexpected leave of absence," she said tersely.

I felt a chill right into my bones. I literally found myself praying that the detective—wherever he was—was still breathing.

It had been so nice not having to think about my father these last several months. But I'd be a fool if I thought he wasn't still thinking of me. Planning, scheming, meddling.

My altercation with Muller had been in a public restaurant. If my father was still having me followed, he would've heard about every detail of it.

"But he's alive?" I asked.

She snorted. "Don't be so dramatic. Of course he's alive. Now please start with why you came to this particular neighborhood at night."

I'd already thought about my answer to this question—even before I'd been asked about it before—and I'd decided to omit the part where I got a message from Zero's phone begging me to come to Stalingrad. It wouldn't help to involve him in any of this.

Besides it was much more believable to the police if I said I didn't have a particular reason for going there at night. Such is their flagrant disrespect for most tourists that they would have no trouble believing that.

"I heard it was exotic," I said. "Especially at night."

Sure enough, the detective snorted and shook her head.

"But when I got there I discovered that Monsieur Ricard had followed me. He was worried about my going into that neighborhood at that time of night."

This of course sounded extremely logical to the detective.

"He and I were talking about the murder of his partner Paolo Rozen. He became upset and then Evelyn Couture showed up and shot him."

"Just like that."

"Pretty much. I'm sure you have people asking her why she might have done that. I'd hate to wager a guess."

"Continue."

"Then Evelyn told me she had a guy breaking into my apartment to kill my ward and his sitter."

"Did she say why?"

"Again, I'm sure you can ask her that, but she told me it was pay back for my American arrogance of thinking I knew all the details about her relationship with Jean-Bernard Simon."

"And what were those details?"

"She said they'd been intimate but she worried he was falling in love with a man."

"*Pardon?*"

"She confessed that she gave Jean-Bernard *krokodil* in pill form when he complained of migraines. Then she tracked down Paolo Rozen, the man she felt had seduced him, and killed him with drops of the same drug in his drink."

"She told you all this?"

"She did."

"Go on."

"Then she showed me a video of my ward and his sitter being threatened at my apartment. I didn't think I had much to lose at that point so I lunged for the gun. She tried to shoot me but the bullet missed. I then disarmed her."

"The medics at the scene said there was significant bruising on her throat."

"I grabbed her by the throat to get her to drop the gun."

Monet raised an eyebrow at me.

"She's still breathing, isn't she?" I asked.

Monet ignored my question which of course wasn't meant to be answered anyway.

"So then you got the gun," she prompted. "What happened next?"

I knew she was asking me how Evelyn ended up with no kneecap. I had to answer this very carefully. With me holding the gun, it was a hard argument to make that I was in fear for my life. I briefly thought about saying I'd had a black-out of some kind but in the end, I was too tired to lie with any embellishment which a lie like that would definitely have required.

"I begged her to tell the man she'd sent to kill my family to stop what he was doing," I said.

Monet's eyebrows shot up.

"And she refused," I said. "So I shot her."

Legally, I had no idea how that was going to go down in France. I made a mental note to research a good defense attorney when I got home later today.

Monet nodded as if what I said was in line with what she thought had happened. She gathered up her notes as I finished off another pastry and felt the sugar rush make my hands shake.

"The gun has disappeared," she said.

I shrugged. "It's a rough part of town. I laid it down and somebody must have scampered off with it."

Detective Monet stood up and used the intercom to ask for a policeman to escort me out. Standing up, I leaned heavily against the table as I waited for my escort to arrive.

"Detective Monet," I said wearily. "Is there any doubt that Evelyn Couture killed Jean-Bernard Simon?"

"Evelyn Couture has confessed to killing both Jean-Bernard Simon and Paolo Rozen," she said.

I felt a rush of relief. I knew this didn't eliminate the trouble I was in for shooting an unarmed woman, but the relief and satisfaction felt overwhelming. My eyes filled with tears.

"And the man who broke into my apartment tonight?" I asked, quickly composing myself. "Did Evelyn admit to sending him?"

"*Non*," she said, walking to the door and turning to look at me. "But the man is blaming Evelyn Couture for his severe concussion and the fact that he is going back to prison. So I feel confident the charge against her will hold."

I smiled as my police escort came into the room to take me home.

58

Two weeks later it was a somewhat warm day for February. Haley and Geneviève had insisted on having our first picnic of the year at Parc Monceau— regardless of the fact that there were no flowers, no ice cream kiosks and no operating carrousels.

Even so, as I sat on a park bench near where Haley had spread a wool Ralph Lauren blanket on top of the pine needles where she and Izzy and Robbie sat I conceded that they might have a point. The picnic of *jambon* sandwiches and sugar crêpes that we'd picked up on the way to the park was spread around them.

I sat between Geneviève and Adele on the park bench and watched Haley and Robbie.

Every time I looked at Haley, I got an image of her in that bathroom, the heavy towel rod over her shoulder, ready to tee up the bad guy's head as soon as he broke through the door. This girl was my hero, not just because she had saved Robbie, but because she'd kept her head in the midst of an unimaginable nightmare. And she was sitting here today smiling and eating ham sandwiches.

Even her parents seemed to have been impressed with what Haley had done that night two weeks ago when a drug-crazed ex-con broke down the bathroom door she was huddled behind trying to protect her charge.

In any case, her parents seemed to be reaching out to her more, listening to her and really trying to hear her. Haley still hadn't talked to her father about what she'd discovered about his extracurriculum activities and a part of me was glad. I was the last person to give advice on fathers, but I would keep a protective eye on her going forward.

Adele shifted on the bench and checked her watch. It was unusual for her to spend so much time without a glass of wine or an ash tray near and I knew she'd probably bolt soon.

"Geneviève said you heard from Gigi?" she asked as she tugged her vintage wool peacoat tighter around her and reached in her Prada bag for a cigarette.

"I did," I said.

Once she was released from police custody, Gigi had gone home to Bayeux to live with her parents. They needed to heal right now and they needed to do that together.

"She says she's doing fine and, since Evelyn Couture has confessed to everything, Berger doesn't even think she needs to come back to Paris for the trial."

"That's a blessing," Geneviève said.

"Of course, it was traumatic losing both Jean-Bernard and Paolo, but she's young. She'll be fine eventually."

When we were finished eating, Haley stood up and helped Robbie into the stroller.

"We're going for a walk around the perimeter," she said as she snapped on Izzy's leash.

I smiled and nodded. It was getting easier and easier to let Robbie out of my sight these days. That was surprising, since you'd think after what happened two weeks ago I'd be even more resistant.

Maybe I was maturing. Ha. At sixty-three, it was about time.

"I heard that Evelyn Couture was being moved to another holding facility outside Paris," Adele said. "She thinks her confessions will enhance her chances at trial."

"I heard that, too," I said. "Good luck to her. The evidence is stacked pretty deep against her."

"I have been meaning to ask you, Claire," Geneviève said. "Was it Madame Couture you heard in the hall that night at your apartment?"

"It was," I said. "I thought it might have been Paolo or even Detective Muller but Evelyn told the police she went to my apartment after killing Paolo thinking she might kill me then too. Guess she felt she was on a roll."

"*Incroyable!*" Geneviève said, aghast.

"Is she trying for an insanity plea?" Adele asked as she blew cigarette smoke away from us. I saw the breeze catch the smoke and snatch it away.

"I don't know," I admitted. "But the more I hear about her the more I think she might qualify."

At that moment my phone began to ring and I saw that it was Julien calling. I excused myself and walked a few steps away from the bench to take the call.

"Hey," I said, answering the phone.

"This is not a bad time?" he asked.

"No, it's good," I said. "How are you feeling?"

The gunshot he'd sustained in the back had fortunately missed all major organs but recovery and rehab still promised to be lengthy.

"I am being discharged today," he said. "My parents are coming up from Lyons to bring me home for a bit."

"I'm glad."

I wanted to tell him I was sorry about getting him shot. Now that I knew he really had just wanted to help, I also knew that if

I'd only trusted him, he wouldn't have felt the need to trail me to that neighborhood.

"Marie-France came to visit me," he said. "She said she's not drinking anymore."

"I guess she's holding your job for you?"

"She offered to. But I told her I wouldn't be coming back."

"Too many bad memories?"

"That, and the fact that I should never have gone there in the first place. I love the law. I'm looking at a few firms in Lyons and I think I'll start updating my CV when I'm on my feet."

"I'm glad, Julien. I think that sounds like a great idea." I paused. "You know, I don't think I ever fully apologized to you, Julien, for thinking you killed Jean-Bernard."

"Apology not necessary. Everyone thought I hated him."

"You'd have to be a saint not to hate him after how he lost your dream job for you," I said.

"But that's just it. He had nothing to do with that. I lost that job all on my own."

"But I thought—"

"I know. Everyone did. Can you imagine if a company could really terminate you over sexual preference? This is the twenty-first century, Claire. And *Paris*."

"But then...?"

"I was young and stupid. I failed a routine drug test after a weekend of partying. It was that ridiculous."

"And it had nothing to do with Jean-Bernard."

"Nothing at all."

"Wow. I really got that wrong."

"But you got a lot of other things right. Gigi is free and Jean-Bernard and Paolo's family have closure," he said. "When I'm next in Paris I'd love to meet you for dinner."

"I'd love that too," I said. "Take care now, Julien."

When I walked back to the bench I could see that Adele was on her feet and ready to leave. Behind her Haley and the stroller were approaching on the long gravel walkway that bisected the park.

"Leaving?" I asked.

"I have a date," Adele said with a shrug.

I grinned at her and she waved me away with a corresponding grin.

"I am not ready to fall in love," she said firmly.

"Naturally not," I said.

We kissed goodbye and Geneviève and I watched her hurry out of the park.

"She is a sweet girl," Geneviève said. "I hope she does find love."

I patted her hand as I watched Haley come nearer with the stroller. Geneviève followed my gaze.

"Have you heard anything more about the lawsuit?" she asked.

"Funny you should ask. I heard from Sabine last night late. Apparently Joelle's lawyer withdrew her petition from the court to fight me for Robbie's adoption."

Geneviève twisted in her seat to face me, a look of surprise and joy on her face.

"*Sérieusement?*" she said. "*C'est merveilleux! Mais pourquoi?*"

"Seems my lawyer had it in hand after all."

"Really? I thought you had lost all faith in her."

"I had. It turns out Sabine was going through something in her personal life so she was incredibly noncommunicative and dour with me so of course I thought she was reacting to my case. She told me she never doubted we'd prevail."

When Sabine called last night and told me that Joelle had decided against pursuing the adoption proceedings on behalf of Emily Bickerstaff, my first thought was that my father was somehow involved. There was just no way Joelle would back away from this fight with me so clearly on the ropes. Honestly, when I thought my father might have a hand in this my first inclination was that I'd rather fight Joelle in court than have him involved.

Geneviève and I watched Haley settle back down on the picnic blanket. Robbie and Izzy were snuggled in the stroller fast asleep. Haley grinned at me, then turned to find another sandwich in the hamper.

"So what happened to make Joelle back down?" Geneviève asked.

"Sabine said that Absalom's case was always just smoke and mirrors."

"How so?"

"She explained to me that as Bob's recognized issue—illegitimate or not—Robbie stood to inherit Bob's estate, along with Catherine. Of course there's nothing to inherit but that's not the point. The point is because France recognizes Robbie's connection to Bob it establishes *my* position—as Bob's widow —as Robbie's legal relative. Closer, in fact, than an aunt or even a sister."

This meant I could also tell Catherine one day that her position as Robbie's half-sibling wouldn't have been germane in deciding who got Robbie if we'd had to go to court.

"So even more so in a French court of law," I said, "I would definitely have won the case *because according to French law I* am Robbie's closest relative."

"That's remarkable, *chérie!* But what about the threat against you for child abduction?"

"That was just Joelle siccing her paid attack dog on me to watch me squirm. Sabine said she assumed I knew the threat was nonsense."

Geneviève clucked in annoyance.

"Why did she assume that?" she asked.

"She said only an idiot would think this was a case of child abduction. So she never bothered reassuring me on that score."

"I think you need a new lawyer, *chérie.*"

"Probably. Anyway, she's immediately fast-tracked Robbie's papers as my legally adopted son and she's petitioning to get his name changed to Baskerville. She doesn't expect there to be any hiccoughs in the process which, now that we're just dealing with one country's adoption court, should be fairly straight-forward."

"It's a miracle," Geneviève said, her eyes misting and looking at the stroller where Robbie slept.

"It kind of is," I said. "Except, trust me, this is just round one with Joelle. I'm pretty sure her obsession with trying to ruin my life isn't finished yet."

"Perhaps," Geneviève said. "But then you will just have to outsmart her again."

"Hopefully," I said. "I guess we'll just have to wait and see."

I felt the sun on my back and suddenly the world felt rosy and wonderful. With Robbie sleeping contentedly in his stroller and me sitting next to my dear friend on a perfect winter day, everything was wonderful in historical, gorgeous, and magical Paris.

59

T hat night it was just me and Robbie on our own again. I'd invited Geneviève to dinner—and Haley of course—but Geneviève had her canasta group and Haley was meeting a couple of new friends to go skateboarding in Parc de Skate. One of the girls told Haley she'd teach her French if Haley could show her how to do wheelies.

I was delighted that Haley agreed to the bargain. She might only be trying to be nice and make friends. Or maybe she was thinking that as long as she was living in France, understanding a little bit of French wasn't such a bad idea.

Because Robbie had had so much fresh air today, he was groggy at dinner and to my delight went down quickly at bedtime.

I made *pot-au-feu* and had just finished putting the leftovers away when I saw I received a text message from Laura Murphy.

Because of Gigi's case, I'd put all my own cases on a back burner. And while I'd expected most of them to drop me and find someone else, I was happily surprised to learn that every single one of them had opted to wait until I was free.

Being the only native English-speaking private investigator

in Paris had its definite advantages.

<Can you meet a new client this week?> Laura had texted.

I was already slammed this coming week but Laura had been patient with me rescheduling some of her best contacts so I knew I needed to make an effort to accommodate her.

<Sure. when and where?>

When I finally took a glass of wine to the living room where Izzy joined me on the couch I found that I was less eager to lose myself in a Netflix drama than I was to just sit in my apartment and enjoy the gentle rumble of the traffic outside my window and the general serenity of my home.

With Robbie sleeping in the next room and no lawsuits hanging over my head, all was currently good with my world. On top of that, Catherine had called this morning apologizing for being out of touch. We'd had a really good conversation about her job, which was becoming more challenging in a good way, and about Cam's teachers who all loved him.

I ran my hand over Izzy's head and she closed her eyes to revel in the caress.

Sometimes when I turn off all my outside stimuli, the computer, the phone, the television set, sometimes my brain goes to a peaceful place of memories from the past. I don't allow myself to go there often because the result is often sadness and remorse. But I don't want to distract myself to the point where I forget to feel or I lose touch with what I am feeling deep down.

Here is the place when I can remember Bob and my life with him and how we raised our amazing daughter together. And those thoughts—good and bitter—I think are necessary for me. Especially in my lifelong quest to forgive him for who he turned out to be.

And then there are the thoughts I have about my father Phillipe Moreau. No matter how evil he proves himself to be I suppose I will always struggle to truly hate him.

As much as I fear my father's involvement in my life, I guess I also fear his lack of involvement. Tonight, thinking of my father made me inevitably think of Vincent Muller.

I'd heard through the grapevine that he was indeed alive but as a result of some compromising sexual information found on his hard drive, he'd been moved to another *préfecture* in Normandy. I was all for bad guys getting their due but there was absolutely no reason to believe that the incriminating information had really been put there by Muller.

The real problem as I saw it was that the guy was a border-line thug. And now he was a borderline thug with an ax to grind.

In a major metropolis like Paris or Marseille, he might not cause too many problems. But in a smaller town he could be serious trouble. It seemed to me, if my father was going to play God, he needed to take responsibility for the situation he'd created and make sure Muller didn't terrorize the new town to which my father had consigned him.

Maybe I'd mention that to my father the next time he popped his head out of his hole.

And of course no introspective evening would be complete without thoughts of Jean-Marc, better known as The One Who Got Away.

Jean-Marc wasn't perfect, God knows. But his flaws were acceptable to me. He wasn't a cheat and he tried very hard to do the right thing. I don't know if I had really fallen in love with him. It's hard to tell now that he's gone and deliberately keeping me at arms-length. There's something about someone who doesn't want to see you that makes them even more entic-ing. I'm aware of that.

But right now, if I hold my breath and ask God to keep things as they are with me healthy and still active, the money coming in, good friends around me, and Robbie and Catherine both happy and healthy, I can see how good my life is.

And then there's the addition of Miss Haley Lewis. When I got home this afternoon after she left I reached out to her folks to invite them to dinner next week. I told Haley I was going to do it and while she didn't love the idea it needed to be done. If she was going to be a part of my new family—and there's no doubt that she is—I need to connect with the people who love her and get to know them.

I looked at my watch and saw it was too early to turn in but I still wasn't interested in turning on the television set. I glanced at Izzy.

"What do you think?" I said to her, prompting that adorable head twist she does when she thinks that repositioning her head will somehow help her to understand me. "Early night tonight?"

Right then the phone rang. When I picked it up I stared at the screen, surprised and instantly discomfited.

It was Jean-Marc.

I clicked *Accept* on my phone. "Hello?" I said cautiously.

"Am I catching you at a bad time?" he asked.

My body immediately reacted to hearing his voice again and I wondered how I could ever have doubted whether or not I'd fallen in love with him.

"No," I said, struggling to sound casual. "Not at all. What's up?"

"Nothing, *chérie*. I was just calling to see how you were doing."

To follow more of Claire's sleuthing and adventures, watch for the release of *Deadly Faux Pas, Book 6 of An American in Paris Mysteries!*

ABOUT THE AUTHOR

USA TODAY Bestselling Author Susan Kiernan-Lewis is the author of *The Maggie Newberry Mysteries,* the post-apocalyptic thriller series *The Irish End Games, The Mia Kazmaroff Mysteries, The Stranded in Provence Mysteries,* and *An American in Paris Mysteries.* If you enjoyed *Killing It In Paris,* please leave a review on your purchase site.

Visit her website at www.susankiernanlewis.com or follow her at Author Susan Kiernan-Lewis on Facebook.

Printed in Great Britain
by Amazon

62500743R00189